NOT THAT COMPLICATED

ISABEL MURRAY

D1361972

NOT THAT COMPLICATED

If this was your classic Cotswolds murder mystery (it's not) and Ray was an amateur detective (he isn't) then when he stumbles across something unexpected under his bedroom floor, he'd investigate the hell out of it.

Hard pass.

Ray's just a thirtysomething graphic designer with a broken heart who doesn't much like his life right now.

And he's already having nightmares about the whole thing, come on. He'd rather not think about it. (Also, the police were kinda mean, and now everyone thinks he's a serial killer.)

Luckily for Ray, the last man in the world he should be interested in has distraction on his mind, and it seems like all Ray can think about is Adam Blake. Adam is everywhere Ray turns. He is too young for Ray, too cool for him, too beautiful for him...and for some bewildering reason, Adam is always there for him when Ray needs him the most.

But Ray's not falling for it. He's not falling for Adam. Definitely not. Because Ray and Adam have a complicated history, and starting something would be a terrible idea.

Not That Complicated is a 74k-word romantic comedy that just so happens to also have some dead guys in it. There are very few details on the correct investigative procedure—not that Ray wants to know—and you can forget about any big reveal to wrap up the case. Ray is tangentially involved in the whole gross business at best, and that suits him fine. This is a romance. Which means there is flirting, awkwardness, some surprising discoveries in the bedroom, awkwardness, misunderstandings, more awkwardness, and the kind of love that changes your life forever.

Wait. No. Ray is *not* falling in love...

Right?

1

*I*t wasn't exactly crowded in the pub, even though it was lunchtime. It was a cold Tuesday in February, in the Cotswolds. We didn't get many tourists at this time of year, and at least half the population of Chipping Fairford had dragged themselves off to the train station at six a.m. for the grim commute into London, while those of us smart enough to work from home were gleefully still in bed.

In other words, there was more than enough room at the bar. So why the guy who'd just blown in on a cold blast of rain-scented air felt it necessary to shove himself right up beside me, I had no idea. He was so close, I could feel his body heat, and smell his rather nice shampoo.

I eased to the side, putting some distance between us, and did my best to catch Lenny the bartender's eye. When Lenny had finished pulling a pint of Guinness for the glum-looking man I thought was my postie, he glanced my way.

And his eyes skimmed right over me to land on the newcomer instead.

I scowled.

For god's sake. It wasn't like we were in a crowded night-club where the hot guys get served first.

Then I turned to the guy beside me and thought, okay. Wow. *He* belongs in a nightclub.

The invitation-only kind, populated by actors, models, minor royals, and Beyonce.

The loose curls of his thick, red-gold hair lay in a sexy, tousled mop that sparkled with scattered raindrops. A fashionably beat-up leather jacket hung open to show a navy t-shirt that clung lovingly to his broad chest and lean torso, and his full lips were curved in a smile as I...

...as I gawked up at him like an idiot.

The smile slowly grew.

Mesmerised, I continued to gawk.

Who knows how long I'd have stayed there, frozen, if Lenny hadn't broken the spell. "Usual for you, Adam?"

At the sound of his name, I recoiled.

You'd think Adam had suddenly lunged at me with bared fangs. I hadn't meant to be dramatic; it was pure protective instinct as my brain finally caught up, put the name together with the face, and I realised exactly who I was gawking at.

It had taken long enough. Then again, the last time I saw Adam was a year ago and he'd looked very different, what with being wet and naked in my shower.

His bright hair, saturated with water, had been a sleek dark bronze. He'd been even more intimidatingly beautiful without clothes on.

And he hadn't been smiling.

Kind of like now.

The smile had dropped clean off his face. "Ray was next," he said to Lenny in a deep voice.

The voice I'd have recognised in an instant. The last

time I'd heard it, he was saying, *Yeah. Like that. Just like that. Deeper. Now suck it. Good.*

He hadn't been saying it to me.

He'd been saying it to my boyfriend.

I was the horrified idiot in the bathroom doorway, home unexpectedly early and struggling to process the fact that my boyfriend was on his knees for the checkout boy from the Co-op.

If you wanted to get technical about it, the last time I heard Adam speak was actually when he showed up on my doorstep the next day with an *I'm so, so sorry*, and an *I didn't know, he said he was single*, and a *Can I please—*

I'd slammed the door in his face.

"Ray?" Lenny said. "*Ray.*"

"Huh?"

Lenny looked from me to Adam and back again with sky-high eyebrows. "What can I get you?" he asked.

"A glass of Chenin Blanc and an IPA, please."

I proceeded to stare at Lenny helplessly as he leaned into his forearms on the bar and reeled off a list of ten different IPAs, with names that ran the gamut from sounding like vaguely threatening sex positions to fantasy novel titles generated by an enthusiastic but confused AI.

I was at the pub for a business lunch with my favourite client, Paulina, who'd stopped in for a rare face-to-face meeting en route to a conference in Milton Keynes. The IPA was for her. I had *no* clue.

"The Hobgoblin is good," Adam said about twenty seconds into my blank silence.

I did my best not to shiver, but the hairs on my arms lifted anyway. "In that case, I'll take the Threshing Orc, thanks," I said, grabbing one at random.

It sounded like an advanced sex position *and* a fantasy

novel. A decent choice for Paulina, who was very much into both of those things.

"Oh-*kay*," Lenny said, looking from me to Adam and back again before he shook his head and ambled off.

I did my very best not to fidget as I waited.

Adam was staring at me. I *knew* he was. I literally felt his attention go up and down my face like a warm stroke. Huffing out a breath of irritation, I tipped my head to glare up at him.

And he—oh. He wasn't glaring back. His expression was wary. Almost...soft?

"Hi, Ray," he said.

"Go fuck yourself, Adam," I said. Oh, shit. Where did that come from?

Adam's hazel eyes flared. "Mm. Already did that twice this morning. Once in bed when I woke up, and once in the shower. Maybe I can fit something in after lunch, though." He ran his gaze over my trembling body. "I'm certainly in the mood for it now."

My eyes bulged, he smiled sweetly, and I strode off.

I'd always known it was likely that I'd see Adam around, since we lived in a small town. But I didn't think we'd actually *talk*. I was utterly unprepared for this.

Why couldn't I have said something cool and polite? Something breezy and distant? Anything at all, other than telling him to go fuck himself.

Because now I was *imagining* it.

Paulina watched me sit down. "I'll get the drinks, shall I?" she said, amused.

I stared at her blankly. Drinks. "Sorry," I said. "I don't know what I... I'll grab them."

"Don't bother," she said. "Here they come."

I looked up in time to watch Adam stroll over with an

insolent, loose-hipped gait, drinks in hand. He set them on the table.

"You forgot these," he said.

"Thank you." Paulina grinned at him.

"No problem." Adam flashed her a smile, and arched a brow at me.

"Thank you," I said. Like a grown-up, professional man taking his favourite client to lunch. "How kind."

Adam held my gaze for a second, his eyes narrowing on mine, and then he lifted his chin, bestowed another devastating smile upon Paulina, and went back to the bar.

"There's a story there," Paulina said, dragging her pint toward her. "I want all the details, especially the filthy ones, because he is gorgeous. Spill it."

"Ha. Not a chance."

She pouted. "Not even if I ask nicely?"

"Nope."

"Not even if I threaten to take my business elsewhere?"

"I will never yield to blackmail. And you wouldn't try it anyway. You love me."

"Damn it." She sighed. "I do love you." To prove it, she left the unwelcome topic of Adam alone.

At least until we'd packed away the fish and chips that The Lion was famous for, and we'd tricked each other into ordering dessert. Everyone knows calories don't count if you both get it.

I scraped up the last smudge of my hot chocolate brownie, determined not to miss a crumb, and managed not to moan with disappointment when I set the spoon on the empty plate.

"Okay but seriously, Ray," Paulina said. "You have to ask him out. Do it now, go on. Run after him. I'll wait. I'm still eating."

"What are you talking about?"

"I'm talking about the hot young thing who practically has *Best Worst Decision Ever* flashing over his beautiful head in three-foot neon lights. He walked past the table when you were busy showing your brownie a good time, and he nearly tripped over his sexy boots."

I blinked at her. "Adam?"

"Oh, that suits him. He looks like an Adam. Go on, quick. He's almost out the door. Run and you can catch him."

"Ugh. I don't want to catch him. He's awful."

"Awfully sexy. Yes. I can see that. If he hadn't been eye-fucking you for the last hour from across the room—and trust me, I've been watching him watch you—I'd have asked him for his number myself. I'm not his type. You're his type. Ray, if you were any more his type, he might have gone ahead and mounted you at the bar. He was standing close enough."

"He *was* standing close, wasn't he?"

She flapped her hands at me. "Go!"

"No. Not even if he was the last man on earth. Not even if it was a case of Adam, or the rest of my life spent alone. Not even if—"

"Too late. He's gone." Paulina gave me a crafty look. "What is your problem with him? If you tell me, I'll let you finish my apple crumble."

"You can't buy me any more than you can blackmail me." Not with apple crumble, anyway. It had fruit in it. It was practically healthy. "I'm not for sale. Besides. It's not a happy story, and I'd rather not talk about it."

"Okay," she said. Paulina was a gossip and she liked to tease, but the moment she hit a boundary she stopped. It was one of the things I loved about her.

And it was a technique that never failed to work on me. "Remember the whole thing a year ago with Fraser?"

She pulled a face. "Yeah," she said flatly. Paulina was not a fan of Fraser. Her eyes widened as she put it together. "Nooo. That little cherub?"

"Cherub? *Adam*?"

If she'd seen what Adam was doing to Fraser, she'd revise that statement one hundred and eighty degrees from angelic cherub to demonic sex beast.

Okay, it was just a blowjob. But the way Adam was holding Fraser, with one hand threaded in Fraser's hair and the other gripping Fraser's jaw, the focus on his hard face as he watched, the growling demand in his voice...

"Ugh," Paulina said. "Fuck him. No, don't. Fuck absolutely anyone else. Pick someone."

"Because it's that easy," I said. "I pick someone."

"How hard can it be? You're a cutie pie. You're a catch. Besides, you know what they say. Best way to get over a man is to get under another one."

"Thanks for the compliments. And the cliché."

"You're welcome."

"I don't need to get under anyone. I am over Fraser. I've been over Fraser for a long time. That's not what's been holding me back. There are slim pickings, hereabouts. I'm not exactly plugged into the social scene. Also, I'm old. I've missed the boat."

She rolled her eyes. "What are you, twenty-eight?"

"Thirty-two." I sighed. "It's all over for me. Downhill from here. Life is done."

"Raymond," Paulina said. "I'm forty-five. Am I over the hill?" She didn't wait for an answer. "No, I'm not. But I won't bully you into dating if you're not ready. There's always Plan P."

"Plan B?"

"*P*. Pity party. Ice cream. Lots of ice cream."

"That wouldn't end well. I'm not technically lactose intolerant, but dairy and I have a very finely balanced agreement. I agree not to eat too much dairy in one sitting, and dairy agrees not to make me sprint for the bathroom."

She swatted me with the menu. "Comfort food of your choice, then. You get my point!"

I did get her point. I still had no intention of indulging myself. I didn't need a pity party. I didn't feel sorry for myself.

At least, I hadn't felt sorry for myself. Until I ran into Adam. That surprise encounter really shook me up.

So, really?

Absolutely everything that happened next was all Adam's fault.

2

I'd thought that I was over the breakdown of my relationship with Fraser. I'd thought that I was cool with it. That I'd shaken it off, moved on.

Apparently, all I'd been doing was repressing. To my absolute disgust, seeing Adam brought it all roaring back to the surface. I was hurt all over again.

It wasn't the loss of Fraser I was mourning. It was the loss of my youthful optimism about love and happily ever after. He'd killed it stone dead. Fraser was an arsehole, and I was relieved to be shot of the bastard. If I never had to lay eyes on or hear from him again, that would be *great*.

He hadn't even tried to fight for me. For us. I wouldn't have taken him back...but he hadn't tried.

That fateful day, I'd walked out of the bathroom and kept on walking, all the way down the stairs and out of the house. I ended up sitting in my car with no memory of getting there. I was staring blankly at the steering wheel, the *please fasten your seat belt* noise binging softly in the background, when the loud slam of the front door wrenched me out of my dazed reverie.

Adam stalked down the drive and stopped right in front of the car.

It was a stupid place to stand. The engine was running, my foot was on the gas pedal, and he was a beautiful boy who had just shattered a (supposedly) stable relationship. I'm not the vindictive type, but *Adam* didn't know that.

We locked eyes through the rain-speckled windscreen.

His face was pale and tight with anger, eyes burning dark. He put out a hand and opened his mouth to say something. I didn't want to hear it.

I backed sharply out of the drive and didn't even look in the rear-view mirror as I drove away.

The initial shock was followed by sheer anger. Fraser agreed to go without any fuss, saying that we'd come to the end of the road anyway, and really, hadn't we been more friends and housemates for the last couple of years?

If we'd been housemates, I'd snapped at him, then he'd have been paying rent rather than letting me carry the mortgage on my own.

Fraser swanned off, rented a flat in town for a couple of months, got a job offer in Wantage, and that was that. I found out about it from Amalie at the coffee shop. Three months after leaving my house, he was all moved in to some other chump's house. And this chump's house had a deck with a hot tub, a garden the size of a small park, and stables.

Whereas here I was, a sucking void of romance, living in my shabby little house in Chipping Fairford where the dating pool, as I had said to Paulina, was barely deep enough to float a paper boat.

Yeah.

A pity party was sounding pretty great right about now.

Since I was feeling spicy, I went with curry.

I should have left it at stuffing my face like a giant pig,

but no. I threw in a few bottles of Cobra beer. I almost never drank, and for good reason. That was my big mistake. Actually, my big mistake was getting into bed with my curry and my beer and my favourite comfort movie, *Pride and Prejudice*.

(Mr Darcy made a big impression on young Ray. I won't apologise for it. It's a rite of passage.)

Two hours, one curry, an enormous coconut naan and three pints of beer later, I was feeling better. I'd given up on my ambitious plan to eat the whole curry, defeated halfway through even though I'd quickly abandoned the rice and prioritised the good stuff. I wallowed in bed, replete and rotund as a manatee, my stomach full with Tandoori Tiffins' award-winning chicken tikka masala and my heart full of wistfulness and defiance.

Fraser? He was no Mr Darcy. He wasn't even a Wickham. He wishes he was a Wickham. No, he was a total Mr Collins. He might be a tall and handsome version of Mr Collins, but inside, he had the soul of the status-grubbing little weasel.

If I'd stayed with Fraser, I'd have been poor Charlotte Lucas, married to the wretched Mr Collins and squeezing what joy she could out of barricading herself in her own private parlour, worrying about her pig, and sucking up to Lady Catherine de Bourgh.

No one wants to be Charlotte.

Everyone wants to be Elizabeth Bennet.

I wanted to be Elizabeth Bennet.

Happily sated and more than a little tipsy, I heaved my tray of half-eaten food and empty bottles onto the floor by the bed, tossed my iPad overboard, and snuggled under my beloved fluffy duvet (replaced since Fraser, the bastard).

I should send Paulina flowers, I thought as I drifted off to sleep. This pity party really hit the spot.

YOU KNOW WHAT'S A DISGUSTING THING TO DO?

Forget that you're a slob of the first degree, get out of bed for the bathroom in the middle of the night, already hungover, and step in a plate of cold curry.

I had no idea what was happening to me. I could not comprehend why, *how*, the floor was cold and squishing under my bed-socked feet.

By the time I'd stopped shrieking and dancing around, and had made it over to the light switch, there was a three-foot blast zone of left-over curry and rice, flung all over the middle of the room, and well ground-in by my panicked gyrations.

Fuck.

The carpet was a light beige. Or, it had been.

Now it was a light beige turning bright, turmeric yellow.

Head pounding and eyes watering in the bright over-head light, I resentfully got onto my hands and knees and did my best to scrape it all up. I sprinkled the remaining soggy patch with the dregs of a sodium bicarbonate tub I dug up from the back of the kitchen cupboard, called it good for the night, and crawled back into bed.

AS IT TURNS OUT, THERE'S A FAIRLY TIGHT WINDOW FOR getting curry stains out of your carpet.

Your best bet is to treat it like the emergency it is. Go fast and go hard.

In other words, I'd half-arsed it, and by the time I gave it the attention it deserved, the turmeric had dyed my beige carpet yellow-orange, and I'd learned a valuable lesson. I could absolutely eat in bed if I wanted, but I had to take the dishes downstairs or pay the price.

I bought some supposedly magical carpet cleaner from Amazon, dutifully followed the instructions, and managed to get the stain out. It was so effective that it also managed to get the original dye out, bleaching the carpet to a crispy white.

Not the result I was looking for.

I called my stepmother, Giselle. Once she'd stopped laughing at me for calling her for domestic advice, she passed me to my father. He told me to dump a bag of cat litter on it to soak up all the wet stuff, and when I told him we were way past that stage, he said get creative with rearranging the furniture or buy a rug to put on top.

Rearranging the furniture was out: I couldn't drop a chest of drawers or a chair right in the middle of the room, it'd look ridiculous. I liked the rug idea, but it wouldn't work, either. The rug would have to be practically as big as the room. The stain wasn't a tidy, contained patch. It was a giant, jellyfish-like patch of wrongness. It had a halo of tentacular splatters around it. It was the Portuguese Man O'War of stains.

And whatever was in the special cleaner was vicious.

After two days, all the bleached fibres started to disintegrate into ashy piles. I hoovered it up. It kept coming. I had a suspicion that the patch was growing.

Worse than looking bad, every time it caught my eye, it reminded me of Fraser, and my pity party, and the reason for my pity party.

Adam Blake.

Wet. Naked.

In the shower, saying, *Yeah. Now suck it. Good.*

My hyperfixation on the last bit was truly tragic, because

he hadn't even been saying it to me, and every time I replayed it in my head...he was saying it to me.

After three days of putting up with my bleached and balding carpet, I decided enough was enough. I measured the room, ordered a basic carpet from John Lewis, and got a recommendation from Lenny at The Lion for a good handyman. By the middle of the next week, my Adam-fixation/stain problem was on the way to being solved.

Craig Henderson—*No Job Too Small!*—showed up at nine a.m. sharp, as he'd said he would, with a big smile, a sturdy-looking sidekick named Kevin, and a can-do attitude.

It all started out so well.

That should have been my first warning.

3

I showed the guys up to my room and left them to it. Settling at my desk, I pulled up the design I was working on that I needed to finish by noon tomorrow, and that was as far as I got before Craig banged back down the stairs and came into my office.

"Right," he said, standing in the doorway and scratching his pepper-and-salt stubbled jaw. "We've got to shift your furniture around a fair bit first. Don't worry if you hear a bit of a racket. We'll pull up the carpet you got there now, bring it down, and then we'll get the new one up the stairs for you and fit it, all right?"

"That sounds great," I said.

I hadn't even bothered trying to drag the new carpet up on my own. I knew my limits. The delivery guys had run it in through the front door, dropped it in the hall, and left before I had the chance to ask them to take it upstairs. I'd rolled it like a log to lie against the wall so I didn't have to keep climbing over it every time I needed to get out of the house, and called it good.

"Should be done by the end of the day," Craig said.

"Marvellous. Thank you." I started to turn back to my monitor, and stopped when Craig smiled at me, brows lifted.

"Cup of tea?" I guessed.

"Lovely."

"...and a biscuit?" I said when he didn't leave.

Craig winked and stomped off.

I made the tea and threw a few Hobnobs onto a plate. After brief consideration, I told myself not to be a selfish arse, and emptied the rest of the packet on there.

I stacked the cups and biscuits on a tray, carried it all upstairs, and swung into my bedroom in time to see Kevin single-handedly hip-thrust my bed past the open doorway. He was hunched over and shoving it for all he was worth, really putting his back and thighs into it. The bed bounced and skittered reluctantly but inevitably over the carpet.

Craig was busy moving the chest of drawers. He simply picked it up in his brawny arms and waddle-walked it to the same side of the room as Kevin had wrangled the bed. Everything else had already been stacked there; bedside table, steamer trunk, the small bookshelf, the laundry basket.

I stood in the doorway, feeling vaguely violated despite their obvious lack of interest in my personal space and effects.

"Ah," Craig said when he spotted me. "Tea break."

They'd been here for fifteen minutes. But, okay.

I headed across the room to set the tray on the chest of drawers. Right in the middle, a board groaned horribly when I trod on it. I stopped, startled. Craig was surveying the cleared side of the room. Kevin's attention had locked onto the tea tray, but he glanced up when I stopped.

I rocked forward half a step and back again.

The board groaned like a pirate ship.

Kevin looked away quickly.

That was new.

I continued over to the chest of drawers, put the tray down, then moseyed on back.

I paused on the creaky board. Once more, it groaned.

Hmm.

I left them to it and jogged back down the stairs to get on with some work.

I *tried* to get on with some work.

Instead of going through my to-do list one item at a time as I should, I sat there and listened to absolutely nothing going on upstairs except, I assumed, tea-drinking and biscuit-eating while they strategised.

I shrugged off my curiosity. I'd paid Craig a flat rate for the day. If they wanted to lounge around and make an outing out of it, that was their business.

After half an hour, I was changing the brand colours for a picky client for the fourth time, and I flinched when all the noise started up.

It sounded like they were fighting up there.

Without realising it, I had half-risen from my chair. I sat back down cautiously, and listened. No one was shouting. It was fine.

I winced when something overhead thumped and shook the ceiling.

It was fine. They were laying carpet, that's all. I was fairly sure.

Maybe I should check, though.

I drifted into the hall and peered up the stairs.

After another great whump, I gave up trying to be a cool and trusting homeowner, the sort who gives the men the whole packet of Hobnobs and lets them do their job in peace, and jogged up the stairs to duck my head in and see what was happening.

Kevin was on all fours by the skirting board at the far wall. Craig stood off to one side, hands on hips, overseeing things.

"Get a good hold, and yank it as hard as you can," Craig said. "Give it some welly."

Kevin got into a squat and hunkered low. He'd shed his grey Under Armour hoodie at some point and was wearing a t-shirt which showcased his thick arms a treat. He did as instructed, got a good hold—of the carpet, I assumed, I couldn't quite see from where I was—and heaved. His neck strained, tendons bulging. He clenched his jaw. His cheeks wobbled. He was giving it his all, but the carpet didn't budge.

Kevin did. He lost his balance and fell backward. The floor shook.

"Oh my god," I said. "Don't hurt yourself, Kevin." I didn't like to think what would happen if he strained any harder. Something might fall out of him.

"He's all right," Craig said, unconcerned. "We're just seeing if he can pull it up or if we need to get the blades out."

"Blades?" I echoed.

"Yup. This is practically welded down," he said. "Come over here and have a look."

I hesitantly crossed the room and stood beside him. He pointed at a thick rubbery seal between the carpet and the base of the skirting board. The carpet had been laid in such a way that the seal was hidden by a fold.

"It's sealed up good," Craig remarked. He bent down, rummaged through in his toolbox, and pulled out a wide, flat chisel. Its thin edge gleamed in the overhead light. "Get started with that," he said to Kevin.

Kevin began working the chisel between the carpet and the skirting board.

"Is this not normal for carpets and underlay?"

Craig scratched the back of his neck. "Not that I've seen, no. Could be a technique from back in the eighties? Or maybe there was a damp problem? Or mould? Mice?"

Lovely.

Kevin grunted as he worked the sharp chisel under the sealant. He made a triumphant noise when he broke through. He got a good grip on it, braced himself for a few more tugs, and I prayed he didn't pop a hernia. He strained, and slowly the carpet tore away from the seal.

Kevin and Craig cheered. I feebly joined in.

"Good job, Kev," Craig said, clapping Kevin on the shoulder. Kevin beamed up at us, sweating happily.

"Won't take us any time now," Craig said with confidence.

I contemplated the sealant. It looked like the waterproof stuff you put around the bath or the sink, but heavy duty. If it *was* from the eighties... "Do you think you should wear dust masks?" I said.

Craig gave me a blank look.

I pointed at the sealant. Now that Kevin was really hacking at it—I didn't even wince when I saw shavings of my skirting board fly up, I wanted this done in one day and I could sand and repaint if necessary—it was coming up in big, friable lumps. If it was a mould issue, could there be spores?

"My Dad works in construction," I said. "He builds conservatories. He's had to tear lots of structures down first before he builds the new one, and the older they are, the higher the risk of toxic materials. You know, asbestos and such."

Craig pursed his mouth in thought. "Nah, it'll be fine," he said.

I wasn't convinced. "Are you sure?"

"Kev. Don't breathe it in," he said.

"Okay." Kevin continued his merry destruction.

Craig gave me a thumbs up. It was a clear dismissal.

I left them to it. I pondered bopping out to the tiny hardware store attached to the newsagents in town and grabbing a couple of dust masks. Before I decided one way or the other, my phone rang, and I got drawn into a polite disagreement with the rebrand client over whether or not he had already passed on the raspberry-and-mint combo. At half eleven, Craig rapped on the office door.

Startled, I smothered a yelp and took my headset off. "Hi. What's up? Are you done already?"

He laughed like I was joking. My hopes of this being a one-day job were fading by the minute. "We're off for a quick bite at the pub, Ray. Lunch."

"Uh. Okay."

"Be careful if you go up there while we're out. Looks a right mess, but it'll tidy up fine, don't you worry."

"Thanks." I had no intention of going up there. I wasn't going to look until it was all back to normal.

"Back in an hour or so," he said, somewhat optimistically.

When they reappeared at two p.m. and had heaved the underlay and new carpet up the stairs, I headed up myself.

"I was wondering if you could do something about the floorboards before you lay the carpet," I said.

"Like what?" Craig asked amiably, coming over to stand beside me.

I stepped on the creaky spot and pushed at it with my toe. "This is going to drive me crazy," I said. "Can you make it not do that?"

"Yeah, no problem. Reason it's creaking is, the nails must have worn loose and the boards have got a bit of space to move. Reckon I can lift a couple for you, nail them back down."

"That'd be fantastic, thanks."

"No worries. Just this spot is it?" He stepped on it and made it creak a few times.

"Let me check?"

Kevin watched while I walked around the room and tested for more creaky boards, trying very hard not to feel like a fusspot.

I completed a circuit and came back to Craig. "Just this spot."

"All right." Craig sank down into a crouch with unexpected grace and grunted at Kevin. Kevin poked around in the toolbox, made a selection and brought it over.

"Huh," Craig said.

"What is it?"

"Floorboards around here are all seated for shit," he said. "No wonder they're creaky. Look." He mapped out about six feet one way and three feet the other, drawing over them with the point of his hammer. "You got pipes or something under here?"

"No? I don't think so, anyway."

"They look like they've been lifted and lowered a fair few times, which is why I can do this." He leaned his weight into his hands and bounced. The boards bowed, popping up a little at the ends. "Let's get in and have a look." He rocked forward onto his knees and efficiently clawed up the nails.

He pulled out the first board and tossed it beside him with a clatter. "Huh."

"Pipes?"

"No. It's a deep cavity, though. Don't usually have the floorboards this high up off the beams."

I looked over his shoulder, then decided to kneel down beside him and have a proper look. It did seem pretty deep. "Modified for extra storage space?"

He shrugged. "Old house, innit? These days they're all built the same, and there's regulations and whatnot, but this house has gotta be about one, two hundred years old? They did what they liked back then. Maybe it was just built that way."

He pulled up another couple of boards and sat back.

"Oh, look." I leaned down and ducked my head in. "I think it *is* being used for storage. There's one of those plastic tubs under here. A big one. It's probably filled with Christmas decorations or something."

Craig pulled up a few more boards, exposing more of the opaque storage tub. It was a very big one, long and deep. It looked old. We all stared down at it.

"You want to get it out?" Craig asked.

It was a tub full of someone else's junk. I'd prefer to leave it where it was, to be honest. I had plenty of my own junk filling up my garage right now. I was about to tell Craig to nail the boards back in place when he leaned over and popped the lid.

Air puffed out.

We both recoiled, and then slowly turned and looked at each other.

"What is it?" Kevin said. He crouched beside me, reached out, and shoved the lid off.

It didn't go far. It didn't even fall all the way off.

It did open wide enough to show that there was a dead guy packed in there, surrounded by greyish-white granules that looked like cat litter.

"Eeeeeeee," Kevin said.

"What the shitting hell is that?" I said, scrambling backward.

Craig didn't say anything.

Unless *hork* counts as a word. He barked that three times as he threw up. Right in the hole.

I was the last out of the room, but only because Kevin had been crouching so he had a head start, and once Craig and I had heaved up off our knees, Craig shoved me aside so he could make it to the door first.

We all thundered down the stairs and ran straight out of the house into the front garden.

Craig kept running. I'd never seen anyone move that fast in my life.

He bolted down the path, beeping his van open as he went, and threw himself in. The engine fired up. Kevin barrelled past me and leaped into the passenger seat. Craig reversed into the road without looking and squealed off into the distance.

It was like a Hollywood action movie. Craig didn't even pause at the junction to check for oncoming traffic. He pulled out, and nearly got t-boned by a DPD van.

My chest was hollow, my heart rattling around in there. I felt my heartbeat reverberating through my body.

"Are you all right, Ray? Ray? *Ray!*" Someone shook me.

Mrs Hughes' face swam into view.

Mrs Hughes lived over the road and two doors down from me with her West Highland terrier, Dougal, who was so old he had to wear arthritis boots whenever she took him for a walk.

They were red.

He looked very sassy in them.

"*Ray.*"

"Hmm? Sorry, what?"

She was gripping my shoulders. "Are you all right?"

I stared at her. "No," I said indignantly. "There's a dead man in my house."

Her grip fell away and she took a step back.

"I didn't kill him," I told her.

"That's good." She took another step back.

"I have to call the police," I said. "Excuse me."

I darted into the house and grabbed my phone from the office, sidling past the bottom of the stairs like the dead man was going to climb out of his tub and come down to say hi if he heard me. I scrambled back out and shut the front door behind me. Mrs Hughes had disappeared. I sank to sit on the cold front step. The stone was vaguely damp but my legs didn't seem to want to hold me up anymore.

I made the call and sat there primly, knees together, until a patrol car pulled up at the bottom of the drive and blocked my car in.

A couple of uniforms strode up the path. They stopped in front of me.

"Ray Underwood?" one of them asked.

In my experience, police officers either looked twelve, or too old for this shit.

The one asking was the twelve-year-old. She had red hair, freckles, and a thousand-yard stare.

"Yes," I said. "That's me."

And the day got worse from there.

4

_____

I held the oversized cup of chamomile tea to my lips. I didn't drink any; I was having trouble swallowing anything. Even water tried to come back up. The warmth from the cup and the lightly fragranced steam was nice, though. It wasn't doing much to calm me down, but then, short of a Valium, I didn't think anything could.

"All right, Mr Underwood. Take me through it one more time."

My eyes slowly focused over the rim of the cup on the man sitting on the other side of the kitchen table.

Detective Chief Inspector Liam Nash was large and solid, with a shock of sandy blond hair, cool blue-grey eyes that seemed to look right into my soul and didn't think much of what they saw, and an annoying habit of asking me the same questions over and over again.

I sighed. "I spilled a curry and ruined the carpet. I bought a new carpet. I hired Craig Henderson to come and lay the new carpet. I asked him to reseat the creaky floorboards while he was at it. We found a tub under the boards.

Kevin pushed the lid off. There was a dead guy in the tub and Craig threw up. The end."

Detective Nash's lips tightened.

I dropped my gaze to the table. "That's really all there is to it," I said. "You can interrogate me another three times if you want, but I don't have anything to add."

Now he sighed. "I'm taking your statement, Mr Underwood, not interrogating you." He gestured at the laptop he'd pulled out of the smart black rucksack he'd brought with him.

"Right." Yes. He'd said something about that earlier, hadn't he? I put my chamomile tea down and got to my feet. "I'm going to make a coffee," I announced. "Would you like one?"

"I'll stick with tea, thank you. Can I convince you to do the same?"

Nope. If I couldn't sedate myself, I may as well try to gain an edge. I felt as if I was coming off a three-day weekend in Brighton, and I mean that in the bad way. Like it was a shitty weekend, everyone else had a great time but me, and I regretted everything. It was shock, probably. And maybe pouring caffeine on top of that wasn't my brightest idea, but I'd rather be wired than woolly and disconnected.

He waited while I fought my Nespresso machine. On a normal day, it was a straightforward process. Insert pod. Press go. Not today, of course. I somehow managed to get the pod in at ninety degrees and had to winkle it out with a butter knife, I forgot to fill the tank so it sputtered to an angry stop with the cup halfway full, and when I triumphantly turned back to Detective Nash with coffee in hand, a floorboard upstairs where the forensics team were moving about creaked particularly loudly. I flinched, and splashed coffee over the rim.

Great. I carried the cup over to the table and sat down. It was almost to my mouth when a crash from upstairs made me twitch again. At least the splash hit the table and not me.

"Okay." Detective Nash leaned over and extracted the cup from my clammy grip. "Let's set this down for a moment, shall we?"

I didn't resist, although usually, trying to separate me from coffee would have me defending it like a starving honey badger defending the carcass of a downed caribou at the end of a hard winter. I am not exaggerating. Luckily for Detective Nash, I'd been distracted by a terrible thought. "Oh. Oh my god."

"What is it? Did you think of something?"

"Yes. I've been doing yoga on top of a dead man for five years."

He gave me a questioning look.

I thrust a finger up at the ceiling and the room above. "That exact spot was literally where I lay my mat. I did downward-facing dog on him." I stared at Detective Nash in horror. "I did *savasana*."

"And that is?"

"In English?" I said, louder than intended. "*Corpse* pose."

He was quick to smother a smile, but not quick enough. I saw it.

"So, what happens now?" I said, trying very hard not to imagine myself lying on top of the dead guy.

"We will continue to process the scene, any evidence will go to the forensics lab, and the body will be taken to a mortuary for further investigation by a forensic pathologist. It's really nothing you need to worry about. My advice is to put it behind you and move on."

"I'll try. I'm not sure how easy that will be. Mentally speaking."

"Well, you have my card if you have any further questions, and the pamphlet I've given you includes some numbers you can call for support."

The pamphlet and his business card were on the table by my elbow. "How long before we know anything?"

"Realistically, the forensics will take months. It doesn't work quite how you see on television or in the movies. These things take time for any case. Given the estimated age of the body and the crime, it's not going to be a priority case. It could be a year. Or longer, depending on how backed up the labs are."

"You're not going to put him in a drawer somewhere and forget about him, are you?" I said.

"No. It's an open investigation. If we can't come up with a solid line of enquiry, the case will get passed to a specialised unit that deals with this sort of thing, but it will be ongoing. He won't be forgotten."

I chewed my lip and stared at the scuffed surface of the table. "Do you...do you think you'll find out who he is? Who m-murdered him? I'm assuming you think it's murder?"

"I doubt he put himself in the tub. Unless we find compelling evidence to the contrary, we'll proceed under the assumption it was murder."

I blinked over at him. "You don't think I did it, do you?"

His lips twitched. "Did you?"

I felt the blood drain from my face. "No!"

"Okay. According to what you told me earlier, you've lived here for five years."

Had I told him? I didn't remember, but I had an uneasy feeling that I'd told him a lot of things. Most of which he hadn't asked about, and didn't need to know. I'd kind of unravelled a bit at the beginning there.

I hoped nobody ever interrogated me for real. I'd give up everything.

"Besides the fact the body appears to be at least partially mummified," Nash was saying, "my roughest guess would put his death some decades ago. I doubt you were even born when he died."

"Phew. Not a suspect." I mimed wiping sweat from my forehead. "Do you think you'll solve it?"

He hesitated.

"I'm not asking for an official answer here. But in your experience in dealing with this sort of thing, pure speculation: what's the likelihood of even finding out who he is, let alone who put him there?"

"Very small," he said. "Considering the apparent age of the body, the condition of the scene, and the circumstances in which we found it, I'd say it's unlikely. Best-case scenario, it could take years. Which is why my advice is to put it behind you, and move on."

I sat there gazing into space and drinking my now unpleasantly cool coffee while Detective Nash popped open his laptop and started typing up my statement.

I'd thought that was something that I was supposed to do myself, and he didn't *quite* nail my narrative voice, but when Detective Nash turned the laptop to me and asked me to read through and sign it if all was in order, he'd got all the facts straight.

I'd also expected to be signing with a pen on paper, but the laptop had a touchscreen. It was like signing for delivery on one of those little handheld devices that delivery people come with. Except using my finger. The squiggle that came out was utterly unreadable as an actual word or signature, but I supposed it didn't matter.

"Do you have somewhere you can stay tonight?" Detective Nash asked, adding his own (much more practiced and legible) signature. He tapped at the laptop a few more times before closing it.

"Uh. In my guest room? Or I'll sleep on the sofa? I hadn't thought."

"Somewhere else," he clarified. "That isn't here. We won't be releasing the scene until tomorrow at the earliest."

"You're kicking me out of my own house?"

"Do you want to be here?" he countered.

Nope.

I rubbed a hand over my face. I was exhausted all of a sudden. It was late, it had been a shitty day, there was a dead guy upstairs. I really didn't want to be here.

I was beginning to wonder if I wanted to be in Chipping Fairford at all.

The thing was, when I broke up with Fraser, he pretty much got the friends in the 'divorce'.

Which was fair. They were his friends to start with. Fraser was a local and I was an incomer. It wasn't as if I was shunned after the breakup. It was painful, that was all.

They'd known.

I never confronted any of them, or asked them, but they had to have known. Nobody had said anything. And nobody made an effort to keep the friendship alive when I threw Fraser out, or even when Fraser had moved to Wantage.

I'd had trust issues going into that relationship. Finding out that Fraser had been hooking up with people the whole time I thought we were securely coupled up and nobody saw fit to mention it did not make me the kind of person to reach out for help with confidence.

While I did have a couple of non-Fraser-related friends in town, none were close enough that I felt comfortable calling them up and inviting myself for a sleepover.

I could go to my parents house, but I didn't want to go through the hour-and-a-half drive it took to get there, or the inevitable fuss and questions I'd face at the end of it.

Or the lecture.

My Dad had been against me buying this house in the first place, saying it didn't have good bones, and it wasn't a sound investment, and why didn't I stay closer to home and get more involved in the family business instead?

I didn't stay closer to home because I didn't want to join the family business. Which he managed to forget over and over again.

There were more than a few guesthouses and B&Bs around, but this was prime tourist country. I refused to pay through the nose for a twee view that I could get by looking out of my own bedroom window.

Detective Nash was watching me have my personal debate. "How about the Premier Lodge?" he suggested eventually. "One of my cousins works there. They often have late room deals." He gave me an encouraging nod.

The Premier Lodge was a local chain hotel. It was a big favourite of tourists who needed the sort of large family room which the cute little cottages-turned-into-B&Bs couldn't provide, and also of people visiting Oxford for the University, or the architecture, or whatever else they kept coming here for.

I wasn't a fan, but it was a good idea. It was cheap. It was efficient. It would do.

It couldn't be worse than staying here, anyway, could it?

The short answer was yes.

Yes.

It could be, and indeed was, worse.

5

I packed an overnight bag, grabbed my laptop because deadlines and clients don't give a shit about personal problems, and left my house in the tender loving care of the Law.

I walked into the Premier Lodge, all unsuspecting, and jerked to a halt at the reception desk.

On the other side of the desk, dressed in a revolting purple uniform that he somehow managed to make look like a deliberate fashion choice, Adam Blake raised his brows.

Adam.

The last guy I wanted to see today.

Well, that wasn't fair.

The last guy I wanted to see today was whoever put the dead body in my floor.

Then it was Fraser.

And *then* Adam.

Regardless of where he ranked on my least-desirable list, I could have done without this particular surprise meeting.

"What are you doing here?" I demanded.

Adam slowly stood. "Working. I work here."

I looked around helplessly. "*Here*, here?"

"Yes, Ray. *Here*, here."

I shifted from one foot to the other and gripped my overnight bag. "Oh."

"Is that a problem?"

"No. I just didn't expect it. Didn't expect to see you. Here."

He regarded me with curiosity. "Where did you expect to see me?"

"I don't know. Behind the till at the Co-op?"

He let out a huff of amusement. "I haven't worked at the Co-op since I was nineteen. Which was four years ago, by the way."

He was twenty-three? I frowned. That couldn't be right. Now that I thought of it, it had been a while since I'd seen him at the supermarket, even before the whole naked-in-my-shower business. And after, I'd stopped patronising the Co-op and driven to the local Sainsburys for my weekly shop instead.

"Four years? Are you sure?" I said.

"Yes. I went away to university, got a degree and everything."

"Oh. Um. Good for you."

I stared at him. His lips curved in that same slow smile I'd seen in the mirror behind the bar before I'd told him to go fuck himself, which I still felt kind of guilty about. Hence me making an effort to be polite rather than yelling, *Give me my key*, and running away with it.

Adam had the most perfect skin I've ever seen in my life. His face was flawless. His cheeks had a delicate peachy-rose blush. He had no pores.

He sat down, propped his chin in his fist, and continued

to smile. "You let me know when you're ready," he said. "I'll be right here. Waiting for you."

"To do what?" I asked stupidly.

He gave an amused snort. His expression was an odd mix I couldn't quite work out. A little fond, which was weird. A little heated. A little...concerned? "To check in, of course," he said. "Unless you dropped by for any other reason?"

"No."

"You'd like to book a room?"

The phone beside him rang. I flinched and came back to myself abruptly. What the hell was I doing, standing there on the other side of the desk gawking at him? Again?

I'd had a shit day. A really shit day. That was all. My house was filled with strangers. I'd been booted out. Adam was the first familiar face I'd seen since Mrs Hughes.

This bizarre urge I was feeling to ask him to come around and wrap me up in his arms and hug me or some such ridiculous thing was perfectly normal.

Understandable.

Inevitable, even.

Although, I didn't know if Adam was a hugger? And maybe he'd read more into the simple, innocent request. Maybe he'd think I wanted more. Or he'd hug me, and then he'd tell me to do something in return for him.

I blushed, hard and furious, at the thought of what he might tell me to do, and met Adam's startled gaze. He'd finished the call and hung up, and was watching me.

"Are you okay?" he said.

"Yes! I'm fine!" I didn't need a hug, and I absolutely would not give him a blowjob for it in return, either.

"You seem to be having quite the mental journey over there."

"It's been a day."

"I heard."

"Really?"

"You're talking about the dead guy under your floorboards, right?"

"How do you know?"

"Small town, Ray. Lots of gossip."

I clenched my jaw at the thought of people talking about me behind my back. "I didn't kill him. When you're gossiping about me next, you can toss that little nugget out if you like."

"Of course you didn't kill him." Adam stood up again and dragged the keyboard toward him. "You couldn't kill a spider. Now, I'm assuming you're here because the police turfed you out? How many nights do you want?"

"One, please."

He paused. "You sure?"

I shrugged. "Start with one. How long can it take to remove the body? He's already, uh. Packed? In a manner of speaking?" I felt the hideous urge to giggle at my poor choice of words.

Adam tilted his head. "Okay."

"Wait. I have to work in the morning. I'm going to need the desk. What time's check out?"

"Ten."

What were the odds I'd be able to go home before ten? Not good. "I think I'd better book it for two nights."

"Two nights it is."

I shifted from one foot to the other. "Aren't you going to ask me about it?"

"I won't lie. I'm curious. Do you want to talk about it, though?"

I shuddered. "No." Preferably never again.

Adam took my information and my credit card and

entered it into the computer. When he'd finished, he stood up and held out the key. My head tipped back. I eyed the length of his arm.

He was big.

I'd got it stuck in my head that he was younger, that he was a boy. I'd tried to get it stuck, in any case. But there was no getting past it. This wasn't a boy.

This was a big man.

A big, confusing man.

I reached out to take the plastic key card. Adam didn't let go. I gave it a gentle tug. Nothing.

"Ray, I didn't know," he said. "You've never given me a chance to tell you properly. I'm telling you now. I didn't know."

I pondered playing dumb for a second or two. But we both knew *I* knew what he was talking about. "Okay."

His fingers tightened on the card. "I suppose I should try apologising again."

"For what? There's no need. You said you didn't know. It's not your fault you were a homewrecker."

An eyebrow twitched. "Homewrecker?"

"Yes. You were also a child. You didn't know better. I accept your apology and I forgive you," I said magnanimously.

His smile sharpened. "I was twenty-two."

"A baby child. Forgiven. Now, is the room this way or...?"

"And I didn't apologise this time."

"You said you *should*. I assumed it was implied."

"It wasn't."

"I forgive you anyway. For your youth and your bad manners." I was uncomfortably aware that my manners weren't exactly a shining example right now. There was something about the way he *looked* at me and *poked* at me that got me all riled up. I was never usually this rude.

"You're very bitter, Ray," he said. "Tell me it's not because you're still pining for Fraser. The guy's a dick. He tried to pass you off as his roommate. Even after you came into the bathroom."

I made an angry noise. Fraser was *such* a dick. "Did you even care, one way or the other?"

"Yes," he said fiercely. "I wouldn't cheat. Ever. Cheating is for wankers."

"I'm glad to hear it. Moral character. Excellent. Carry on."

The smile that had been flirting over his expressive mouth burst into full bloom. "Moral character, huh?"

"Was that right or left? For the room? Do I go along the corridors swiping my card until I hit the jackpot? Or do I have to call your manager and get them to show me?"

"Call my manager?" Adam was unimpressed. "You're better than that, Ray."

"Nice that you think so," I said. "But no."

"In that case," he said, "*Sir*. Your room is on the second floor. If you'd like to take the lift, it's the first right and all the way to the end of the corridor."

"*Sir*," I mused, giving the word the same weighting he had but leaving out the sarcasm. I tapped the edge of the key card on the desk. "I like that."

"Yes. I'm rather partial to being called sir myself."

My eyes widened.

I had the feeling that he didn't mean that in a customer-service kind of way.

Partly because of the tone of his voice, which carried an authority that no one so young should possess, but mostly because of the way he dropped his gaze down to my lips, then dragged it slowly back up.

I clutched my bag tightly and blinked.

His perfect face remained distant and blank.

My skin prickled over with goosebumps.

What was happening?

I was being psyched out—sexually and otherwise—by the manchild my boyfriend cheated on me with.

And I was getting hard about it.

There was only one thing to do.

Retreat.

I'm almost sure I didn't break into a run.

FIVE HOURS LATER, I WAS BACK AT THE FRONT DESK. I'D HOPED that Adam's shift would be over and he'd be gone.

Today was still not my day.

I'd spent hours trying to sleep. It wasn't the emotional fallout of unexpectedly finding a dead body in my house keeping me awake. It wasn't even the unsettling encounter with Adam. It was the noise from the room next door.

Dear god, the noise.

I pulled a hoodie on over my faded *Fraggle Rock* t-shirt, sweatpants on over my boxers, and stuffed my socked feet into Adidas flip-flops.

The lift doors opened directly facing the desk, or I'd have turned back the moment I spotted Adam, and put up with the noise instead.

Once he'd noticed me, I felt honour-bound to see it through. He watched me all the way across the foyer.

"You did it on purpose, didn't you?" I snapped, bellying

right up to the desk. Going on the offensive. Taking control of the conversation from the start.

I could do this.

"Good evening, Ray," Adam said.

"It is very much not a good evening, which I suspect you very well know."

"Mm-hmm. What are you doing down here?" His eyes gleamed. "Are you bored?"

"No, I'm—"

"Looking for company?"

"Almost never." I was an independent man, damn it.

"Looking for reassurance after the shock of finding a dead guy in your house?"

I mean, I didn't *need* it or anything, what with being an independent man, but since he'd brought it up—

"Or did you come here to flirt with me some more?"

"Absolutely not. I have *no* interest in flirting with you. I am here about the sex!"

He raised a brow. "Cutting right to it, are we? All right. I like a man who asks for what he wants. I'm off in an hour. Can you keep it together until then?"

I growled. "I can't sleep because of all the sex that the couple next door to me are having."

"Are the honeymooners in the room beside yours?" he said. "I had no idea."

Like hell he didn't, the little shit. "I would like to change my room, please," I said stiffly.

"I'm afraid we're booked up." He didn't even look at the computer.

"Will you please check?"

"I don't need to check. I filled the last room twenty minutes ago. Nice lady. Dr Ridley. She's a regular. Comes to do research at the Bodleian Library. Specialises in the Norse sagas." Adam was loving this. Every second of it.

I wrinkled my nose. "Who regularly chooses to stay at a Premier Lodge?"

"People who aren't entitled snobs and can get by with clean rooms, decent amenities, breakfast included, and have no burning need to post the whole thing as an Instagram story?"

"Are you calling me a snob?" My voice went high with indignation.

Adam considered me thoughtfully. "Yes."

I bumped up against the front desk and poked a finger into the shiny wood between us. "I'll have you know I have lived and stayed in all sorts of places. All sorts!"

"Doesn't make you not a snob."

"It...does. It does! I once stayed six months in an off-grid cabin in Wales, sleeping on the floor."

"I'll bet it cost you two hundred pounds a night."

"It did not!"

"I bet you were glamping."

I sucked in a breath and went up on my toes, leaning into my widespread hands. "How dare you."

"Very easily."

"I'm not a snob!"

"I know. I also know that you are incredibly easy to manipulate."

"Bollocks."

"It took me about ten seconds to distract you from whingeing about your room. You're so wound up you're almost climbing over the desk to get to me. Another ten seconds and I'll have you all the way over here, begging me to distract you with my lips."

I couldn't argue with that, even if I wanted to.

I dropped my gaze to his smug, smiling mouth and back up to his knowing face. "Make it two seconds," I said.

For a moment I thought he'd laugh at me and make me die of embarrassment on the spot. For a moment only.

He slid a hand over my jaw to curl it around the back of my neck. He nudged my chin up and lowered his lips to mine.

I've made some bad decisions in my life; buying a house with a dead body in it was the current number one.

Kissing Adam Blake in the deserted foyer of the Premier Lodge was a strong contender for number two. I was sure I'd regret it any minute.

But not quite yet.

Adam was one hell of a kisser. His lips were firm, his hold was gentle but in control, and he had a gift for gauging how much pressure I needed, and not letting me have it.

He stroked his mouth over mine in teasing brushes, pushing then withdrawing. I hadn't had even a hint of tongue yet and I was half hard.

"Yeah," he whispered against my lips as I opened up helplessly. He pulled me a fraction of an inch closer, licked into my mouth to make me moan, then...he let me go.

I dropped back onto my heels with a jolt, stunned. I gaped at Adam.

He held the phone to his ear with one hand and tapped at the keyboard with the other. His mouth was red and damp and he had a hint of colour in that peach-perfect skin, but otherwise he showed no sign that until the phone rang he had me up on my toes, his tongue in my mouth and his hands cupping my face while he kissed me like he was off to war.

"Yes, we have a room free," he was saying. "Would you like a single or a double?"

I was sweating lightly as my racing heart slowed.

Hold on.

He'd told me Dr Ridley had the last room.

"Would that be for tonight or more than one night? Yes, three nights, not a problem."

Adam must have sensed the pulsing beat of my ire. He cut me a glance and paused, attention arrested on my face.

I snatched up the pen and notepad from beside the bell on the desk. In block capitals, I wrote *ARSEHOLE!!!*

With a flourish I tore the flimsy sheet off the pad, slapped it down in front of Adam, and stalked back to my room.

$\mathcal{I}$t will come as no surprise to hear that I was utterly incapable of sleep that night. I lay in bed, staring at the ceiling, for hours.

I couldn't even blame the dead body or the squawking honeymooners in the room next door, whose enthusiastic shagging eventually simmered down to a dull, background roar.

Both were excellent reasons.

And yet full responsibility lay with Adam Blake.

Adam Blake, and the way he kissed me, riled me up, and then left me drowning in self-loathing for a) kissing such a manipulative and annoying shit in the first place, and for b) kissing a twenty-three-year-old.

By the time six a.m. rolled around, I was gritty-eyed with exhaustion and exceedingly cranky.

I took a long, hot shower in the tiny cubicle and used up all the free toiletries, having forgotten to bring my own. When I was done, I was squeaky clean and hotel scented from top to bottom.

I bundled myself into cosy sweatpants, thick socks, and a

jumper. The air con in the room was set to meat locker. I would rather freeze to death than call the front desk and ask Adam for help. I'd had a cautious fiddle with the dial the night before, and gave up when the thing had threatened to come off in my hand.

I made coffee from a packet of disgusting freeze-dried instant provided on a little tray with a tiny kettle. The hotel had also provided a miniature packet of biscuits, which were just about big enough to wake up your appetite and make you yearn for a Hobnob. I choked down the coffee, scoffed the biscuits, and grudgingly set my computer up at the desk.

Ninety-nine percent of the time, I loved being my own boss. On days like this, though, it would have been great to be able to call in sick and have someone cover for me.

I couldn't even say screw it, I'll take the morning off and work late, since I had a deadline and there was a client out there expecting files to be sent over by lunchtime. I buckled down and got the job done, then poked about online until I received confirmation of receipt from the satisfied client, and staggered back to the bed.

Now I could sleep.

Hopefully.

OF COURSE, AS SOON AS I DROPPED OFF, I WAS STARTLED awake by the shrill demand of my iPhone, which I'd left sitting on the desk across the room. My Apple watch took up the slack and did its best to shock me awake by having an actual fit on my wrist.

I hauled the pillow over my head and fumblingly removed the watch. I tossed it in the general direction of the bedside table, and carried on with the important business at hand: sweet oblivion.

My nap extended all the way to five p.m. Even though I'd needed the rest, I was horrified at myself for sleeping the day away.

I might not be a morning person, but I did consider myself to be a day person.

I tried to tell myself it was okay, a nap was completely understandable due to the stress of Adam catching up with me—oh, and the corpse—but it didn't make me feel any better, and great. I was back to thinking about Adam again.

The text message and brusque voicemail I found waiting for me from Detective Nash didn't make me feel much better.

I slumped on the edge of the rumpled bed and called him back at the number provided, wondering what fresh horror he had for me.

"Nash," he said.

"Hello, Detective. This is Ray Underwood, returning your call."

In a dramatic change from how things were going thus far, Nash had good news for me.

"...and that's it?" I said. My tired gaze had drifted around the room while Nash was talking, and had landed on the generic landscape that hung on the wall opposite the window. It hurt my graphic designer's soul. It probably hurt everyone's soul. "I can go home?"

"That's it," he confirmed.

"Huh."

"You're welcome."

"Right. Thank you for letting me know. And for removing the body."

"All part of the job."

"Where...where is he?"

"At the hospital mortuary."

Something other than Adam and the honeymooners had kept me awake last night. I didn't want to ask in case I didn't like the answer, but on balance, not knowing was worse. "Was he murdered *there*? In my room?"

"I'm not at liberty to say."

"Are you at liberty to hint?"

"No." Nash cleared his throat. "You can go ahead and return home whenever you like."

I clutched the phone, pressing it hard against my face. I knew better. I kept hanging up on people or randomly opening apps with my cheekbones.

But I was freaking out a bit here, okay? It had taken a while for it to sink in that not only was the poor guy stuffed in a tub and nailed under my bedroom floorboards, but he could have expired right there.

Things like that left a mark on the world, didn't they? They had to. What if...what if he was restless? A restless spirit?

I didn't realise I'd spoken the last bit out loud until Nash sighed in my ear. "Are you talking about ghosts?"

"Yes!"

"I'm sorry, Mr Underwood, but ghosts are not in my job description. You know who to call."

My face twisted in suspicion. "*Ghostbusters*? Was that a joke? Are you making fun of me?"

"Absolutely not. I am a police officer. I have no sense of humour whatsoever. Mr Underwood, I'm off duty, and I really don't have any more information for you."

"Oh. Of course, sorry. You'll keep me updated on how it goes, then?"

"Yes. Although you should be aware that, as you are not

personally involved in the crime, there are limits to what I can share."

"I feel pretty involved, detective. I've been living with the man for five years. My house was a crime scene."

"Thank you for your co-operation. Goodbye, Mr Underwood."

"Good—oh." He was gone.

I stared at the landscape picture a bit longer.

It was growing on me.

Eventually, I packed up my overnight bag, which seemed to have exploded and flung its contents everywhere, and headed down to Reception.

Adam stood behind the desk.

"Exactly how long are your shifts, anyway?" I said with a scowl.

His attention flickered to my bag and back. "Checking out early?" he asked. "You'll still be charged for the room overnight."

"Yes, yes, I know. And yes, I'm checking out."

"Issues at home resolved, are they?" He turned to the screen and tapped at the keyboard.

Issues at home. That was one way of putting it. "If you mean have they moved the crime scene tape and can I go back in, then yes."

"And the dead guy?"

"They took him away yesterday. I don't know why I even had to leave. It's not like I'd just killed him and they had blood spatter patterns to photograph and skin cells to scrape up. It wasn't that kind of crime scene."

"If they thought you'd killed the guy, Ray, you'd have spent the night in custody while they were gathering evidence, not the Premier Lodge."

"Bet the coffee's better in prison."

"Ah. You're a snob about coffee as well as hotels. How very unsurprising."

"I am not a snob about anything, will you stop saying that?"

"Our coffee is perfectly decent."

"Your coffee comes in freeze-dried granules, in little sachets. That's not decent. It's a travesty."

His lips twitched. "You are very high maintenance."

I strode forward and bumped into the desk, even though I knew it was what he wanted me to do. I could tell by the way his hazel eyes glinted. "I am incredibly laidback and easy to please!"

"If you say so."

"I do say so! I am laidback!"

He ran his gaze over me in that distant, assessing way that should not have made me as hot as it did. His cheeks were tinted faintly pink. "I haven't seen any evidence of that," he said. "Perhaps I should lay you on your back and find out for myself quite how easy to please you are."

That was a terrible, terrible line. It was awful. I wasn't aroused by it at all. I was staring at him wordlessly from being stunned at how embarrassed I was for him, coming out with a line that bad.

Okay, fine. My brain just vaporised.

For whatever reason, being in Adam's presence lowered my IQ. I was perpetually flustered. It was probably his flawless beauty. I was probably too close to it, that was what was wrong, and it was warping reality. Once again, I was mashed up against the desk, all but climbing over it as I vibrated up at him in anger.

"Do you wear makeup?" I said suddenly.

Case in point. That was not a normal thing to ask a man

you didn't know, regardless of how unnaturally even and poreless his skin was.

Adam gave a tiny huff of amusement and his cheeks bunched under his eyes, which sparkled.

He was practically anime.

"On occasion," he said.

Which I hadn't expected, at all, despite my stupid question, and now the thought of it was *doing* things to me.

I shifted from one foot to the other." Are you wearing any now?"

I had a sneaking suspicion that my obsession over Adam's appearance was an avoidance tactic, but I was embracing it. Hard. Like a barnacle. The way I thought of it was like this: I could stare at Adam's beautiful face, or I could keep getting flashbacks to staring down into the hole in the floorboards and seeing an infinitely less beautiful face.

I chose Adam.

"No," he said. "I'm not."

"Are you sure?"

"Yes."

I gave him a sceptical look.

"You don't believe me?" He was highly amused.

"I think you're caked in Maybelline. In fact, it's a bit patchy. You might want to blend. Right here." I gestured at his jawline.

Adam caught my hand. I froze. He carried my hand over the distance between us, eyes intent on mine, and pressed it to his cheek.

I was...cupping his face.

His cool fingers slipped down to circle my wrist. My gaze dropped from his and I stared at my hand on him.

He really was like a freaking peach.

I realised I'd said it out loud when he replied, "Thank you. You should feel my arse sometime."

It took a second for his words to percolate. As soon as they did, it was like a sucker punch of want low in my belly.

"Well?" he said.

"What? I..."

"Clean skin," he said, and rubbed his cheek against my palm. Tauntingly. "I always hated having to wear foundation," he said.

"Who...why would you wear foundation? Who made you?"

He seemed annoyed at himself for a moment and answered flatly, "Photographers."

"You're a model." Water is wet, the sky is blue. Adam is a model. It all tracked.

"Was. I did some stuff. A while ago. It doesn't matter. I never wear foundation, that's the point." He distracted me by rubbing into my palm again.

I don't *think* I moaned. "What do you wear, then?" My voice was thin and breathless

"A bit of mascara on occasion. Sometimes lip balm. Sometimes tinted lip balm."

My gaze went from his long tawny lashes to his mouth. Like he knew it would. He smirked, and then very slowly licked his plump bottom lip.

My hand twitched. I wanted to trace the damp, smiling curve of it with my thumb. Adam expected me to, I could tell.

So I didn't.

I pulled my hand away and took a long step back from the desk. "Congratulations on the excellent genes, I suppose," I said. I pulled my laptop bag around to cover the absolutely disgraceful boner that was going to make walking out of here uncomfortable.

To my ego's delight, I wasn't the only one thwarted. Adam's peachy cheeks (his face cheeks, I fumed at myself, don't you dare think of his naked arse) flushed with a delicious wash of subtle rose. He glared at me, then his attention cut to the couple coming in.

"If you'll step aside and let me check in these guests, I'll process you after—"

"Nope." I tapped the desk. "Nice try, though. I'm here first." I turned to the new arrivals. "You guys aren't going to push in front of me or anything, are you?"

"Of course not!" the woman said, scandalised.

Adam sent everyone a tight smile.

Hah, I thought. A point for Ray. Suck it, sunshine.

For a horrifying moment, and based on the calculating look Adam shot me, I thought that once again I'd spoken out loud.

A quick check on the murmuring couple waiting at a polite distance behind me showed them unbothered.

"There we go, sir," Adam said. "All checked out." He slid a small folder with the receipt in over the desk. He kept a hand on it until I looked up. Holding my gaze, he slipped a business card inside. "If there's anything else you need from us, please don't hesitate to get in touch."

His expression was bland. His eyes were intense.

I dragged the receipt out from under his hand. "Thanks," I said. "But I can't imagine needing your services again."

"Hmm," he said.

I'd moved away but at that smug, irritating hum I ducked back to add, "Sweet of you, though. But I won't."

"We'll see."

"Ha ha. No, we won't."

"Enjoy sleeping in a gravesite."

"*What?*"

"Hope you don't get haunted. Restless spirits. Disturbed resting place. Angry ghosts and all that." He plastered a professional smile on his stupid face and waved the couple up to the desk. "Good evening, madam. How may I help you?"

"You absolute fucking arsehole," I said, wonderingly.

The couple gasped.

I stormed out.

7

The crime scene tape had been removed, which was a promising start. I still hesitated on the doorstep. I jiggled my house keys nervously and glanced around.

I felt like I was about to break the law, which was ridiculous. It was my house. I had permission and a legal right to go in there. I just didn't want to.

At all.

My fingers tightened around the handle of my overnight bag.

Either I manned up and went in there, or I had to go crawling back to Adam. To the Premier Lodge, I mean.

I couldn't get my key in the lock quickly enough.

This was fine. I could do this. It was fine.

I let myself in, closed the door, and stood there with my back pressed to it, clutching my bag to my chest.

It smelled like other people in here. Like forensics specialists and policemen. Like the Law.

I also detected a faint mustiness that I told myself was

definitely my imagination and absolutely was not what a mummy smelled like.

Even if it was horrifyingly similar to the air in the Egyptian gallery in the Ashmolean Museum.

Because *that* was the smell of a specially filtered and temperature-controlled environment, not old dead people.

It was my imagination, I told myself, again, and lit every single scented candle I possessed. Which was a lot. I'm a nightmare to buy presents for. Everyone always seems to default to candles. And handmade journals. Usually from Italy, for some reason.

I puttered around in the kitchen for a bit. After supper I did a little work to make up for my lack of focus (nap) earlier in the day. I was feeling stout and brave all the way up to nine p.m., at which point I glumly concluded that I couldn't avoid it any longer.

One way or another, I had to go upstairs.

I couldn't spend the night sleeping on the sofa. Not if I wanted to walk upright the next day.

I switched on all the lights and stomped up the stairs. Before I could chicken out, I hung a left into my bedroom and stopped abruptly.

"You bastards," I said blankly.

Was it *so* outrageous of me to have expected them to put things back in order? Was it?

They didn't have to finish laying the carpet, or shove the bed back into place and make it for me, but come on. Could they not have at least put the floorboards back?

Two long narrow planks were all that had been levered up when Craig and Kevin and I found the body.

Now, practically the whole damn room had been pulled up. The majority of my bedroom floor was a ragged hole.

I hoped they had a complaint form or a suggestion box

at the station, because I planned on being down there first thing in the morning.

The air was sour with old dust and chilled damp creeping up from the exposed underfloor. Craig's tools and toolbox were still there, along with the tea tray with empty mugs and a crumb-strewn plate. Floorboards had been shoved to the edges of the room, piled up any old how. It was a wreck.

I left my cosy eighty-bloody-quid-a-night room at the Premier Lodge for this?

I flung around, slapped the light off as I went, then thought better of it and smacked it back on again. Leaving it burning, I took myself and my overnight bag into the small guest room next door.

I got into my pjs, did the usual in the bathroom, changed the sheets on the bed because I couldn't remember when I last had, and slid under the covers with a sigh. I clasped my hands over my stomach and stared up at the ceiling.

I'd left the Velux blind open for the ambient light, not wanting to lie there in complete darkness. Soft silver moonlight filtered through the trees outside and dappled my bed.

So calm. *So* calm. Is what I was.

There was no need to be anything other than calm, really. He'd been there under the boards the whole time I'd lived here, hadn't he? The dead man? Nothing bad had happened before. There was no reason to think anything bad would happen now.

I pondered writing a strongly worded letter to the surveyor who had inspected the property before I closed on it. He'd given a hearty thumbs up. Okay, checking for dead bodies probably wasn't part of the process.

But it should be.

I couldn't help but wonder what else he'd missed. Wood-worm? Black mould?

A portal to Hell?

A board creaked in the room next door.

Every hair on my body prickled to quivering attention. My clasped hands spasmed, my heart pounded, and my head whipped to face the closed door.

My eyes locked onto the door handle.

If it moved, I was going to shit myself. No question.

I shouldn't have closed the door, should I? It had seemed like the right move when I did it. The way the bed was placed, I had a view straight out onto the landing from where I lay. I'd closed the door because I didn't want to be staring out there waiting for movement to flicker in the corner of my eye.

But now I was lying here thinking that a ghost was standing on the other side.

I'd once read that the anticipation of a jump-scare was worse than the scare itself.

Can confirm.

My breathing picked up, hot and desperate.

This room was at the very top of the house. I had two options for escape. I could go out the door—thus having to pass through any spectral beings loitering on the landing—or I could go out the window.

It opened onto the flat roof of my bathroom. Knowing my luck, if I climbed out onto it, I'd fall through and get stuck at the waist, legs kicking in the bathroom below, and the ghost coming at me from above.

I strained my ears, staring at the door until it wavered like a heat shimmer on a summer road.

Nothing happened.

Of course nothing happened. The boards always

creaked. It had never bothered me before. It was an old house kind of thing.

It was also possible that nerves were making me extra dramatic right now.

First I ran into Adam at The Lion. Then I gazed down into the floor of my bedroom and saw a dead guy in a tub, like the last biscuit in the tin no one wanted. Then I walked into the Premier Lodge only to be confronted once again with the beautiful boy who was better than me in every possible way, and my genius response was to kiss him.

I was a man on the edge, clearly.

In the room next door, another board creaked.

I gripped my hands tighter together and looked away from the door long enough to glance at my phone on the bedside table.

You know who to call, Detective Nash had said, making his shitty *Ghostbusters* joke.

Joke was on him: I had his number in my phone, and very little pride right now.

I was calling him if I got even a fraction more freaked out.

The peace of the night was shattered by a shrill blare of jangling sound.

I flailed under the covers, yanking them over my head. My ears roared with a rush of adrenaline-spiked blood. My heart raced. I panted into the blackness.

The noise continued.

A faint glow seeped between the crack made between the mattress and duvet when I bravely lifted it a millimetre.

For fuck's sake.

I tossed the covers back and lunged for my phone. Sitting up, I pushed my hair back off my hot face and stared at the screen.

I didn't recognise the number. It wasn't in my contacts.

Normally, I wouldn't answer an unknown caller, based on the theory that if it was important enough, they'd leave a voicemail.

But, you know. Times were not normal. I answered.

"Hello?" I said cautiously.

"Hey."

"Hi."

"Hello."

"If this is a prank call you need to work on your material," I snapped.

"It's not a prank call, Ray."

Adam. My stomach tightened in visceral recognition at the sound of my name in his deep voice. "*Adam*?"

Someone rang my doorbell.

I scrambled up onto my knees. "Is that you?"

He laughed. "Yes, it's me. I'm on your doorstep. Come down here and let me in."

I was already halfway down the stairs.

8

"What are you even doing here?" I said into the phone as I went to open the door. I gave it a tug, but of course it was locked. "Hang on." I hung up, snagged my house keys, and unlocked the door. The deadbolt. The Yale lock. The second deadbolt.

"That's a lot of locks," Adam remarked, smiling down at me. "Hi."

I didn't know why I was happy to see him, considering I'd been calling him an arsehole not that long ago, but happy I was. "Hi." I swallowed. He'd looked hot in his stupid uniform—in spite of his stupid uniform—but in his own clothes it was worse.

Ripped jeans, heavy boots, his leather jacket.

A motorcycle helmet dangled from his fingers.

"You have a bike," I said. "Why am I not surprised?"

"It's cheaper than a car."

"It's also more likely to kill you."

"Nice of you to care. My bank balance doesn't." Adam nudged me gently backward, waited a split second to see if I was going to put up a fuss—and I might have, if he'd waited the actual whole second—and muscled inside.

He dropped his helmet on the hall table beneath the mirror, ran his hands through his bright hair with a critical look, and turned to me.

"Your hair is fine," I said dryly.

He cocked his head then tilted it downward at an exaggerated angle. "Why are you so short?" he said.

"Because I'm barefoot and those boots give you at least another two inches? You may as well be wearing heels." Two inches was an exaggeration, but they weren't exactly ballet flats. They were closer to construction worker's boots.

He snorted. Holding my gaze, he unzipped his boots and pulled them off. He set them alongside mine under the hall table. He stepped into me, stopping before our bodies touched. "Still short."

"You're a beanpole," I said, holding out a hand for the jacket he shrugged off. I hung it on a spare coat hook. "Have you even stopped growing yet?" I headed for the kitchen.

"Yes, Ray, I am fully matured." He followed me.

"Do you want coffee? No, it's too late for coffee. I don't have decaf. Hot chocolate?" I busied myself filling the kettle.

"Hot chocolate works," he said.

I fussed around, taking down mugs and spooning in the hot chocolate while the kettle boiled, feeling his curious eyes tracking me all the while. "How do you have my number?"

"How do you think? I got it off your hotel booking."

"That sounds very illegal."

"It is."

He was utterly unrepentant.

"Let's make it fair," he said. He lifted his hips and took

his phone out of his back pocket. Holding it up at an angle, he pulled a ridiculous face and snapped a photo. His fingers flew, and from out in the hallway where I'd left my own phone, I heard a faint ping. "There's my number *and* a great photo for your contacts."

I gave a nervous laugh and turned back to my very important drink making preparations.

My heart was still racing. There was some lingering fear from earlier in there, but I wasn't kidding myself. It was ninety-five percent Adam-induced.

This didn't happen to me. Hot guys tracking me down at arse-o-clock in the morning for...oh. *Ohhh.*

Was this a booty call?

I'd never really done the booty call thing. How would I know?

...did I want it to be a booty call?

"Everything okay over there?"

I jumped at Adam's voice. "Everything is great," I said breezily.

"Mm-hmm. The reason I ask is because you've been staring at the kettle for two minutes. It's already boiled."

"Right." I clapped my hands together. "Yes! Hot chocolate, coming up."

I added the water and stirred until I couldn't put it off any longer, stiffened my backbone, and carried the mugs over to the table. Adam lounged at his leisure, looking all princely with his hair and his face and everything, completely relaxed.

I'd have been irritated by how much more at home he was in my kitchen than me, except his eyes were soft as he watched me cross the room.

"Here you go," I said. "Now, it's not freeze-dried, like I

know you prefer your beverages, but it *is* powdered and it *did* come out of a jar. Enjoy."

Adam grinned as I passed him a mug. It was my very best Cornishware, with distinctive thick bands of blue and white, and I was not trying to impress him.

If I was trying to impress him, I'd have offered him some marshmallows.

"So," I said, sitting opposite him. "What can I do for you at one o'clock in the morning?"

If he said blow job…I was probably going to give him one.

"It's more a case of what I can do for you, actually," he said.

If *I* said blow job, would he…?

Eyes on mine, Adam set his full lips to the rim of the cup and took a long sip of the hot chocolate. He made a strangled noise and lunged for the sink. He spat it out, ran the tap, and drank from it.

I followed him over to the sink and dithered beside him. "Are you okay?" He grunted and gave me a short nod, but he didn't stop drinking from the tap.

I laid a tentative hand on his back and rubbed it in soothing circles.

Adam turned off the tap. Slowly, he straightened, dragged his sleeve over his wet mouth and jaw, and stared at me.

"It's called *hot* chocolate for a reason," I told him. "You're supposed to blow on it—"

Adam's eyes flashed, he pushed me up against the counter, held my face, and kissed me.

"Ow, fuck," he said, pulling back.

I winced. "I'm pretty sure first aid for a burned tongue is not to stick it in someone else's mouth—mmph!"

He kissed me again, and whimpered. "Ow, *fuck*."

"Adam." I pressed my hand to his lips when he tried again and shook my head. "No," I said. "Stop hurting yourself."

He fumed silently, then removed my hand. "Fine," he grumbled. "I'll kiss you without tongue."

I gave him a sceptical look. "I'm not sure you'll be able to control yourself," I said. And I didn't want him to hurt himself again.

"Let me try."

I narrowed my eyes at him. Adam squeezed my hips, which he was holding between his big hands, and lightly bumped his pelvis into mine.

We were both very clearly into it. And yet...

"Why are you here?" I said. "I thought maybe you came to taunt me some more, maybe to indulge in a spot more emotional torture as a nice way to relax after your workday. Now I'm thinking...?"

"Are you finishing that sentence? Because, Ray, trust me when I say I have no idea what you're thinking. I can't tell if you want to slap me or shag me. You like my face, I can tell that much. But a lot of people like my stupid face, so it's not all that helpful."

"You're not too far off the mark," I said, squirming out from between Adam and the counter. "I do want to slap you half the time."

"And the other thing?"

I shot him a glare.

He returned it with a cocky grin.

"Where do you get your confidence?" I marvelled. "You're not smooth. Two minutes ago, you were drinking from my tap like Mrs Hughes's Westie, Dougal, drinks from the garden hose. Your t-shirt is soaked, you made such a mess."

"Yes," he said, "but I did it sexy."

I didn't even bother to argue. Yes. Somehow, he had indeed managed to make lapping water from the tap with his head all but stuffed in my sink sexy.

I sat at the table and sipped my hot (now lukewarm) chocolate with a deliberate display of caution.

"Can I have a glass of milk to soothe the burn?" he asked, then waved me down with a tut of irritation when I half-stood. "I can get it, Ray." He leaned over and opened the cupboard where I kept my glasses, snagged one, and took it to the fridge to fill it with milk.

At the fearsome scowl on my face when he turned back to the table, Adam hesitated.

Firming his jaw, he strode over, kicked the chair out, and threw himself into it.

Neither of us spoke. Adam drank the whole glass in long, slow pulls, his eyes on me, and set it down with a clink.

"You have a milk moustache," I said into the ringing silence.

"Come here and kiss it off."

"Ew."

He laughed at that, licked it away without even trying to be sexy—I mean, he still really, really was—and slumped.

"I came to apologise, Ray," he said.

"For what?" I said. "For being an arsehole today? Or for being an arsehole last year?" I pointed accusingly at the cupboard. "It did not escape my attention that you know where the glasses are kept. You went straight there. I didn't even have to tell you."

Adam shoved his chair back and got to his feet. He stalked around the table.

Reaching down, he grabbed my chin and held it firmly as his eyes bored into me. From this close, I could see that the golden hazel had a thick black limbal ring around the irises. He slid his thumb along my jaw, and nudged my chin higher.

My hands went up and held his wrist. I didn't try to pull him away. I held on.

Adam smiled at me. It was heated and bitter. "I thought this was Fraser's house. I thought he lived here alone. I thought he was free, single, and down to fuck."

Well, that was crude.

"I was furious when I learned about you."

"At the competition?" I said.

"God, you're obtuse." He sank into a crouch with fluid grace and placed his hands on my thighs. He dug in his fingers.

The view looking down into his upturned face really was something. I couldn't help it. I touched his cheek, fleetingly. He turned into it but I'd already drawn away.

He heaved another of those sighs. It was a mix of eye-rolling youth and world-weary man, and I didn't know what to do with it.

He squeezed my thighs, still balancing on his toes. "Let's get this back on track. Ray, I'm here to apologise for scaring you earlier," he said.

What did he mean, earlier?

"Earlier when we were at the hotel," he clarified.

My stomach lurched. How humiliating. I *knew* he'd been able to tell that he'd psyched me out and thrown me into a sexual panic. "Oh, I wasn't afraid." Like hell was I going to admit it. "I'm confident. I'm a confident sexual man. You didn't scare me even a bit. It was a kiss and some banter. I can handle you."

He hummed thoughtfully. "I wish you *would* handle me. I wasn't talking about erotic fear, though."

My mouth dropped open a little at his words. *Erotic fear?* It was the perfect description, but good lord. I was aroused, intimidated, and scared all over again.

Adam's eyes tracked down to my mouth and back up. His lips curled. "I meant for freaking you out about the dead guy, not for flirting with you at the hotel."

"Oh. Yeah. That was shitty."

"Which is why I'm here." He rubbed my thighs then stood up. He did it slowly, sinuously, giving me aaaall the time I needed to get a jolly good look at his lithe, flexing body. My gaze came to rest at his groin, which was, most conveniently, at eye level.

I stared.

He was definitely hard.

I stared some more and managed to tear my gaze away when he stepped back. He shot me an amused, heated look from under his lashes.

Freed from his proximity and the sheer magnetism no one so young should have, my head cleared. I was about to cordially invite him to leave when he said, "Let's see the crime scene, then. Where is it?"

I shuddered. "There isn't much to see, you vulture. As I said at the hotel, it's not like there's blood splatter everywhere. It's a ragged hole in the floor. Very uninteresting. Also, should we be calling it a crime scene? There was no crime committed there."

"Let's see the grave, then. Where is it?"

I stared up at him, horrified. The *grave*.

In my bedroom floor.

"Ray."

"Huh? Oh. It's in the master bedroom."

"Yikes," Adam said with a wince.

"Yeah."

"Come on."

"Wait," I called after him. "Adam!"

It was too late. He was already out of the kitchen and heading for the stairs.

chased after him. "You coming here was a ruse to get a look at a grisly true-crime location, wasn't it?" I said to his beautiful round arse as I followed him up the stairs.

He snorted and to my surprise went the wrong way, walking straight into the guest room. Hands on hips, he stared at the bed. The covers were tossed aside from when I'd scrambled down to answer the door, and the pillows were askew. "Ray, did you tidy up the crime scene and re-lay the carpet? Were you allowed to?"

"No. I don't know if I'm allowed to. I think I am? Detective Nash said the scene was 'released', anyway. You're in the wrong room. This isn't the master bedroom."

"It's not?"

"No. It's the guest room." Thank goodness. If Adam thought this was the master bedroom, it meant that Fraser hadn't been crass enough to have sex with his boy toy in our bed.

Wait.

If they didn't do it in my bedroom then they must have

had sex in... My attention tracked over to the guest bed and I bristled.

Adam blocked my view, turned me around by the shoulders, and manhandled me out onto the landing.

"Did you—" I began indignantly.

"Nope. Of course we didn't. Come on."

"I was *just* in—"

"In here? Let's go." He pushed me into my room, reaching over my shoulder and groping for the light switch. Adam walked right up to the hole and peered down. I bumped into his back but kept him between it and me.

"He was right there?" Adam said.

"The whole time I've been living here," I confirmed. "I used to do my yoga there."

Adam let out a noise that sounded dangerously close to a giggle. "Unfortunate," was all he said.

"Yeah."

"Do you believe in ghosts?" When I didn't reply, he added, "If you do, you must be soooo embarrassed."

"Stop talking," I growled. "Or you're going in the hole."

"Think about what that poor guy has seen. Think about what he's heard."

It had crossed my mind.

I'd decided for my sanity and in the service of absolute denial that I didn't believe in ghosts as such, but a person's bedroom was their private place. Their inner sanctum. It was where you should be able to do whatever you want. Snore, cry, be vulnerable. Have an ill-fated pity party.

Be intimate.

All of the above without an uninvited audience.

"Think how many times he's had to hear you having a wank," Adam said, and yelped when I poked him in the kidney.

"And how many times he had to watch you bounce around on my boyfriend like a cowboy on a wild mustang, homewrecker."

Adam whirled around to clutch at me when I poked him, like we were kids pretending to push each other into a puddle or something.

"If only the ghost had been able to communicate," I said with a dramatic sigh. "Think of the pain that could have been spared."

Adam was holding my upper arms, his head at a curious angle. "Even if the corpse in your bedroom floor could have communicated with you, Ray, he'd never have told you about me bouncing around on your boyfriend."

I chewed my lip. "You think he was on Fraser's side? He preferred Fraser?" I said.

Most people did, even after he weaselled off to Wantage and I was left living in a place that suddenly made me feel like a stranger. Unfortunately, all of my financial assets were sunk into the house. Whether I belonged or not, here I would remain.

Possibly forever, because how the hell was I going to offload a murder house?

I glared up at Adam.

He returned my glare with amusement. He bumped me and proceeded to back me out of the room. "I meant that I never rode your boyfriend like a cowboy, Ray." He bent down and bit my lip gently. "I'm a top."

Until that moment, I didn't think that I could have wanted Adam more.

Apparently, I could.

The idea of having Adam under me, of looking down into his beautiful face and tenderly taking him as a worldly wise and experienced older lover had been clamouring for my attention for longer than I cared to admit.

The idea of having Adam hold me down while he moved in me, over me, hit me with all the subtlety of an unexpected slap to the balls.

I was violently aroused.

"Thought it was Fraser fucking me, did you?" he said with an edge. "What on earth gave you that impression? Because I'm younger than him? Because I'm prettier? You do know that's not how it works, don't you?"

We'd made it into the guest room and he'd been inexorably backing me across the room. My legs hit the bed and I glanced down. He reclaimed my attention with a soft *ah* noise and a finger under my chin.

I jerked my chin up. "What on earth gave you the impression that I know how any of this works?" I said. I'd intended it to come out as sassy. It sounded lost.

"Then allow me to educate you, Ray," Adam said, and pushed me backward. I hit the bed.

He crawled over me, somehow managing to get an arm beneath me and slide me up the mattress. I was breathless with the show of strength and, oh god, that confidence again. I'd say arrogance, but...it wasn't.

It was certainty.

There were few things I found more attractive than self-assurance and certainty.

I gazed up into his face. "Fraser never let me fuck him," I said.

Adam's mouth was soft, his eyes sympathetic yet guarded. "Did you want to?" He settled his weight on me and I relaxed under it with a wash of relief.

"Sometimes."

Adam looked at me.

"Fine. Once. I didn't... I prefer..."

"You finishing that sentence?"

"No, actually. I have no idea what I'm saying. I have no idea what I'm doing. What *am* I doing? I'm lying under a hotel receptionist preparing to share my sexual preferences." My breathing was fast and ragged. "Adam. None of this was on my calendar. This is *not* how my Tuesday was supposed to go."

Adam pressed more of his weight into me. My arms came up and locked around his waist.

"Yesterday morning, my biggest problem was whether or not Craig would get the job done in one day or if it would end up being a two-day thing, and would I have to go and buy more Hobnobs. Then he pulled up the floorboards, an exceedingly unlikely chain of events ensued, and somehow I'm here."

"I'd say things are on the up," Adam murmured.

I squinted at him. "You're talking about my dick, aren't you?"

He laughed, open and honest. "No. I mean, yeah, it's up —" he rolled his hips into mine and I moaned, "—but I meant the body's gone, it's all been dealt with, and you can move on."

"Adam," I said.

"Hmm?" He rocked into me again.

"Why are you here?"

He stilled. "Really, Ray? You're really asking me that? I'm lying between your thighs right now. You can't guess?"

I didn't know Adam well. Or, you know, at all. But it struck me that he got extra sarcastic when he didn't want to give me an answer.

To distract me further, he shifted over me again. It was a

slow, slooooow drag of his hips over mine; my hands grabbed for his arse.

"Oh," he said, pleased.

He was less pleased when I let go and pinched one taut cheek instead. "This is a pity fuck, isn't it?" I said. "You feel sorry for me."

"I felt bad for scaring you about ghosts and I decided to check up on you."

"You felt guilty."

"Not actual guilt," he said with a smile. It was a patient, sweet smile. And condescending.

Also radiant.

His lean muscles pressed down against my so, so very slightly softer body. His hair shone. His skin glowed. Why did I fixate on it so much? Did I have a skin fetish? Kink? Was that a thing? I'd be telling him to rub lotion on any minute.

A flash fire of heat scorched through me at the thought of Adam and lotion.

I shoved that particular image way, way down.

Adam was so out of my league it was insane.

And I didn't even subscribe to the idea of *leagues* of hotness or nonsense like that.

I had robust enough self-esteem. I was an average-looking guy. I had nice brown eyes and a decent body. Personality-wise, I was a harder sell. I could be fussy. People tend to run out of patience sooner rather than later. But on the surface at least, I was a nice guy.

Average, you know?

There was not one thing about me that should attract the attention of someone like Adam.

He couldn't want me for me.

He felt guilty for the Fraser thing, he felt guilty for the

ghost thing, and I was obviously out of my depth and smitten with him. Why *wouldn't* he come here for a quick orgasm after work?

You know what? I had my pride, dammit. I wanted to be wanted for me. Not as an apology, a duty, a convenience.

"I don't want a pity fuck, thank you all the same," I said. "Or a guilty fuck."

Adam's eyes narrowed. "I already told you that's not why I'm here."

"I don't believe you." I shoved at him. He caught my wrists and pulled my arms over my head.

Oh no.

The sexy pinning move.

I was in so much trouble.

Adam gave me a smug smile. I heaved up against him.

"Settle," he told me.

Okay, now Adam was in trouble. I made a noise like an angry cat. "Listen, Junior—"

He ducked down and sucked a hard kiss on my mouth. "Don't call me that."

"Listen," I gasped when he pulled back, eyes dark, "*Junior*. We need to get one thing straight."

"Do not call me that, Ray," he said.

"Or what?" I scoffed.

"I'll spank you."

My vision wavered. I heard a high-pitched whistling in my ears. Every cell in my body realigned itself with Adam as the magnetic pole.

I'd never been spanked in my life.

I'd never even thought about being spanked.

"What?" I said feebly. "You will not."

"You'll have to ask me very, very nicely."

"Which I will not do! Ever!"

"We'll see."

"Ever! I have absolutely zero desire to be spanked by a...a...an adolescent."

"That was weak." He stroked a hand down the side of my heaving ribs and held my waist with a firm hand. "We both know I'm in my twenties."

"Barely! By a matter of months!"

"Thirty-six, actually."

"What?"

"Thirty-six months into my twenties, Ray." He smiled. "Are you counting?"

I was trying.

"Oh." I gasped when he rocked down into me, then smacked him on the shoulder. "I'm not in a maths headspace right now."

"It was more logic than maths," Adam said. "And you started it. Never mind. I hear your cognitive abilities begin to fade as you get old."

I hitched a leg up and around his hip. He was moving with intent, flexing his spine and pushing rhythmically into me. And I was pushing back.

I'd stop him any minute now.

"I don't want your pity sex," I said.

"It's not pity sex or guilt sex."

"Then I really don't know why you're here."

"You really don't?"

"No," I said.

His face had frozen into a distant, beautiful mask.

"Unless it's for the convenience," I said in a small voice. I had an uncomfortable feeling that I'd offended and disappointed him.

"You're hard work, Ray," he said. "There's not one thing convenient about you."

"Okay, ouch." Now I was offended. I'd heard a variation on that more than once.

We had a glare-off.

"How about some hate sex?" Adam said. We were still sliding against each other. His hips ground into me with steady pulses. He pushed in hard then moved in tiny, taunting circles.

My neck arched, fingers scrabbling at his back.

"That sounds—" like a terrible idea, "—doable?" My voice quavered up at the end. "Wait. Oh, shit." He'd snatched his t-shirt off already. That was fast. "Nothing too intimate," I said.

"Wouldn't want that."

"You can't...I don't want you to fuck me."

Lie. I wanted it so badly.

But if we stopped to get our clothes off, or at least get our pants down and the condoms out, I'd come to my senses, and an orgasm was barrelling down on me.

"Fine." Adam hauled my t-shirt up, got it shoved up under my armpits, and bent down to bite a nipple.

"Hhnn," I said.

"Yeah. That's what I thought."

I pushed and pushed at his shoulders. He snatched my wrists and pinned my arms again, thumping my hands either side of my head. He stared down at me.

"We can just rub off on each other," I told him.

"I got it."

Our bare stomachs slid together. I was definitely getting the better part of the deal; I was in sweatpants, and he was still in jeans.

"It's just friction," I said. "You could be anyone."

"What the hell, Ray?"

"I mean we're both here for the orgasm. As long as everyone's clear, it doesn't matter if that's all it is."

He shook his head. "You should probably stop talking, or I'm gonna leave you high and dry."

He was shaking against me. I didn't think he could stop right now for anything. I knew I couldn't.

"Maybe you'd better stop me talking, then." I was not so subtly angling for a kiss. Adam pushed my wrists harder into the mattress and leaned back when I went for it.

"No," he said. "I want you saying my name when I make you come. I want you to know who's here with you. I'm not having you pretend. You're not going to close your eyes and pretend I'm anyone."

"I know who you are," I said.

Adam's breath feathered over my lips. He angled his head and dropped a soft kiss into my waiting mouth.

He slowed down.

"No, no," I said." Noooo. Keep going. What are you doing?"

He moved against me in fluid thrusts, but his urgency had faded. Mine had ratcheted up. My need to orgasm was clawing at me like an animal. If he didn't get back up to speed, *I'd* be clawing at Adam like an animal, and then I'd have no self-respect left at all.

"I'm taking my time, Ray," he said.

"Okay, but can we get back on track? Because some of us have to work tomorrow. It's late. I need sleep."

He gazed down at me. "We'll go at my pace," he said, and kissed me tenderly.

I seethed with a mix of physical need, indignation at his dominating attitude—*we'll go at my pace*, who did he think he was?—even greater indignation that I didn't laugh in his face about it, and more of that fear.

Erotic fear, yes.

But worse. Emotional fear.

He was staring into my eyes. Right in. He was staring at me like he could see everything, like I was lying there and giving it all up.

And I couldn't read him for shit.

I closed my eyes.

"Look at me, Ray,"

"No, thank you."

"Don't you think I'm pretty?" He kissed me and murmured against my lips, "I know you do. I'm blushing for you, Ray. Don't you want to see my pretty blush?"

My eyes popped open. "That was low." He knew I was bedazzled by him. He'd sounded resigned, amused, a bit bitter about it. "You are very manipulative."

Also, that wasn't a blush. You had to feel at least a grain of self-consciousness for it to be a blush, and he didn't have it in him. It was a sex flush.

He hummed. "I do what I must to get what I want. And I always get what I want. I'll use any tool necessary."

"Wow," I said, eyes wide. "Unsettling."

He flashed me a bright grin, wide and dimpled. "True, though."

"Uh-huh. Well, you want an orgasm, I'm right here to use. Come on, Junior. Let's get this show on the road." I got a good grip on his arse and hauled him against me, hard.

Adam went rigid above me.

His smile had vanished. His face was once again that distant and intimidating mask of perfection. He caught my jaw, pressed his thumb into my lower lip and glared down his nose at me.

The air in the room was charged and crackling. My hands fluttered up to lie flat on his chest, his skin scorching hot beneath my palms, his heart pounding. I wasn't pushing him away. I wasn't drawing him back down, either.

"Uh—" I said.

He dipped his head and kissed me. His tongue pushed into my mouth and twisted over mine, his lips worked hard. He took a sharp breath in through his nose and broke away.

"I told you not to call me that," he said.

"What?"

"Three times. You need to listen, Ray."

I gaped at him.

Adam pushed up and off me, then rolled off the bed. He stood looking at me. "Are you scared?" he snapped.

"I mean, a little? If I'm honest?"

He shoved his hands into his hair.

"I can't help it. You're intense! I'm not used to this kind of —" I flapped a hand between us. "This is not as straightfor- ward as I'm used to."

Adam froze. "I didn't mean are you scared of *me*!"

"Oh." Awkward.

"Christ, what do you think of me?" He firmed his jaw. "Are you scared to be alone, Ray?"

"Sometimes. I suppose. Everyone gets lonely, though. I don't need to be with someone to be validated. I'm an inde- pendent—"

Adam made a strangled sound of frustration. "Right now. I meant right now. Here, alone in your murder house at night! Not for the rest of your life, what the fuck."

"In that case, no! "I yelled it at him. "I'm fine!"

"Are you sure!" he yelled back.

He closed the distance between us. I was up on my knees on the mattress. We were inches away from each other. "Yes!"

"Then sleep well. I'll see you around. Maybe."

"Wait—"

"If you get scared," he ground out, "call me. If you want to finish this—" he reached out and grasped my erection. I gasped and bucked my hips into his hand. He gave me a vicious smile, "—you're on your own."

"Has anyone ever told you that you're a drama queen?" I said. "Anyone? Ever?"

He dragged his lower lip in between his teeth and bit down. His nostrils flared.

"Because you are." I shoved a hand down the front of my sweatpants, holding his gaze. I gave myself a hard stroke. I didn't even mean to make the questioning moan that came out of me. I didn't hate it.

Neither did Adam. His sex flush darkened.

I stroked myself again, and I made it showy. "Are you going to watch?" I said politely.

Adam's burning gaze flicked up from my dick to my face. "No, thank you. I'll leave that to the ghost."

He stalked out.

I reached back, grabbed a pillow, and winged it at the back of his head.

I missed.

*D*enial. Sometimes, it's the only way to go.

This was definitely one of those times.

I wanted to put this whole nightmare behind me and pretend it never happened. It was proving impossible to do when there was a hole in my bedroom floor and the carpet I'd spent a fortune on—it was from John Lewis, but it wasn't cheap—was still rolled up nice and tight in its plastic shroud.

Wrapping.

In its plastic wrapping.

At first, once I'd grabbed a week's worth of clothes from my drawers and carried them into the guest room where I now lived, I kept the door to the master bedroom shut.

That just drew my attention to it whenever I was upstairs, achieving the opposite of what I wanted.

I called Detective Nash to double-check and see whether or not they were going to come and fix it.

He informed me that the police weren't the ones to make the hole. I was on my own.

Okay, they hadn't made it but they *had* widened it.

As soon as I had the go-ahead to fix it, I ended the call with Detective Nash and called Craig Henderson.

The phone rang a good few times before it went to voice mail. I left a message. I left another message the next day, and then again the next, backed up with a text.

After a full week, I'd stopped asking him to return my call at his convenience, and left a message saying that, as he had apparently finished the job, I was going to go ahead and leave him a review, how did that sound?

He called me back within ten minutes.

"Craig," I said. "What a delightful surprise." I wouldn't really have left him a shitty review. Craig didn't know that.

"Ray," he said. "How's it going?"

"Not great. There's a hole in my bedroom floor and a carpet waiting to be laid, and I wanted to get a timeline on when that's going to be taken care of."

"Uh. Sort of up to you, isn't it?"

"It is? Oh, good." And here I'd thought he was going to be a dick about it. You are a bitter man, Ray Underwood, I told myself. Have a little faith in humanity. He's been waiting for you to reschedule. "In that case can you get here by nine tomorrow?"

"Uh, no."

"Day after?"

"No as in I ain't coming back, Ray."

I blinked at my computer screen. "You're going to leave me with a big hole in my floor?"

"Yes. And I don't care what review you post." His voice took on a belligerent edge. "No one would blame me."

"I think a few people might."

"No one wants to work in a murder house, Ray."

"It's not a murder house!" It was one thing for me to call

it a murder house. When Craig said it, it was rude. "No one was murdered."

"That we know of. Unless you heard something from the police? They say anything?"

"Are you going to come and fix the hole if I tell you?"

"No."

"Then they didn't say anything."

"They did! What did they say?"

"Come and fix the hole and I'll spill."

"I can't do it, Ray. I'm sorry, but I can't. It's damaging to my wellbeing."

"Okay, and it's damaging to my household budget because I already paid you a deposit, and it was for you to lay a carpet, not make a hole in my bedroom floor!"

"I only did that because you asked me to. That was me being nice."

He had a point.

"What I'm going to do, Ray, is this. I'll refund you the deposit and we'll call it square. And I'm the one getting the raw end of this deal, what with me having wasted a whole day hard at work and getting nothing out of it."

He'd got a packet of Hobnobs out of it, which is not bad going for the actual hour and ten minutes of work they squeezed into the five hours they were here. Also, "My bedroom is unusable. I assure you I have the raw end of the deal here."

"I dunno what else to tell you, Ray. I'm refunding you the money. And because I'm a good guy—and your review, if you leave one, should definitely mention this—I'll give you the number of a buddy of mine. Mason will do anything for a couple of hundred."

With that somewhat unsettling recommendation, he read out a number I scrambled to jot down and hung up.

I wanted to be angrier than I was, but Craig hadn't signed up for discovering a body any more than I had. Unlike me, he could walk away.

I rang Craig's buddy, Mason. He showed up the very next day at eight a.m. and resurrected my faith in all contractors.

He was a complete dick who glared at me like I'd insulted his mother. He made a hell of a noise, used the bathroom eight times and only flushed once, and made me genuinely uncomfortable. But he packed up at the end of the day with the job done.

Most importantly, he got it done without throwing up.

And he didn't find a dead body.

"All right?" he grunted at me, having commanded me to come upstairs and check before he left.

I was impressed.

It was perfect. There wasn't a single ripple in the carpet. It flowed from one side of the room to the other, melding with the skirting boards without a gap to be seen, and he'd even hoovered it. He was a magician.

"It's great," I said. "Thank you so much!"

My big smile withered under his unrelenting glare, and I trailed him awkwardly out of the room and down the stairs.

When I said I'd call him with any other jobs that cropped up, he grimly instructed me not to, he didn't like murder houses any more than poor old Craig did, and that was that.

I SOON REALISED WHY CRAIG HADN'T BEEN TOO BOTHERED AT the idea of me leaving a shitty review. He'd got ahead of the problem by leaving me one first.

Sort of.

I was in the newsagents opposite The Chipped Cup Coffee Shop to buy some batteries, some chewing gum, and a Cadbury Creme Egg because I was worth it, damn it. I stood in the queue behind a woman I didn't know but often saw cycling her two kids to school in the morning, and my eye fell upon the local paper.

I was not a reader of the *Chipping Fairford Inquirer*, and had politely declined when a nervous and enthusiastic-sounding reporter had called to ask for an interview. It was pure luck that I even saw it.

But there they were in a large front-page photo: Craig and Kevin, doing their best to look suitably haunted by their trauma but both clearly loving the attention.

Above it was a poorly worded headline: LOCAL HANDYMEN DISCOVER BODY IN LOCAL MURDER HOUSE, by J.C. Connolly.

Against my better judgment, I grabbed a copy, and stood outside the newsagents scanning it while I ate my Creme Egg.

The article was histrionic, inaccurate, and full of grammatical errors. A good seventy-five percent of it was dedicated to a long, drawn-out play-by-play of The Gruesome Discovery, as it was referred to over and over again.

It seemed that Craig's experience and mine were somewhat different.

The way I remembered it, Craig had knocked me out of the way and was out of the house and burning rubber under a minute after he'd thrown up everywhere.

The way Craig told it, I had a fit of hysterics, leaving him to take charge of the scene. He gallantly escorted me to a safe place, where I continued to be hysterical while Craig called the police and was all-round heroic and pragmatic about things.

I pondered whether or not it was legal for the paper to print such inaccuracies. Since I was only briefly mentioned, and the bulk of the story was about how stoic Craig and—to a significantly lesser degree—Kevin were, I decided to let it go.

I worried for a while that the story would get picked up and printed in the Oxford papers. I hated the idea of being talked about. The real worry was whether or not it made it to the national papers, and hence into the orbit of my parents.

I'd made the executive decision not to tell them about the whole nightmare. Dad would say, *I told you not to buy that house, Ray.* Giselle, would rush down here to burn sage and throw crystals around or some such nonsense. I didn't feel up to it.

In the end, it must not have been important or exciting enough to get picked up nationally. This wasn't a surprise. It was a cold case, and there was more than enough present-day crime happening to keep people entertained. I'd have preferred it if no one at all knew, but thanks to the ridiculous article, I ended up fielding a few calls from anyone who saw the local paper.

Including, to my astonishment and indignation, Fraser.

He texted, and I was foolish enough to open it. I'd removed him from my contact list and his number came up as unknown. I had to check it, as it could have been a prospective client. I didn't read the whole thing—the moment I realised who it was, I hit delete.

I didn't want to talk about it with anyone, let alone Fraser.

So. Denial.

I ignored it, I ignored the curious looks I got for a few days as I went about my business running errands in town, and crazy though it seemed, that was it. Drama over.

When I was ten years old, Giselle moved in with us. Her huge Norwegian forest cat, Holly Golightly, also moved in. Holly was nearing the end of her long life and she did very little other than nap in the sun and occasionally kill something if it wandered too close. Apart from her bottomless appetite for death, I thought she pretty much had it made.

I loved that cat. That cat loved me. A little too much; she flat-out dumped Giselle as the recipient of her love gifts and started leaving them for me instead.

I never did get used to waking up to dead mice on my pillow. Or birds, toads, and on one memorable occasion a slow worm, which I thought was a small bronze snake. Whenever this happened, I would scream, Giselle would roll her eyes and take care of it, I'd change my pillow case, and all was forgotten until the next corpse showed up.

It felt wrong that discovering an actual human being in my house should play out the same as coming nose to nose with one of Holly's presents, but that's how it went.

It was distressingly easy to get over. In fact, a month later, I didn't even think of it at all.

That wasn't the problem.

Adam was.

I could *not* stop thinking about him.

It was one thing to replay that disastrous night when he'd left me high and dry, obsessing about every little detail and imagining how else it could have gone. I was a champion overthinker. That was par for the course.

But when I caught myself daydreaming about him—about his smile, about that frisson of panic/lust I felt whenever he looked at me, about the heat of his body hovering over mine—that was when I began to think I had a problem.

It got worse.

Even if I was the sort of man who was well-adjusted enough to actually be able to control his thoughts, it wouldn't have helped.

Adam was everywhere.

Sometimes it was a random sighting. I'd see him idling at the pedestrian crossing on his Triumph, or catch a glimpse of him in the Sainsburys car park, striding on his long legs toward the shop, or I'd walk past him having a pint outside The Lion with a group of friends.

Mostly, though, I saw him at the coffee shop. Which was weird.

I went to The Chipped Cup every day at eleven for a latte. I loved my job and I loved working from home, but if I didn't make the effort to get out and interact with people in real life, days could pass with no social contact beyond Zoom meetings and phone calls and emails.

I'd been making that effort like clockwork for five years. I'd never once seen Adam there.

I'd have noticed him.

You couldn't *not* notice him, sitting in his loose-limbed and graceful sprawl, his lean body obnoxiously relaxed, like he owned the place and everyone in it. If he didn't arrive with friends, someone would inevitably show up or rush over to join him. He drew the light itself to him. It refracted off his cheekbones, off his laughing smile, off his shiny red-gold hair in its ghastly perfect curls.

The first time I saw him, I'd been sketching furiously on my iPad, trying to shake loose some ideas. I paused for a sip of coffee, glanced up, and my eyes clashed with his.

He stood with his back to the counter while the barista, Amalie, made his coffee. He had his elbows propped on the counter and pelvis tilted out in a casual stance that displayed every one of his aesthetically pleasing angles to perfection.

It displayed more than his angles. He was wearing extremely tight jeans.

When he caught me looking, he smirked at me.

He did it mean.

Sexy-mean.

All hot, narrowed eyes, with an arrogant curl to his lip and an arched eyebrow.

I tore my gaze away, cheeks scorching with heat.

He must have really liked The Chipped Cup's coffee. Even when he was on shift, based on his stupid uniform, he'd at least duck in and grab one to go. Even when he must have just come off the night shift, he was there.

I once caught him snoozing over his Americano.

He'd been there a while; he had two cups in front of him, one drained and one still steaming. It was a cold and rainy day but his coat, which he'd slung on the back of his chair, was dry. Full-on, actual sleep was happening. He was slumped and his head was held in a way that gave him an unflattering double chin, and still he glowed.

I ordered my latte, gulped it down—not because I was a coward but because I had a Zoom meeting scheduled for noon, thank you very much—and gathered my stuff to head out.

Adam was still sleeping. As I passed by, I noticed that he'd dropped his beanie on the floor by his chair. Without thinking, I crouched down to pick it up.

When I glanced up, he was looking down at me in confusion.

He rubbed at one eye crankily. His skin was flushed a delicate rosy peach. "Ray?" he said. "What are you—"

"Shh." I patted his thigh. "You're dreaming. Go back to sleep. It's a dream."

He snorted faintly and closed his eyes.

I stood up, knees cracking. Great. I put his beanie on the table by his cup and scurried out.

After two months of it, I had to accept that I wasn't infatuated with him.

I was, in fact, obsessed. Like the ageing, hopeless romantic I was.

Adam was out there, living his life, always smiling whenever I saw him. Always with people, enjoying himself.

I was always alone. Working.

And sometimes guiltily opening up our text conversation that had never gone past the photo that Adam had taken in my kitchen and sent to me along with a delightful text that read, *For your spank bank*.

Eventually, it started to affect my mood. I'm an independent man, but that didn't mean I didn't get lonely. It had been creeping up on me for a while, I guessed.

If I could admit that I was obsessed with a beautiful boy who more than likely never even noticed me back, I could admit that I was lonely. I could admit that I was ready for romance.

I was ready to move on.

I was going to renovate my murder house until it was such a cute little Cotswolds cottage that prospective buyers wouldn't give a crap about the dead body. When I wasn't busy doing that, I was going to renovate my love life.

Unfortunately for me, neither of these excellent intentions panned out, and I once again found myself flat on my back beneath Adam.

11

*U*nlike almost everyone I knew, I hadn't done the dating app thing before. I wasn't sure if that made me a giant weirdo, or damn lucky.

I signed up to Grindr over a bottle of Prosecco and my three hundredth viewing of *While You Were Sleeping*. I didn't actually look at the app until I was waiting in line at the Post Office.

It was Giselle's birthday next week. I was sending her a silk scarf I'd designed and had screen-printed by a friend.

Giselle was the artsy type. She was passionate about art and crafts and poetry and dance and such, and had no talent whatsoever in any of those areas. She proclaimed it cheerfully, and didn't let it get in the way of her enjoyment of it, her patronage of it, or the wide-eyed, optimistic adoption of every new artistic hobby she came across.

Last I heard, it was weaving baskets out of willows.

The only thing Giselle liked more than discovering a new creative passion was when I presented her with something I'd designed for her.

She was going to lose her mind over the scarf.

She'd wear it every damn chance she got, and she'd tell everyone who inquired that her son the *artist* had *envisioned* it for her. She'd tell them whether or not they asked.

The Post Office was jammed and I fidgeted in the queue, swiping back and forth through my apps. Contemplating Giselle's joy and her tendency to big me up could only occupy me for so long.

The couple in line ahead were standing close together. The young woman slipped her hand into her boyfriend's back pocket. She rested her hand on the curve of his arse with a comfortable familiarity and grinned up at him when he shot her an amused, sideways smile.

That was what I wanted, I thought, with a sudden hollow feeling in my chest.

That sort of closeness with someone.

That sort of sweet, casual intimacy, the kind that could only be built on a secure relationship with unshakeable foundations.

On my way home, I ducked into The Chipped Cup. I had a client call in half an hour, which gave me enough time to pick up some caffeine on the way home. Since it was hot, and May, I planned on getting a frappe rather than my usual latte, and I swore I'd lift weights to work it off. I was sure I had some in the garage. Somewhere.

It was even busier in here than in the Post Office, and I once again found myself at the back of the queue. I woke up my phone to check my email, and hesitated. Taking a deep breath, I ignored the email app with its double-digit notification of unread messages, swiped to the third screen of my cluttered phone, and opened up Grindr.

I immediately had to back out and open up Google.

I asked Google how best to do this thing, skimmed a couple of advice blogs on what sort of photo to put up and how to showcase your interesting life. Then I flipped back into the app and stared at everything I had to fill in.

Wow.

I mean, someone has to be the least popular profile on Grindr, statistically speaking.

But I didn't have to volunteer.

This was a mistake, wasn't it? Yes, it was. I was going to go ahead and delete it. My thumb was hovering over the button when a bright laugh caught my attention.

Like a well-conditioned lab rat, and before I even registered that it was Adam's laugh, I glanced over.

A tall, muscular guy in athletic shorts and an obscenely tight t-shirt instructing the viewer to *WORK IT!!!* pinched Adam's chin and bent down to give him a loud, smacking kiss.

Adam turned his head at the last minute and the guy ended up smooching his cheek. Adam's eyes were half closed. A smile curled his mouth.

He was looking right at me.

I gripped my phone tighter. Adam tilted his head and his eyes glinted.

I raised my phone to clutch it against my chest and glared.

He glared back.

Gym boy looked from Adam to me and back again with interest.

Thankfully, Amalie behind the counter broke the standoff by calling my name.

"Oi, Ray. What d'you want?"

"I'd like a caramel frappe to go, please, Amalie," I said whirling away from Adam to face her instead. "And out of curiosity, what would you say my best feature is?"

Amalie stuck a cup under the ice machine, turned it on,

and yelled over it, "Your eyes, mate. Why? And d'you want cream on that?"

"My eyes?" They were so boring. Plain, boring brown.

She came over, leaned her elbows on the counter and fluttered her lashes at me. "They're like gingerbread," she said.

Gingerbread? "They're brown."

"Yeah, but like a lovely velvety brown. And you've got all those little gold bits in them." She gestured at my face. "They sparkle."

I gave her a look.

"Dunno why you can't see it," she said. "You being an artist and all."

"Graphic designer," I corrected. She was as bad as Giselle.

"Whatever. You work with colour, don'tcha?" Amalie shoved up and off the counter, and went to slap the machine, which was gagging dramatically on an ice cube. "Why d'you ask? You looking for compliments? You've got a nice arse, too."

I blushed. She'd bellowed it over the death rattle of the ice machine. Behind me, a couple of people laughed.

"Oh," she said, voice unnecessarily loud now that she'd turned the machine off. She'd spotted the phone. She banged the frappe down in front of me. "Dating profile, is it?" She winked, gave the whipped cream canister a showy shake and squirted an obscene amount through the hole in my frappe cup.

I felt eyes boring into the back of my head. "Um. Yes."

"Want anything else?" Amalie said. "Biscuit? A blondie brownie? Got some fresh out of the oven."

"Nope. Blondie brownies are spawned from the same

hell as white chocolate and I would rather eat sand. Besides, I have to go. I have a meeting."

"Right. That'll be three pound seventy-five. And if you need any help with the profile, you let me know. I'm great at that shit. Marketing degree," she said with a sigh.

"I don't—"

"Bring your dates here," she said. "Support your local coffee shop. Fuck Starbucks."

"Absolutely," I said, ignoring the cranked-up intensity of attention on the back of my neck.

"Eyes and arse," she reminded me, tapping the counter with an authoritative forefinger. I was released from my humiliation when she waved me along and said to the person in the queue behind, "What d'you want?"

I knew better than to look at Adam, but I did it anyway.

Oh. He wasn't paying me any attention after all. He was too busy soul-gazing with his muscular buddy to notice anyone else.

Mrs Hughes was sitting at a table behind Adam. Dougal was tucked under her chair, up to the whiskers in his weekly puppuccino (warm frothy milk). She gave me two thumbs up.

I returned it, and headed home.

Eyes and arse were listed as my best features, and I was officially doing this.

Two days later, I had a date.

With Detective Nash.

12

"Is this legal, Detective Nash?" I asked, flipping a hand between us. We were at The Lion. He'd taken my order and come back with a glass of wine for me and a Guinness for him.

"Call me Liam," he said. "And is what legal?" He slid onto the chair opposite me, kicked out his long legs, and drank damn near half his pint in one long pull.

I felt my eyes go wide.

He winked over the rim of his glass.

Was I...was I into it?

Nash licked the foam off his upper lip.

I flashed back to Adam, sitting at my kitchen table at one a.m. with a stupid milk moustache, telling me to come over there and kiss it off.

I was into it, I told myself firmly. *It* being Liam Nash, the thirtysomething, rugby-playing, mountain-biking, rugged man who asked me on a date.

Not the dominating twink who thought I'd roll over for him just because he told me to.

"You're allowed to date me, right?" I said.

"Yes. But I'm intrigued to know why you think we might be breaking the law."

"Dating the witness and all that."

"Do you have a crime to report, Mr Underwood? Because if so, you should contact the police through official channels. Not Grindr."

"I didn't do anything. Or see anything. I'm innocent."

He grunted and took a sip. "You have no idea how many times people have confessed their innocence to me."

He'd dressed for our date in dark indigo jeans and a cashmere burgundy sweater. A manly dusting of gingery blond stubble glinted in the low lights of the pub, and his sandy blond hair was artfully tousled, with a faint curl to it.

"Is it more or less than how many times people ask you to handcuff them to the bed?" I said.

He blinked.

"Which I am not asking you to do. For the record. Just...curious. Um." I did my best to get things back on track. "The dead body. An issue, or...? No?"

"Are you talking about the one in your bedroom? Or another one?"

"The one in my room. God, could you imagine me finding another?" I shivered theatrically.

He smiled. "The odds of that never happening are very much on your side. And the first body was unfortunate, but it's not an issue. You're not a witness or a suspect. It's a cold case."

"Do you think you'll ever solve it?"

"I won't, since I'm no longer on the case. It's been punted over to another department." He leaned back in his chair and gazed at me. "Is that why you wanted to meet for a beer? Trying to pump me for information?"

"I'd probably go about it differently if I wanted to extract information," I said.

His gaze sharpened with interest even as he said, "Because I'm not talking about it with you."

"We'll see," I said breezily. "For all you know, I'm incredibly subtle and I'm extracting information as we speak."

He smiled. "I mean it, Ray."

"I know. I'm messing with you."

"He likes to do that," a deep voice said behind me as a hand dropped onto the back of my chair. "Mess with people."

I stiffened. Nash's expression didn't shift.

"Adam," I said, twisting to glare up at him.

Oh, great. He had what I was calling his *model face* on. Hard, and aloof. The planes and angles of his cheekbones and strong, elegant jaw caught the light and slapped it disdainfully away. He was so close, I could smell his laundry detergent, his body wash, and his skin.

"Ray," he said. He glanced over to Nash. "Liam. Be careful with this one." He ran a familiar hand up the back of my neck, and playfully tugged my hair. "He's a bit of a tease."

Heat rushed through me. A good fifty percent of it was arousal. Who knew I liked my hair pulled? Not me. The other fifty was fury. I twisted away.

"Do you mind?" I said. "I'm on a date."

Adam's eyes bored into mine. "How's it going?"

"It was going fine until you showed up," I said. "Any time you'd like to leave would be good."

"You're not going to invite me to join you?" He shifted, putting his hard, flat belly in line with my eyes.

"For a threesome?" I whisper-shrieked. "No! This is our

first date! A bit early to open up the relationship, don't you think?"

Nash made a gagging noise. "Gross, Adam."

Adam's lips twitched. "I meant for a pint," he said. He stuck out his tongue at Nash.

Nash shuddered.

"Nice to see you're not everyone's type," I said, feeling oddly triumphant as I smiled over at Nash.

At *Liam*.

Adam shifted again, drawing my attention back to him. "Interesting to hear that you're up for a threesome so long as it's after the first date."

"I didn't say that." I sort of had, hadn't I? "I did not say that."

Adam pursed his lips consideringly. "It sounded that way to me."

"You're reaching. And you're dreaming. I'd never have a threesome with you."

"I know. You'd want all my attention to yourself." Keeping his eyes on mine, he said to Nash, "He's a bit of an attention ho, Liam. Very demanding."

"Excuse you?" I said. "You were the one making all the demands, if I recall. And the reason we won't all be jumping into bed together is because out of the two of us, you're the attention ho." I waved my hands incoherently at him. I'd shuffled around in my seat and somehow Adam had ended up standing between my knees, smiling down at me with an evil glint in his hazel eyes. Or soft. No, evil. *Evil.* "Look at you, in your...your—" I flicked his thigh, "—stupid tight jeans. And you're wearing glitter, aren't you?"

"Your jeans are pretty tight, Adam," Liam said.

Adam ignored him. "I'm not wearing glitter. It's youthful radiance, oozing out of my pores."

I growled. "Well, you..."

"I...?"

Why? Why did my IQ plunge like this whenever he was near?

I groped desperately for the thread of our conversation. Attention ho. Right. "And as well as being an attention ho," I said, "you are way too bossy for a threesome. That's a given. You'd lie around, telling people what to do, giving them orders and making everyone *service* you or whatever."

"I do like giving orders, Ray, but you know very well that I'm not the type to lie around."

"You probably wouldn't even let anyone else have an orgasm."

"Let?" Nash said wonderingly.

"Could I stop you, though?" Adam said. "You do get yourself worked up."

"You, me and Nash? Not happening. Right?" I said to Liam.

"Yeah," he said. "But mostly because Adam's my cousin. I'd have to arrest myself."

"*Oh.*" I smacked Adam's thigh. "Are you depraved? Stop trying to sleep with everyone, what is the matter with you? He's your *cousin*! Do you need help?"

"If you're offering—"

"Adam," Liam interrupted. "Go away, will you?"

I glanced over at Liam, suddenly and sickeningly aware of how badly I was behaving.

"In a minute." Adam's cool fingers caught my chin and turned my face to his. Startled, I held on to his wrist.

"Adam," Liam complained. "Come on."

"Dibs," Adam said to Liam. His eyes were steady on mine.

"You can't call dibs on a grown man," Liam said.

"Can. Did."

"You can't call dibs on me," I said with dignity, "because of your boyfriend."

"I don't have a boyfriend," Adam said.

"Then who was the buff guy from the coffee shop you were soul-gazing with?"

He tilted his head, eyes intense on mine. "A friend." He ran his thumb along the edge of my jaw. My lips parted.

"Adam, hands off my date." Liam was starting to sound pissed off, and less like his depraved younger cousin was amusing him.

It might have something to do with the way I was staring up at Adam, transfixed. And the way he was staring back.

Very slowly, I moved his hand, squeezing his wrist. "Stop being rude," I said. To him and to myself. My voice sounded weird. Almost vulnerable.

"Fine." Adam's face shuttered and he stepped back. "Enjoy your evening." As he stalked past Liam, he ducked down and said, "I'm telling Grandma you're dating again. She'll be thrilled. You'll have to bring Ray to family dinner."

Liam blanched. "Don't you fucking dare. Or I'll tell her you tried to sleep with me."

Adam paused. "You wouldn't."

"Keep inserting yourself into my love life and I will."

"Mutual destruction?"

"Agreed."

Adam lifted his chin and went to join the group of young cool people standing by the bar, leaving me and Liam sitting in ringing silence.

"This is going well," I said, and fidgeted with my wine glass. "Yes?"

Liam sighed. "You and Adam?"

"It's complicated."

"Didn't look all that complicated from where I'm sitting. What it looked like was foreplay. It also didn't look like it was over."

"What? No, it's not over. It can't be over, we never...we're not together. We never even hooked up!" Almost. But nobody had an orgasm.

Okay, I did, but Adam had stormed off by then. It didn't count.

"He seems to know you pretty well."

I snorted.

"He knows that you're demanding. That you get yourself worked up."

"I am not demanding, for starters. I am very easy-going and extremely laidback."

His face remained blank.

Right. I was talking to a man trained in detecting lies.

"I *can* be easy-going and laidback." Only if I'd had a Valium because of a dentist's appointment. I didn't see any point in sharing that with Liam. "And we didn't hook up. Did we skate close to the edge? Yes. I will confess to that much. But we came to our senses, or at least I did, what with being mature and responsible, and called the whole thing off. Besides. He is way too young for me. Don't you think? It's not quite a decade, but it's close enough. A decade is too much. Isn't it? We're practically of a different generation. I couldn't be his father or anything but still. And look at him. I mean..." I flapped a hand at Adam. He leaned against the bar, head tipped back, laughing. "Does it look as if I belong over there? With them? In any way?"

At some point while I was busy unravelling, Liam had picked up his pint glass. He finished it, and set it down with a click and a hint of irritation. "Yeah. There's nothing between you at all. I'm convinced." Liam's voice was flat.

I was not going to let Adam Blake ruin another relationship. And, true, Liam and I didn't have a relationship yet.

But we could have.

Liam was big and burly. He had some bulk to him, and I was here for it. He had a kind face—when he wasn't interrogating you. He had nice eyes, and a smile—when he did smile—that wasn't evil at all. It was a touch stern, granted. I was also here for it. When he looked at me it was with cool interest. I got no *I'm about to fuck with you*, Ray, vibes from him at all.

I also got very little in the way of *I absolutely want to fuck you, Ray*, either, but I wasn't too concerned about that.

I'd had enough of all those vibes from Adam, thanks. He'd reignited my need for companionship and, yes, orgasms from another person. Starting something with Adam was too much of a risk. He'd chew me up and spit me out.

Starting something with Liam, on the other hand...? I let myself imagine it.

His rugged eyebrows furrowed. "You all right, mate?" he said.

"Yes. Yes I am."

Liam smiled slowly.

And there it was. A warm glow of attraction.

Which was doused by a cascade of bright laughter from the bar, Adam's deep voice in the mix.

"I know we were only going to have a quick get-to-know-you pint," I said. "But out of interest, where do you stand on the idea of extending it to a get-to-know-you dinner?"

"I can always eat."

More excited by the idea of food than me. That was fine.

I tossed back the last of my wine and stood up.

I knew Adam was watching. I knew he'd love it if I

caught his eye. I ignored him as I shrugged on my coat and waited for Liam to come around the table. We left together and went to The Star, The Lion's main competitor.

We had fun. He ordered the steak. I ordered my usual beer-battered fish and chips and chocolate brownie, and vowed to go for an extra-long run every day for the rest of the week. We hit it off. Conversation was easy. The evening was perfect.

Liam walked me to my front door like a proper grown-up on a date, rather than ringing my doorbell at one a.m. He said, "This was nice," and kissed me.

It was a good kiss. It was.

He was firm but not demanding. Technically skilled. He pushed me up against the door. I spread my legs enough for him to lean in and opened up to it.

But he didn't spin me around, tell me to open the door, wrangle me inside and say, *Which way's the bedroom?*

Instead, he pulled back, smiled kindly at me, and said, "I've got to be up early tomorrow. I can't come in."

"Okay," I said.

He'd already sauntered off before I gathered my wits enough to think that what I should have said was, "I didn't invite you in." I whirled around and scrambled inside before he got the idea I was gazing after him with hearts in my eyes or something.

I was annoyed at the offhand way he'd assumed that coming inside was a given, if only he had been on a later shift. Was arrogance stuck to the Blake/Nash genetic code, I wondered? Or was it me? Did I come across as that available?

No, it was them. Arrogance, for sure. I found myself smiling, thinking about how Adam would react if I called myself available in his presence.

He'd be so torn.

He'd want to scoff and make a big, bitchy deal about how difficult I was. And at the same time, he'd want to do something tauntingly sexual to show me exactly how available I was.

I realised that I was standing in my hall with my back to the door, gazing into the middle distance with what was no doubt a ridiculous look on my face, thinking about a man who was *not* the man who'd just had his mouth on mine.

I scowled.

I would not let him cockblock me. Heartblock me. Whatever. Get in my romantic life.

I was starting something with Liam Nash, and that was all there was to it.

APPARENTLY, LIAM DIDN'T GET THE MEMO ABOUT OUR BRAND-new relationship, I thought, glumly poking at my phone a week later.

He hadn't called to arrange another date. He hadn't called at all. Or messaged. I checked the app notification settings, and I got Giselle to text me in case my iPhone was having another timeout. It had developed a personality since that time I'd dropped it into the toilet bowl. It still worked. It just had the odd mood swing every now and then.

Giselle's texts came through. It was working.

Liam didn't message.

Was I supposed to message him, I wondered? Were we playing chicken? Challenging for the top spot in the relationship? Did I care?

On reflection, no. I did not.

Maybe I'd take the initiative and message him in another week. As for everyone else on Grindr, meh. They were all like Liam. Mid-thirties to forties. Busy, professional men.

I didn't think I had all that much to offer them.

I didn't want to have a one-night stand, I didn't want an FWB, and I wasn't ready to commit to middle age like some of these comfortable-looking guys were.

I wanted to live first.

IN THE END, I DID TAKE THE INITIATIVE AND CALL LIAM.

Unfortunately, it was on a professional basis.

13

ork was going great, but it wasn't all that challenging. Perhaps I did need to branch out. I should start calling myself a graphic designer *and* an artist, think about taking up painting again. There were only so many logos, websites and brochures you could design, you know?

While work was steady, my emotions were all over the place. Adam had picked up my calm (boring) life like a shiny glass bauble and tossed it carelessly to the floor. I found myself wanting things I couldn't name, and everything was deeply, desperately, unsatisfying.

The dating experiment had turned out to be a bust. Screw the love life renovation. I decided to focus all my energy on getting my house in order.

The new carpet in my bedroom looked fabulous, and made me want to repaint the dingy off-white walls. The new, cheery primrose-yellow walls demanded a new chest of drawers in a soft cream with a slate-grey top, and a wardrobe to match.

I framed one of my best paintings back from my art college days, and hung it on the wall.

For the finale, a new bed. I'd replaced the mattress after Fraser left, and now it was time for a new frame.

My room was perfect.

I didn't stop there.

The guest room was next.

I repainted first. I didn't bother to put down a drop cloth since I was going to replace the carpet after. And I decided to save some money and do it myself rather than try to cajole Craig into doing it or, worse, get the other guy, Mason. Although I was fairly sure they'd both turn me down flat.

A sweaty, grunt-filled hour in, I conceded that pulling up carpet was a lot harder than Craig and Kevin had made it look, and they hadn't made it look easy. I was prepared for the thick rubber sealant and carefully scraped a Stanley knife all around the perimeter of the room, detaching the carpet as best I could first before I started yanking.

Craig and Kevin must be so freaking strong. My arms were buzzing and felt like overcooked spaghetti. I managed, though.

I rolled the old carpet and flaking underlay to the far side under the windows, and it dawned on me that I'd also have to wrestle it out of the room, down the stairs and off to the recycling centre by myself. I could always cut it up into smaller, more manageable pieces.

That was a problem for Future Ray.

As for today, I had most definitely earned myself a pizza. With two sides. Garlic bread and cookies.

I moseyed over to the bed to grab my phone where I'd tossed it after pulling up Spotify and starting a peppy playlist to accompany my labours. The boards creaked under me.

I stopped and glanced around, vaguely surprised. They hadn't creaked before. Then again, the bed used to be here. I hadn't walked over these boards before.

I shuffled through my modest toolbox and grabbed a claw hammer and a box of nails. Fixing boards: something else I knew how to do.

Forget branching out into art as a side hustle. I should go into the handyman business.

I got down onto my hands and knees and bounced my palms on the boards as I'd seen Craig do. Yep. Definitely loose.

Humming to myself, I dug around to catch the head of the loose nail and levered it up.

I could get into this. I tugged out the second nail. Be some competition for Craig.

The third nail came out. The fourth was pounded in flat. I wrestled with the board, wiggling it, getting a flathead screwdriver in the crack and easing it up. I worked the nail loose enough to catch it with the hammer, yanked it out, and pulled up the board.

The board either side and ahead were also loose, and I...

Froze.

I froze.

Very, very slowly, I pushed back to my heels, then to my knees, and then I rolled up to my feet. Never once taking my eyes off the hole I'd opened up in the floor.

Like a moron.

I backed up to the bed, flailed around until my fingers brushed the cold hard casing of the phone, and only then did I glance away.

It was the looking away that did it.

Panic, shock, fear. It all punched me in the chest at once.

I bolted out of the room, slammed the door behind me

and shot down the stairs. I ran out into the back garden and raised my phone, double-fisting it in shaking hands. It took me three goes to navigate to my contacts, and two to hit the call button and press it to my ear.

"Hello, Ray," Liam said, sounding surprised but pleased. Also a little smug. "You called."

"A-a-n other," I gasped out.

"Ray, you sound out of breath. Are you okay?"

"Another one!" I yelled.

"You want another date?"

"Dead guy. Body. Dead body guy. *Jesus*."

"What?"

"I found another one!"

"What?"

I held my phone in front of me with both hands and yelled at it, "I found another dead guy in my house!"

"Okay, that's a police matter—"

"You're the police!"

"This is my private number, you have to report—"

"Dead guy! In my house! Liam!"

"Yep." I heard the faint jingle of keys. "I'm on my way."

IT TOOK LIAM AND HIS PARTNER TWENTY MINUTES TO SHOW up. I can say with all confidence that those were the longest twenty minutes of my life.

I paced up and down in the back garden, avoiding looking at the house. In particular avoiding looking at the window of the guest room. If I saw movement—which I would not, because that guy was so very dead—but if I *did* see movement, I would expire on the spot.

And then I'd be haunting this place, too.

Liam didn't have his siren on, but I heard the tires chirp on the road as he came to a fast stop and saw the splash of electric blue light between my house and next door thrown up by his car. He pounded on the front door.

I scurried around to the side gate and shot into the drive.

"Hello!" I called out, and waved. "Over here!"

Liam and DS Patel were standing on my doorstep. Patel saw me first, and nudged Liam.

"Mr Underwood," she said, briskly coming my way.

"Yep. That's me." I recognised her from last time. I smiled but she didn't give me anything. All business. Pretty daunting, actually. She was about five feet six, had an unlined face but a wicked cool streak of iron grey in her thick mahogany hair, and a flat professional detachment in her steady gaze. "Hello," I said. "Hi, Liam."

"Mr Underwood." He gave a curt nod. "Shall we go in?"

"Must we go in? Can't we chat in the back garden?" I looked around. "Where are the forensics guys?"

"We'll call them when the body has been verified."

I cocked a hip and said to Liam, "Tell me you don't think I'm making it up."

"Inside, Mr Underwood?"

"Can you call me Ray, please? *Liam*? You're freaking me out."

Liam's lips tightened. "Ray."

I tipped my head. "Come on around the back. I don't have my door keys with me. I just ran out the house. Sorry." They dutifully followed me.

I was getting some serious fuck-off vibes from Liam. Rude. He'd sounded happy enough to hear from me before I mentioned the dead guy.

I dithered in the kitchen. "Tea, anyone? Or...?"

Patel gave Liam a knowing look, edged with a hint of exasperation. Liam pinched the bridge of his nose.

I squinted at him, then I gasped. "You *do* think I'm making it up."

"We have to check all calls," Liam said.

What a fantastic non-answer. "Why would I make it up?"

"Nobody's saying you're making it up, Mr Underwood," Patel said in a wonderful deadpan. "Would you like to show us the body?"

"*Like* is overstating it, but okay. We'd better get it done."

"Where is it?"

I shifted my weight. "Bedroom."

"Which bedroom is that?" Patel asked.

And that struck me as an odd question. I only had two bedrooms up there. They'd checked the master bedroom for more bodies when processing the scene last time. I had assumed. "You did check the rest of the master bedroom underfloor, right?" I said suspiciously.

"For what?" Liam said. "More bodies?"

"No, Liam, for woodworm."

"Sarcasm isn't helpful, Mr Underwood."

"Stop calling me that. It's *Ray*. We all know you've had your tongue in my mouth, or the pair of you wouldn't be thinking this is some desperate lonely housewife/policeman porn. *Oh, officer,* do *check my bedroom*."

Patel arched an eyebrow at Nash. "Do you need to recuse yourself, detective?"

I liked her.

"I had a pint with the guy."

Liam, I did not like. "The *guy*?" I said. "A *pint*?"

"I know him socially," Liam ploughed on. "We're not dating."

"So very not," I told her crisply. "He's not that great of a kisser."

Patel cracked a smile.

"You did check, though?" I said. "For other bodies? Because I got the boards relaid and the new carpet's down and everything."

"I think someone shone a torch under there," Liam said.

"A torch? Is that all? It was a crime scene. It's not standard procedure to investigate a little harder than shining a torch?"

"I assure you that all correct protocols were followed, Mr Underwood," Patel said. "And it was a body disposal site, not a crime scene."

"If I'd known, I'd have checked myself," I muttered, lying through my teeth, as I led them out of the kitchen and up the stairs. I slowed as we reached the top, and hesitated at the guest room door. I bravely opened it and stepped back. "He's in there," I said, pointing.

Liam nudged me forward with a hand at the small of my back.

I threw my arms out and gripped the edges of the doorframe, starfishing. "I'm not going in there and you can't make me. You go ahead. You can't miss him. He's right there in his tub in the hole."

"Fine." Liam shuffled me out of the way and strode in, his shoes striking the bare boards loudly.

He stood and stared down into the hole. "Huh."

Patel headed downstairs, already on her radio.

Hands on hips, Liam cut a look my way.

My I-told-you-so smile slipped at his thoughtful expression. "What?" I said.

14

I took a deep breath and dialled.

"Hello, Premier Lodge," the voice at the other end said. "How can I help you?"

"Hi," I said brightly. "Is Adam there?"

"No, he—"

"Great. Thanks." I hung up.

After the shitshow of a day I'd had, I didn't want to talk anymore, which was a bad sign for me. I was a talker. And I knew for sure that I couldn't handle Adam.

Checking to make sure he wasn't there and then booking a room online took care of both of those things.

I got the room cheap because it was late by the time Liam let me go, and once again I booked it for two nights rather than one. I didn't know how long it would be before I could get back in the house, but I could tell by the way Liam had taken me to the station and kept me there for six hours of uncomfortable conversation that the situation was more complicated.

At least I knew the deal now.

I packed an overnight bag, my running kit, and my

laptop. I remembered my toiletries so I didn't have to use the hotel stuff again. I even remembered ear plugs, in case of honeymooners.

I had a plan, and it looked like sleeping as long as I wanted, eating crappy room service, and deleting Liam Nash from my contacts list.

And Grindr.

I marched into the Premier Lodge as night was falling, made a beeline for the front desk, and stutter-stepped to a dismayed halt when Adam looked up with a professional smile.

"Oh," I said, and glanced around crossly. "You're not supposed to be here."

Adam leaned his elbows on the desk and said in his deep voice, "I work here. And I was on a break when you called. I'm assuming that was you? Prank-calling an hour ago, asking for me then hanging up? I was on a break. But I'm here now. How can I help you this evening, Mr Underwood?"

This family really knew how to weaponise surnames.

I felt guilty, okay? Yes, I'd called to see if Adam was there for the sole purpose of avoiding him. I was feeling emotionally fragile and very much not up to going head-to-head with Adam. Mano a mano. Any body part to any body part.

"I'd like to check in, please," I said politely.

"You'd like to book a room?" Adam said. "Of course. Let me check availability. Although I warn you, I suspect we are fully booked."

"Yes, and one of those bookings is me. I'm all paid up. Gimme the key card, and I'll be out of your hair."

Adam slanted me a distracted smile, eyes on the computer screen. "No," he said. "No record of that, I'm afraid."

"Ha ha." I poked the counter with a forefinger. "Not tonight."

"This does happen from time to time," he said. He sat down in his spinny chair and turned it toward me. Slow and deliberate. Like a Bond villain.

I growled. "Check again."

Eyes on mine, Adam reached out and tapped the spacebar. "Nope. Nothing."

I popped my jaw. "I hate your entire family," I said.

"That's a bit much, Ray."

"Is it? Is it? Ha ha, no." I stabbed at my phone, bringing up my online banking app. "You know where I've been for the last six hours?"

"No, but I sense that you're going to tell me."

"I have spent the last six hours with your demanding beast of a cousin, completely at his mercy, while he did nothing but work me over. Hard. See if I ever accept an invitation to 'go somewhere quiet' with him again."

"What?" Adam snapped. "I didn't think you were dating? And he was doing *what* to you?"

I wished it *had* been a date. Even though Liam was a dick. "To be fair, he let me have a break for a snack and a bottle of water about halfway through the whole ordeal. Otherwise? He was *on* me. That man is relentless."

"Then you *are* dating?" Adam's expression darkened, eyebrows pulling low and lips flattening to a hard, tight line. "What did he do to you?"

"The usual. You know how these things go. He didn't bring out the handcuffs, but trust me. It was on the table." I gazed off into the distance. "I suppose I should count myself lucky he didn't throw *me* on the table the minute he got me in his lair. Bend me over it. Start screaming at me to give it up. He is not a subtle man when he wants something from you."

Adam's jaw clenched so hard I saw the muscles jump.

"Safe to say, after that unpleasant encounter, he has been deleted from my dating app."

"Did he hurt you?" Adam said in a low, vibrating voice.

I'd entered my passcode wrong while ranting. "Hmm? He did hurt my feelings a bit. There's no need to be rude about these things."

Adam stared at me. "I'm gonna kill him."

"Mm-hmm." I got my passcode entered, and checked my app. "You shit," I said, seeing the cancelled payment. My phone had dinged in my pocket an hour ago. I'd ignored it. I hadn't been in a phone-checking mood. I'd been in a fantasizing-about-throttling-Liam-Nash mood.

Adam held up a finger, eyes blazing as he grabbed his own phone.

"Could you at least try to be professional?" I sighed. "For once in your life? Like your cousin? Li-"

"Liam, what the fuck did you do to Ray!"

Woah. I blinked at the fury rolling off Adam.

He snarled into the phone, "Because if you're going to date him, you can't treat him like one of your hook-ups, he's *sensitive*, and—what?"

"I am not sensitive," I protested. "What are you talking about? And hook-ups? Dating?"

"Are you serious?" Adam said to the phone.

"I'm empathetic," I said. "I'm an artist. Well. Graphic designer. Also, what was that about Liam's hook-ups?"

"Shh, Ray. I'm not talking to you."

I slapped Adam's hand out of the air when he went to lay a finger on my lips.

"Good grief," I said.

Adam leaned over the desk and put a hand over my mouth. And, yes. I could have stepped back. But I didn't.

"Right," he said. "Okay. Got to go." He hung up. He moved his hand slowly, ghosting his fingers down the side of my neck before getting out of my personal space.

I was *not* disappointed.

"Liam arrested you?" he said, for some reason sounding amused.

"No! How dare you, he——"

"When you said he took you to his lair and worked you over hard, my mind went somewhere else entirely."

It took me a second. "Oh, ew. No."

Adam laughed. "Ew? I'm telling him you said that."

"I doubt he'd care. Your cousin and me? No. Never. Turns out he's as much of a dick as you are."

"Ah. We've circled back to the insults, have we?" Adam said mildly.

"I think it must be genetic. Your general dickishness. That's my theory, anyway."

"Uh-huh."

"I'm a person of interest."

"Definitely are."

"To Nash," I said, "not you."

"I'm assuming you mean legally."

"Weren't you listening? He's an arsehole. I wasn't a person of interest for the first body. Why now?"

Adam smiled.

"I am offended," I said. My voice quavered.

"I can tell."

It wasn't offence making me shaky. An official interview had been perfectly in order. Two bodies. If it was someone other than me, I'd have been all for it.

I wasn't offended, I was unsettled. I was scared.

"Here." Adam held out a key card.

"My booking suddenly reappeared, did it?" I said.

"No. But have a luxury suite upgrade as an apology for the mix-up. We like to keep our repeat customers happy."

I searched his face but he seemed to mean it. "That's very kind." I took the key card, then narrowed my eyes at him. "Same price, though?" I said, "You're not tricking me into spending five hundred pounds on a Premier Lodge room, are you?"

"No, you snob."

"I'm not a snob." I whisked the card out of his hand.

Maybe I was a little bit of a snob. Mostly, though, if I was going to spend hundreds of pounds a night or for two nights, it wouldn't be somewhere within walking distance of my house. You know. My murder house.

It would have a view of the ocean, bare minimum.

"Ray."

"Yes?"

Adam's eyes were on mine. There was something cautious in them. "Are you okay?"

Right. I was staring off into space, thinking about a room with an ocean view. "Me?" I said, "Oh, yeah. I'm great." I shot him two thumbs up, caught the strap of my laptop bag when it slipped off my shoulder, fumbled the key card, and rushed off.

I hesitated at the lifts, wondering which floor my room was on. I looked back at the desk.

Adam was watching. He silently held up three fingers.

Third floor. Got it. Finger guns.

As I stood there waiting for the lift to arrive, my phone vibrated. I jumped, forgetting I'd stuffed it in my front pocket. Yeah, no, I thought. It can wait.

It went to voicemail after ten rings. Then it began again.

Oh, fine. I grabbed it, went to turn it off, then saw Adam's contact photo on my screen.

"What?" I said, turning to glare at Adam. He was leaning on the front desk, phone held to his ear.

"If you need to talk about it..." he said.

I waited for the punchline when he left a pause. The lift arrived and I lunged in.

"I'm available." Adam hung up.

I shoved my phone back in my pocket. That was unexpectedly nice of him. I looked up and caught sight of my reflection. I flinched. Yow.

My face was starkly pale, with streaks of hectic red on the crests of my cheeks. My eyes were wide and haunted. I made a worried sound and tried to smooth the furrows out of my brow before they settled in for the long haul.

I...did not look great.

The lift dinged and the door opened. I couldn't get away from all the mirrors quickly enough. I let myself into the room and nodded with appreciation. I'd been hasty dismissing the place. It was no Barbadian love nest on the beach, but it was a few steps up from the single I'd booked last time.

And that I'd booked this time, in fact.

Would Adam get in trouble for upgrading me? Was it ethical?

Did I care?

To my consternation, I did care.

I didn't like the idea of some nameless superior yelling at Adam for essentially giving me an upgraded room at mates rates. I mean, it was a thing. Late rooms and all that. It was a business model.

Then again, I couldn't really imagine Adam being all that bothered by someone attempting to tell him off. I couldn't really imagine Adam considering anyone his superior, regardless of who was signing his pay cheque at the end of the month. He'd probably stand there and smile at them until they gave up.

Net gain: lovely big bed for me. I wasn't mad about it.

I was still surrounded by the hotel's lurid purple livery, but you can't win them all.

I flopped down onto the bed face first and groaned as I sank and sank into the fluffy duvet.

What the hell was going on with my life right now?

I rolled over to blink up at the ceiling. There was a smudge in the corner. A tiny cobweb. I should call Adam and complain. Get him to come up here with a feather duster.

My amusement at the idea faded as I thought about my house. When Liam—make that Detective Nash—had me escorted me out, it had taken a moment to realise what was happening.

The forensics van had pulled up in my drive. Curtains were twitching in houses the length of the street. Mrs Hughes and Dougal were standing in her front garden. Neither of them were even pretending not to look.

And okay, Liam—*Detective Nash!*—hadn't thrown me down over the bonnet of his patrol car and read me my rights, but he'd had a *very* firm grip on my arm.

And he'd put me in the back seat.

He'd done the head thing. Hand on the top of my head. It wasn't a chivalrous move, either. It was a prevent-a-lawsuit move.

Were they all still at my house?

Were there cordons?

Were there *journalists*? Blech.

I hopped up and strode through to the bathroom. I

swished some water around the tub, stuck the plug in, and ran myself an indulgently deep bath.

After the first dead body, I'd had trouble sleeping, and not just that night Adam had left me high and dry, either. This time, I was smart about it.

One of the larger local farms had expanded a few years ago into producing a range of products from their lavender fields. They'd hired me to design the packaging, and I was proud of it. That pride hadn't extended to opening or using any of it, but I'd had their lavender bath oils along with lavender moisturiser, soap, room spray and candle on display in my bathroom for long enough. Lavender was good for de-stressing. It was soothing. It would chill me out.

Right?

I'd grabbed the bath oils and moisturiser from my bathroom shelf on the way out of the house. The real reason I hadn't used the bath oils before was because cleaning the tub was my least favourite chore. But since I wasn't going to be cleaning this tub, and I was stressed out to the max, it was the perfect opportunity.

The theory was sound. In practice, I was heavy-handed with the oil, went overboard, and ended up with watering eyes and nose.

It didn't make me any less stressed. I gave myself a point for trying, though.

I crawled into bed and lay there with the lights on, and I mean all of them, not just the soft and romantic bedside lamp. My heart was racing like I was coming into the final stretch of a marathon.

Could I be allergic to the lavender? Was I going into anaphylactic shock?

No. It was probably the stress of finding another body.

And low blood sugar. I hadn't had a chance to eat or drink anything between the police station and here.

I rolled over and reached for the hotel phone.

This is stupid, I said to myself. This is a terrible idea. He's going to make everything worse. Don't do it.

I dialled the front desk.

15

"Good evening," someone who was not Adam said. "How can I help you?"

For some idiot reason I'd assumed that Adam would be there just because I wanted him to be.

"Oh," I said. "Is...uh. Is Adam there at all? I mean...can I speak to Adam please?"

"Adam's shift ended about ten minutes ago, sir, but I'd be happy to—*ow*."

They cut off with a yelp. In the background, I heard an indignant voice complaining. I didn't pay any attention. Because in my ear, a familiar voice was saying, "This is Adam. How can I help you?"

My throat creaked. I hung up.

Great.

Good, Ray. Smooth. Everything's better. Well done.

Three minutes later there was a soft knock at the door. I startled, but recovered quickly. I knew who it was even before I opened the door.

Adam had changed out of his hideous uniform. He was wearing his usual tight jeans and motorcycle boots, and had paired it with a comfortably oversized sweatshirt that read *Cambridge University* in blocky white letters against the plain grey. He'd shoved his sleeves up to mid-forearm, showing strong wrists and a few beaded bracelets.

I looked him up and down and got stuck on his thighs. "Are those jeggings?" I said.

He grinned. To my mortification, I actually took a step back. Holy crap. What a smile.

Adam tipped his head a fraction and the raw amusement softened at the edges. "I can't wear jeggings in public," he said. "People walk into walls. Fall off bicycles. Traffic piles up. It's not right." The smile softened further when I failed to come up with a sassy response. "Am I coming in?" he said.

I reached out, tangled my fingers in the loose, body-warm fabric of his sweatshirt, and tugged nervously.

Somehow I forgot to stop tugging, until he was in my room, he'd kicked the door shut behind him, and our bodies were plastered together. His arms came up and around me and held on.

I pressed my face into his shoulder and clung and clung until the low-level tremble of anxiety that had been sending shockwaves through me for the last ten hours finally faded.

"Come on," Adam said. The low rumble of his voice dispersed the last vestiges of my anxiety. He nudged me with his hips. "Let's go." With one hand at the small of my back and one cupping the nape of my neck, he slowly walked me backward until I hit the bed.

I didn't know what I expected. I didn't know why I'd called in the first place. I was mildly surprised—although not displeased—to find myself rolled under the duvet and efficiently tucked in while Adam sat on the edge by my hip and picked up the phone to order food.

"Do not order the steak," I said with a shudder. "I think I'm going vegetarian."

Adam tried not to laugh.

"You're the worst," I told him as he ordered the pizza. "Maybe not the absolute worst," I amended when he ordered the chocolate fudge cake and the cheesecake.

"Shuffle over," he said. His words were muffled as he bent over and unzipped his motorcycle boots. He kicked them off and swung his legs up onto the bed. He was wearing mint-green socks with fluffy white sheep on them. He shifted around until he was comfortable. I complained when I was jostled, but only for the look of things.

He stretched out his long, long legs, and crossed his ankles.

Unable to resist temptation, I poked his solid thigh, then attempted to pinch the fabric of his jeans between my thumb and forefinger. "They're so tight," I marvelled.

"Ray, you are obsessed with my jeans."

I was obsessed with what was *in* his jeans. But sure. Let him think I was into his fashion choices.

"How do you even get in them without straining something?"

"One leg at a time. Like everyone else who pays basic attention to fashion and wears jeans that fit rather than shopping in the Sad Dads section of Marks & Spencer." He couldn't even keep his face straight while he got that out.

"I can't help it if I am too much man to pack into your teenager clothes."

He smiled down at me. Somehow—it must have been when he was jostling me about as he climbed on the bed, it was the only possible reason—I had ended up curled into his side. He gently squeezed the arm he had around my shoulders. "Don't feel bad. Your arse isn't that big."

I pinched his thigh. "I meant my...my stuff. My giant dick."

He laughed at that. "Oh, honey," he said.

I shoved myself upright. "Excuse me?"

"So cute." He chucked my chin, eyes sparkling.

"I have a proper man-sized dick, I'll have you know, which needs adult-sized clothing that won't strangle it to death."

"Okay."

Yes. It was ridiculous. Adam was bigger than me in every way. Even though I hadn't seen his dick in the wild, I'd felt it against me. I already knew it was bigger than mine.

I flipped out a hand and gestured at him. "Are you not being choked as we speak?"

"I'm touched at your concern for my cock. But there is Lycra in these jeans. Modern technology is a wonderful thing. And I'm quite comfortable. More than I would be in the stiff old-man jeans I've seen you wearing."

He had a point. There was a reason I wore sweatpants unless I had to go out and about in public. My jeans *were* stiff. There was very little give to them, very little stretch.

The only good thing about them was, they were baggy enough that, should the situation very clearly arising in Adam's jeans right before my eyes occur, no one would notice.

Unlike me. Right now. With my eyes locked on Adam's lap.

My hand was still on his thigh. His was resting on top. He squeezed my fingers, encouraging me to look up. When I did, he removed his hand and arched his back the tiniest bit. Enough to slip down the bed by half an inch.

Offering.

I glanced back down at the area rapidly filling out. Fascinated, I slid my hand higher up his thigh.

Adam took a deep breath but he didn't move—not until the loud knock at the door.

I flinched, he heaved an exasperated sigh, then rolled off the bed and strode to answer it.

I flopped back under the covers and tugged the duvet over my head.

Great.

Adam answered the door to my room, and now his co-worker would clock the monster erection in Adam's tight jeans, go back to the kitchen, and they'd have a big laugh about the sad old man in the luxury suite being seduced by Adam. The gossip would be all around town by mid-morning.

I yelped when Adam tweaked my foot through the covers. "Come out, Ray," he said.

I listened to the muffled sounds of plates and cutlery being arranged. I didn't move. After a short silence, the duvet was tugged off and Adam smiled down into my flushed face. "Food," he said.

My stomach rumbled on cue.

He waited patiently while I scooted up to lean against the headboard and cross my legs. He passed me a plate that was almost buried under an enormous slice of pizza.

My appetite had come roaring back once Adam showed up. I fell on the pizza like I hadn't eaten in days.

"Do you want to talk about it?" he said when I'd demolished half the slice. He shook his head when I offered him a bite.

"Not really," I mumbled through a mouthful of sourdough crust and fragrant tomato sauce. Sexy. Oh. Sexy? Adam reached out and swiped at a string of mozzarella that was connecting me and the pizza. He twisted his wrist to twirl it around his finger, then he stuck his finger in my mouth.

I didn't even think. I sucked.

His eyes darkened.

I pulled off with a pop, dropped my gaze and said, "So, the dead guy."

That should puncture the sudden ramping-up of sexual tension that had slowed time down and turned the air heavy.

The bulge in Adam's jeans didn't go anywhere.

Maybe not.

"Mm," Adam said. "Liam mentioned something about another body. Same kind of scenario? Tub, cat litter, floorboards?"

"Yep." The pizza lodged in my throat.

"Finish your food, Ray. Then you can tell me about it. If you want. I'm here to listen."

I pulled a face but obediently finished the pizza and started eyeing up the cake.

"Chocolate or cheesecake?" Adam asked. He took my empty plate off my lap, set it on the bedside table, and held out the dessert plates, one in either hand.

"Guess."

He passed me the chocolate and dug into the cheesecake himself.

I moaned at the delicious moist cake. It was dense and sticky and perfect. "Oh my god. Have you tried this?" It was even better than the brownie at The Lion, and that thing had won awards. Local, to be fair, but an award was an award. Did people know about this cake? Because they should.

Adam pulled the fork slowly out of his mouth, eyes on

mine, before replying, "I have, yes. I didn't like it quite that much."

"I'm not even sorry." I moaned again. "It deserves acknowledgement."

"Very much a sweets guy, aren't you?"

"If I could get away with it, I'd have dessert for breakfast, lunch, and supper."

I couldn't get away with it. Which was why I'd ended up buying dad jeans from M&S. It wasn't my extra dick inches I was accommodating.

Adam forked up the last of his cheesecake and held it out to me.

"Don't mind if I do," I said, leaned forward and took it. I didn't mean to make eye contact with him any more than I'd meant to moan again. But I did both. I didn't look away as he drew the fork back, the metal sliding smooth and warm over my lips.

I swallowed hard a few times then weakly said, "Want some chocolate cake?"

I was being polite. I really hoped he said no. It was amazing cake.

"Don't mind if I do." Adam leaned forward and gently kissed me.

My muscles relaxed all at once. He cupped the back of my head, smiled against my mouth, and touched his tongue to my lips once before pulling back. "Mm."

I stared at him.

He stared back.

I broke first, obviously. I shovelled the last mouthful of chocolate cake in my mouth and surrendered the plate when he motioned for it.

I heard the crack of a plastic seal, then Adam was holding out a bottle of water.

"Thank you. I must say, you're much better at feeding and watering people than your cousin." I drained half the bottle and tried to give it back. He shook his head and nudged it back to me again. "Liam winged a packet of peanuts from the vending machine at me, and that was it."

"I'm better at everything," Adam said, watching intently while I finished the water.

"You're about equal when it comes to ego, though."

He laughed, delighted.

"I have to brush my teeth," I said suddenly, and rolled out of bed.

Adam gave an amused grunt behind me. He followed me into the bathroom, and raised an eyebrow at my big-eyed glare.

"What are you doing?" I said around my toothbrush and a mouthful of minty foam.

He unwrapped the free toothbrush but ignored the hotel-supplied tiny tube of toothpaste and helped himself to mine. "I take cavities very seriously, Ray."

Fair enough. We stood side by side and brushed. The size difference between us was more noticeable standing like this, and somehow worse with me once again in my pjs and him fully dressed.

"Are you staying the night?" I blurted, and banged the toothbrush briskly on the edge of the sink. It was something I'd seen my dad do when I was growing up and I'd inherited the habit.

Adam spat, rinsed his brush and stuck it beside mine in one of the water glasses. "Yes."

If he'd asked to, I'd probably have said no, contrary creature that I was. But his confidence was as reassuring as it was attractive, and I didn't want to be alone.

"Get into bed," he said. "I'm going to have a quick shower."

"Okay." I headed off but turned and ducked back into the bathroom as Adam whipped his shirt off. He turned to me, casually unbuttoning his fly with one hand. "No sex, though," I said.

He tilted his head in that considering way he had. It used to make me feel like a weird little insect when he did it. Now, it made me feel interesting.

I'd rather feel like a weird little insect. Less pressure.

"Are you telling me not to masturbate, Ray?"

"What?" Well, that came out much higher than necessary.

"Is it no sex with myself that I'm not allowed to have, or no sex with you?"

"Me!" I said, lightheaded. "Sex with me. No, *no* sex with me, I mean. I can't stop you...doing..." I trailed off into silence.

Adam unzipped his jeans. I bolted.

16

*H*e left the door open, the absolute shit.

The water came on with a hiss and a splatter into the tub. I imagined Adam standing there, wrangling his tight jeans off, waiting for the spray to heat up.

And then I remembered that I'd had a soak with bath oils.

I chewed my lip.

He'd be fine. I'd swilled the tub out. He was a grown man. He wouldn't slip.

Skid backwards.

Hit his head and die.

Yeah, Liam wouldn't buy it if I was anywhere near connected to another body, ever, let alone hours after he cut me loose, let alone if that body was his cousin.

I sat up. "Adam!" I called. "Be careful of the tub!"

"What?" The extractor fan hummed and water splashed.

I raised my voice. "The tub! Be careful! Don't slip!"

"I can't hear you, Ray. If you want to tell me something, you'd better come in here."

He'd be *fine*.

I heard the squeak of flesh on porcelain.

"Be careful you don't slip!" I yelled as I darted across the room. The water shut off and Adam appeared in the doorway.

He wasn't wearing the towel wrapped around his waist like a normal person. Oh no. He'd bunched it up in one fist and casually held it in front of his groin.

Like a big white fig leaf.

The fact that it left his lean, muscled flanks right there for my viewing pleasure was coincidental, I was sure. I could see his narrow hips, the grooves of his Adonis belt, the outer edges of his thighs...

"What?" he said with a bemused laugh.

I reached out and almost touched his naked chest. "I used bath oils earlier. I don't want you to slip in the tub."

"Okay. Ray?" He caught my hovering hand and enfolded it in his own, warm and damp. "You've been through it today. But you're safe. Your blood sugar is—well, thanks to the cake it's not what you could call stabilised, but it isn't low, and it should be steadying. You're hydrated. I'm here. You can sleep. It's all fine. It's okay to freak out but right now, you're safe."

"I know, I just don't want you to slip and die. Your cousin would definitely arrest me."

"I'm capable of taking a shower."

"Now that you've been warned."

"I saw that the tub was used. I'm taking the appropriate cautionary measures."

"You're welcome."

His beautiful lips curled up in amusement. "You're very highly strung."

"Thanks for the random criticism."

"It's not criticism. I like it. I like that you're a ball of anxiety, because I know how to calm you down."

"Me not wanting you to slip in the tub doesn't mean I'm a ball of anxiety, Adam. It means I'm a decent human being, that's all."

"I'm going to make you feel better in a minute. Hop into bed while I shower—with extreme caution—and then I'll come and lie on top of you."

I gaped at him.

"Don't worry. I'm going to have a quick wank first so you don't get too freaked out about my dick."

I gaped harder as he turned and sauntered back into the bathroom. I hurriedly looked away before I got caught staring at his arse.

The water hissed on as I got back into bed. It pattered against the tub for a few seconds, then it quieted.

Adam must have stepped under the flow, I thought.

He'd be blocking it with his body. The water would cascade over his broad shoulders and wide, firm chest before lovingly dripping down the curves of those sleek muscles I'd seen, and—oh no.

I squirmed against the mattress.

I was getting hard.

This was terrible timing.

I hadn't had even a twitch earlier when I was bundled up in his arms, or when I was sucking on his finger or his cutlery. My chest had hollowed out with arousal and my heart had spasmed once or twice, but an erection had been very much not on the cards. I was thirty-two, stressed out to the max, had been brutally interrogated (fine, very firmly interviewed) and left hanging around in a police station for hours, and whenever I closed my eyes, I saw the dead guy.

None of the aforementioned was conducive to sexy thoughts, even with Adam's warmth and proximity.

It was one thing when he was eating cheesecake in his baggy sweatshirt and his socks with fluffy sheep on then. That was safe. The sexuality was contained. Well, as contained as Adam's sexuality ever got, which wasn't saying much.

But now it was unleashed. Now, he was dripping wet and naked in the shower.

Possibly having a wank.

I strained my ears, even while telling myself not to be such a pervert.

If he was doing anything, I concluded after hearing nothing more than the gentle fall of water, he was being remarkably quiet about it.

He'd said it to wind me up, hadn't he? I—

My scurrying thoughts screeched to a halt when I heard a faint gasp.

...did I?

It came again. I had to listen hard to catch it, but yes. There. A deep, heavy breath, pulled up short with an abrupt hitch. I sat up, eyes wide.

He really was in there pleasuring himself, wasn't he?

A soft, shuddering moan drifted from the bathroom. A rumbling *mmm*. My cheeks scorched with heat. My stomach tightened.

"Ah," he gasped softly. "Ah, ah, ahh."

Oh my god.

The water shut off.

I dived under the cover and dragged a pillow over my face. All was dark, muffled and quiet. Despite this, I was so electrified and aware of Adam that I didn't even startle when he sat on the bed by my hip, rolling me toward him.

"Are you naked?" I asked.

He pulled lightly at the pillow. "If you want to talk to me, you'll have to come out from under there."

I flung the pillow off but kept my eyes closed. "Are you naked?"

"Stark bollock naked."

I looked. Okay? I looked. "You liar."

He grinned. The large fluffy white towel was properly applied, wrapped low around his hips. Low enough that I was treated to the sight of his flat, muscled abdomen and the trail of coppery gold hair that started below his belly button. "Do you want me to be naked, Ray?" He set his palms flat on the mattress and leaned back.

If he was naked in the bed with me, I would absolutely have sex with him. Which was a terrible idea. "I have clean boxers you can sleep in," I said.

"Cool." If he was disappointed, he didn't show it. He went over to my open duffle on the luggage stand. "As long as you didn't get them from the dads' section of M&S. I have standards."

"I did get them from there," I said. "Enjoy."

I was starting to get worried. *Was* there a dads' section of M&S? Had I been inadvertently shopping in it? Or was this Adam being mean?

He rummaged around and came up with a pair of cotton plaid boxers. Dangling them from a forefinger, he gave me a judgemental look.

I saw where all the comments were coming from. Those boxers were a cheap multipack statement that sex was very low on the priority list. Or a distant memory of a youth long gone.

"Not everyone likes to dress in lace and leopard print," I said.

"They're missing out," Adam said. "Although not leopard print. I'm lace, all the way." He turned his back, unwrapped the towel, and tossed it over the back of the desk chair, giving me an uninterrupted view of his high, round arse.

Then he bent over to step into the boxers.

I must have squeaked or something, because his voice was heavy with amusement when he said, "Did you faint?"

I tried to say something grown up and witty, like, *pshaw*. But all that happened was another ungodly noise of startlement and want as he straightened and dragged the boxers slowly up his thighs.

He stopped with the elastic cupping the lower curve of his buttocks and he sort of...tugged, making the two globes bounce. "How about now?" he said.

I grabbed the base of my dick and squeezed viciously hard. It was that, or come from his ridiculous antics.

"I have to say, Ray, I admire your self-control." Adam strolled over to the bed, switching off the desk lamp en route. He climbed in. "Most guys wouldn't be able to resist."

"I am not most guys," was all I managed

Kudos to me, I sounded pretty detached.

"That's for sure." Adam lay on his side facing me, and slipped a hand over my waist. He let it rest there, a solid weight. "Want me to lie on top of you?" he said quietly.

"What? No. No sex. I can't." I could. I wanted to. But it would be the worst idea.

"I know," he murmured. "It's good for anxiety."

Flat on my back, primly clutching the duvet to my chin, I blinked at the ceiling. He'd mentioned this before. I rolled my head to look at him. "I don't have anxiety."

Flushed from the hot shower, Adam's cheeks were that beautiful rose peach I couldn't look away from. He dipped his gaze with a soft hum.

"Do you think I do?" I said.

He hesitated.

I flopped over onto my side until we were nose to nose. "Is that what this evening has been about?" I smacked his chest with the back of my hand. "It's pity again, isn't it? A pity cuddle?"

Pure frustration flashed over his face. "No. I don't do anything out of pity. I'm not that nice. I wish you'd get that through your head."

Was it me? Was I such a sad creature he felt compelled to *do* something about it? Like an abandoned kitten in the rain? Or did he have some sort of kink that made him—

Adam rolled me over onto my stomach and slid on top of me.

17

"I don't pity you, Ray," he said into my ear. "I don't feel guilty for breaking up your relationship because I didn't know. It's not that complicated. I like you, okay?"

I didn't even flail. I let him manhandle me as if he had the right to, as if I'd given it to him. I lay there, stretched flat in the dark and relaxed under him. I turned my head to one side.

Adam smoothed my hair off my forehead with a warm hand. "Is this okay?" he asked.

"Yes," I said. It took some effort to say it. My voice came out slow and heavy. "'S nice."

"I'm buying you a weighted blanket," he said.

"I don't need one. I don't have anxiety."

He shifted over me, resettling.

There was that hesitation again.

I arched my back in an irritated hump. "There's nothing wrong with having anxiety," I said, "I'm not, like, being a dick about it. I just don't have it." That I was aware of.

"I'm not telling you that you do," he said carefully.

"Although fair to say anyone would be shaken by discovering a dead body."

I murmured agreement.

"And you're highly strung."

I couldn't argue with him there, either. I'd had that complaint before.

"You are all over the place," Adam said. He let out a shuddering breath. "Makes me want to contain you." His arms tucked in tight to my body. His chest was against my back. His legs were to the outside of mine. I'd say he was doing a pretty good job of containing me, actually.

I squirmed under him, enjoying his weight and the slide of his soft skin, marvelling at his confidence.

I'd been a mess of a human being at twenty-three.

I hadn't had a fraction of Adam's maturity or steadfastness. He was so certain in his opinions and in who and what he wanted.

Twenty-three-year-old Ray went where the wind blew him, and as for his sexual confidence? His experience, skills? I'd been entry-level at best. I messed around, I wasn't inexperienced or shy about it. But I didn't have a clue what I wanted. I went along with what the other guy—and on one memorable occasion, woman—wanted and it was all good.

But Adam was *handling* me. He'd done it from the start, and he got better at it each time we clashed.

Although, I didn't think clashed was the right word.

He'd shown up, hugged me, fed and hydrated me, tucked me up, and was now cuddling me.

I had no idea what he was getting out of this deal, but he was right. I was highly strung, I'd definitely been feeling some anxiety, and my muscles were relaxing under his steady, solid weight, the stress falling like dominoes.

"Why do I keep finding dead people?" I said. Adam

shook with laughter. I giggled. "Why are they all in my house?"

"I don't know," he murmured.

"I never expected to see a dead person. Except on TV. It's quite upsetting, to be honest. I think less than if, you know, they'd just expired. But...yeah. Unexpected."

He hummed.

"I feel like I should be doing something about it."

"Something like what?"

"I don't know. There's a whole shelf in the second-hand bookshop in town dedicated to cosy Cotswolds murder mysteries. They're called things like, *Murder in the Cotswolds*, and *Slay Bells: A Cotswold Bellringer Mystery,* or, *Cotswolds Carnage*. I feel like I am failing to live up to expectations. Shouldn't I be investigating, instead of lying in bed in the Premier Lodge? Shouldn't I be running around, being a maverick amateur sleuth? Poking the bear? Stirring up a hornet's nest. Cracking the case wide open and all that." I ran out of cliches.

"While 'all that' sounds like a spectacular way to piss Liam off and thus I am very much in favour, Ray, I hate to break this to you, but you couldn't find your arse with both hands."

"Hey," I said, and reached back.

"Yeah, see?" Adam breathed. "That's my arse you're fondling."

"Is it?" I squeezed. "Are you sure?"

His hips hitched into mine. "Yes."

I reluctantly stopped fondling him, and shoved my hands under the pillow instead. "What do you think is going to happen next?"

He hummed again. "The police will look for more bodies."

"They didn't last time."

"One's a surprise. Two is a pattern."

"Oh no." I writhed and squirmed under him until he lifted up enough to let me turn over. I enjoyed every minute of our bodies sliding together. He settled back on top of me. "It's not a murder house anymore, is it? It's a serial killer house."

We stared at each other.

"Do you think?" I said.

"Ray, I don't know the exact number of bodies you need to make it a serial killer house, but I don't think it's two. I can ask Liam."

"I'd managed to forget, you know? I mean, I haven't managed to get back to sleeping in the master bedroom yet, but on the whole I'd got used to it. I redecorated, by the way. It looks fabulous."

"I'd like to see that. You should invite me over."

"Are they going to tear the house apart? Will I be allowed to live there? Do I want to live there? I'll have to. I can't afford a hotel room for long. Even your shitty basic rooms." My words were coming faster and higher. "I'll have to live out of my car. Or with the ghosts. I'll...no, I'll never be able to sell it. If it was one body, sure. Anyone could overlook that, right? But it's two bodies. It could be more. I'm stuck with it forever! Who would buy a serial killer house? Well, me. But I didn't *know*. Who would buy one if they knew?"

"Shh. Ray." He'd been saying it for a while but I was too busy unspooling with panic to pay any attention. Adam laid a firm palm on my cheek, fingers curling around my jaw. "Ray. You don't have to worry about any of that right now."

I stared at him. "Must you be *so calm*? What is *wrong* with you? Stop being reasonable!" I shoved him.

Adam caught my wrists and gently pushed my hands down until they were held into the pillow by my head. I resorted to bucking my hips up. My breath was still coming fast, catching at the top of each inhale.

"You're here with me right now," Adam said. "It's just you and me. No dead guys, no ghosts, no detectives. That can all wait until morning. Okay?"

Yes. Focus on the now. I should revel in the quiet, the late hour, the luxury bed, and the smoking hot twentysomething with a giant erection throbbing against my stomach. Be present. Be in the moment.

"You know," I said, "I've tried the whole yoga and meditating thing. A lot. A *lot*."

"Maybe practice some more?"

"It doesn't stick. It's not for me. I've given it my best shot. Meditating makes me want to scream."

He drew his bottom lip in between his teeth and let it out slowly. "So highly strung," he said on a happy sigh.

"I do still do yoga. Which I've been doing on top of a dead guy for the last five years." I shuddered at the thought. Adam stroked my ribs. "It bores me to tears. I keep at it, though. Unlike the meditation, it does have obvious advantages."

"Such as?"

"Keeps me limber." I got my legs up and around Adam's hips. After a bit more thrashing and heaving, I had him on his back.

He probably let me do it.

Yeah, I thought, looking down into his calm, warm face. He's humouring me.

I wrestled my way up to straddling him, palms flat on his chest. "I need a distraction," I said. "Distract me."

"Okay." Adam gazed up at me. "Did you know that the

green woodpecker's tongue is so long that it wraps up and around the back of its skull before it comes out of its mouth?"

"Wha—?"

"And it's about a third as long as the woodpecker's body? Imagine having a tongue like that."

"With sex!" I said. "Distract me with sex, not random and frankly horrifying scientific facts." I ground down onto him.

Adam's amused, patient expression turned sharp.

"Yeah?" I said, and rocked down.

His hands came to my thighs and gripped hard. "This isn't a good idea, Ray."

"Correction: it's a fantastic idea. I practically pass out after an orgasm. Sounds awesome to me right now."

His grip readjusted, gliding up until he was holding my hips. Holding me still.

"Come on, Adam" I said. "Distract me."

"No."

"You were all for it last time we were in a bed together—"

"You weren't hysterical last time."

"How dare you. I'm not hysterical now."

"Mm-hmm."

"For god's sake. Am I supposed to beg?"

"One day, yes. I very much intend to make you beg. Twenty minutes ago, you told me no sex, and you meant it."

"Wow. Okay, I changed my mind. I mean it. I want it."

He didn't make a move. "Unless you don't," I said, and went to scramble off, mortified by my behaviour.

Because I didn't want it.

He had an erection. I was in a position to know. I was still sitting on it, after all. I, on the other hand, despite where

I was and despite my earlier problem when he was in the shower, was bewilderingly unaroused. Adam was cupping my cock with a gentle hand. He gave it a soft, meaningful squeeze.

"You've got that the wrong way around," he said. "Of course I want you. I always have. From the first moment I saw you. But as I said, I like you. I'm not going to take advantage of you, what kind of man does that?"

"I've known a few."

He gave me an arrested look and said, "Huh."

My breathing had slowed. Adam was holding my hands now, our fingers laced together.

"Come back down here," he said with a firm tug, "and I'll kiss you silly."

I already felt silly. But why not give him a shot? I sank down and stretched out over him.

"I hate my life right now," I said dolefully into his warm throat.

"Yeah," he said, then drew me up with cool fingers at the nape of my neck and kissed me softly.

"Sucks," I said when he pulled back.

"Oh yeah?" He rearranged us until we were lying on our sides. His mouth brushed over mine. "How about now?"

"Be better if you fucked me."

His hips twitched involuntarily, pushing into me. He was still hard. I still was not. "I'm not giving you another reason to hate me, Ray," he said. His kiss was still soft but edged with urgency, his lips grazing mine lightly then deepening the pressure. I opened to it. He slid his tongue over mine once, twice, then withdrew.

"I don't hate you," I said with surprise.

"Right." He lazily stroked my back.

"I don't! You didn't know about me and Fraser."

"You believe me?" He sounded surprised.

"Yes, of course." I kissed him. He moaned sweetly when I nipped his bottom lip and sucked on it." I wouldn't let a man who I thought was an adulterer in my bed," I said.

And then I froze.

Wait. Hang on. I straight-armed him backward when he went to chase my lips.

"Are you...oh my god. You're making *me* the adulterer, aren't you?"

"What?" Adam sounded dazed. His voice sharpened. "What?" he snapped.

"Exactly. What about Mr. Muscles?"

"Who?"

"Gym boy. Big guy from the coffee shop. Your soul-gazing partner."

After a beat of hesitation, he said, "Jasper?"

"His name is *Jasper*?"

"He's my personal trainer. And he's a friend. We've been over this."

"What's he training you in? It looked very personal from where I was standing."

Adam glared at me. "I know what you're doing, Ray. You're picking a fight, and it's not going to work." He hooked a thigh over mine and dragged me closer with the power of his magnificent quads alone. "I am not in a relationship with Jasper or anyone. I am a free man who can kiss or fuck anyone he wants and for some shit-brained reason—" he sounded strangled with fury, "—that's *you*. And you drive me absolutely *crazy*." He dragged me even closer. "You're not pushing me away with your nonsense."

"How—

He kissed me ferociously, driving past all my defences and owning my mouth like it was his to take. He didn't stop until I was shaking. Then he held my face between his hands and stared at me. "Go to sleep. I don't care how mad you make me, you're not pushing me away and I will not leave you alone after a day like this."

"You did last time," I muttered.

"Yeah, well, unlike some idiots—" he flicked my forehead, "—I reflect and learn."

"Bet I could piss you off enough to make you leave," I said.

"You can't out-stubborn me, and I won't leave when you need me. Or someone," he said bitterly.

"Adam."

"I will gag you."

"But—"

"Zip it." He rolled me over, lay on top of me again, and I zipped it.

It took a while, but my heart rate slowed and synchronised with his. God, he smelled good. He smelled great. Warm and sweet like honey, the fancy Manuka kind from New Zealand which is organic and costs fifty quid a jar and you can't stop eating it by the spoonful.

Embarrassment tinged the edges of my relaxation. Yes, I could be forgiven for freaking out. I could be forgiven for directing it at Adam. It didn't make me any less of an arsehole.

I languidly reached back to slide my fingers into his hair. "I'm sorry," I whispered.

He sighed, kissed my wrist, and rolled off me. He dragged me into the cradle of his long, solid body and spooned me like I'd never been spooned before.

I had a falling sensation in my chest.

I thought that perhaps he really did like me. And maybe I could admit that I liked him back.

More than liked.

I pushed into his warmth. His arm tightened around me. He murmured something indistinct into my neck as I drifted off.

He was gone in the morning.

18

$\mathcal{I}$ woke up alone with a headache, an erection, and an impending sense of doom. I took care of the headache (ibuprofen) and the erection (in the shower) but I couldn't shake the doom.

Along with the general horror and stress of finding a body, and then semi-willingly accompanying an almost-ex to the police station for a 'friendly' chat, I had low-level, queasy feeling of discomfort.

I'd exposed all my vulnerable parts to Adam. I'd exposed more to Adam in one night than I'd ever exposed to anyone. Ever.

I'm a private person, and I'd handed it all over to Adam without even realising it. With ten hours of sleep behind me, I was realising the hell out of it.

I was just grateful that one of us had been grown up enough to keep sex out of the mix.

I was disappointed, and yet unsurprised, that it hadn't been me.

Every time we ran into each other, I liked Adam more. For god's sake, I'd slept in his arms.

I am a terrible sleeper. I fidget, I talk—or so I've been told—and I once sleep-punched a guy and gave him a nosebleed.

The sheet and dented pillow where Adam had slept held a faint, lingering echo of his warmth when I ran my hand over them. He'd stayed with me the whole night.

This all obviously had to stop.

I didn't want a fling. I was done with short-term relationships. I'd been done for a while, which was why I'd asked Fraser to move in with me. In retrospect, that had been too fast. We'd only been dating for a few months.

I'd thought that I was making a statement: share my space. This is for the long term. I'm serious about us.

Fraser had read something else into it. Something along the lines of: hey, man. Want a sweet pad with a roommate dumb enough to give you a pass on the rent, regular sex, and not nag you about chipping in for groceries while you're busy seducing all the hot boys?

Starting anything with Adam had a short expiry date at best. Men like him didn't stick around. He was an ex-model who'd graduated from Cambridge University, and was temporarily working at the Premier Lodge to put together enough money for his future.

It was doubtful that Adam's dream future included a highly strung, thirtysomething graphic designer with trust issues that ran as deep as the Mariana Trench, and a serial killer house.

It had been a big deal for me to put down roots in Chipping Fairford. I'd researched the area, the pros and cons of buying versus renting, of buying an old house versus a new house. I'd read blogs and articles, listened to podcasts. I had a Pinterest board. I collected advice on what to do about rising damp, black mould, leaky roofs, and anything else a new homeowner could want to know about.

I never once came across any advice on what to do when dead bodies show up.

Should I Google it?

No, nope, *no*. With my luck, Liam Nash would find out, I didn't know how but *somehow*, and before you knew it, I'd be back in the station having a chat. It wouldn't be remotely friendly. And there would definitely be handcuffs.

I moaned in despair as I sat on the side of the bed and dug the heels of my hands into my eyes.

Coffee.

Coffee always helped. I eyed the coffee-making facilities on the desk across the room. This might be the luxury suite, but the set-up was the same. A tiny kettle on a dinky tray with cups and biscuits and freeze-dried packets of coffee. The only difference was, the kettle was shinier, and the cups had roses on them.

I made myself a cup, opened up my laptop to see which deadlines were screaming for immediate attention, and managed to distract myself with work for two whole hours.

Who needed athletic Adam-sex?

I'd become a workaholic.

You can't think about corpses and police officers when you're trying to satisfy a client who has the vaguest idea of what they want, but they do know that they want it by the end of the week.

After two hours, the headache was back and I was seriously in need of a proper coffee—I hadn't managed to choke down more than a mouthful of the freeze-dried stuff.

I was a snob, wasn't I?

Whatever. I wanted the good stuff, and I wasn't ashamed.

I grabbed my coat, stuffed my laptop into the bag along with the power cord, and headed out.

I stopped abruptly in the foyer and stared at Adam behind the desk.

I mean...

"Are you always here? Do you *live* here?"

"Good morning, Ray."

"But...always? Aren't there child labour laws?"

"We're not doing this today," he said crisply, getting to his feet and leaning over the desk. To my astonishment, he slid his fingers along my jaw, tilted my face up and kissed me. Quick and dirty. "Good morning, Ray. And no, I don't live here. I live with my mother." He smiled at the surprise that must have shown on my face. "Moving home after university is not exactly ideal, but she needs the help. She had a pacemaker operation while I was finishing up my degree, and since I'm still deciding what to do, I came home. In case you were wondering, working here isn't my end game."

"You didn't get a degree in hotel management, then?"

"Less managing them, more designing them. Architecture degree."

My father would *love* him. If Dad had even an inkling of Adam's existence and of Adam being interested in my existence, he would try to bribe Adam to marry me, just so he could have a son who was into building things.

"Beauty and brains," I said. "Lucky you."

"Mm-hmm."

"Is your mum okay?" I said, fidgeting. "She's doing well?"

"She's doing great. Loving life. I'm here to slow her down and stop her taking on too much too soon, really."

I nodded a few times, oddly reluctant to leave. I wanted to know more about Adam. I wanted to know everything. I was fairly sure he had my number by this point, especially after last night. He, on the other hand, was still a mystery.

He was watching me, his eyes thoughtful and assessing.

I should go.

I didn't. "Um. So. End game. What does that look like?"

"I'm not sure," he said slowly. "Things have a way of changing unexpectedly, you know?"

"No," I said, deadpan. "I have no experience of that whatsoever."

He huffed a laugh. "Do I do a post grad? Apprentice? Do I want to be an architect, or do something else entirely? Whatever I choose, I need to build up some capital." He tapped the desk. "Hence working here."

"You could probably build enough capital in a week to buy a yacht if you modelled again."

"Yeah." His face shuttered. "I could. Except I don't want a yacht. And I prefer this."

"Why?" If I looked like Adam, and people would pay for the privilege of looking at me, I'd be tempted.

"You never know who you'll run into, working in a job like this," he said, giving me a heavy look.

I pointed at myself. "You mean me?"

"Yes, Ray. That's what I mean."

"Well, you won't find me on the set of a photo shoot, that's for sure."

"No," Adam said softly. "You won't."

He reached out and touched my chin. I leaned into it, into him, only to jerk back when the phone on the desk rang.

"Excuse me, I have to get that." Adam answered the phone. He gave it his full attention, ignoring me completely.

I stood there feeling bereft because I didn't get my kiss, and indignant that he could shake me up so easily, then switch straight into business mode while I was left buzzing and off-balance.

After a minute, Adam turned to look at me with a raised eyebrow.

I hurried off.

I was still turning it over in my head as I strode to the coffee shop. The sky was blue, the sun was shining. It wasn't too busy. Yes. This was what I needed. Fresh air.

I felt better already.

It was later than I usually went to The Chipped Cup, but I was fairly confident that I'd find a seat and a power outlet. I strode briskly on, a bounce in my step.

Then I walked into the shop and the comforting noise, a blend of crockery clattering, steam hissing and people talking, cut out.

Everyone stared at me, judgement in their eyes.

I felt my own eyes widen in response, and I clutched my laptop bag tighter. My eyelid twitched. Nobody moved.

Fuck.

They all knew about me and Adam, didn't they? I knew I shouldn't have let Adam and his boner answer the room service. How did it even get around town so fast? I blamed Facebook. No, WhatsApp. No. *TikTok*.

They were judging me for being an ageing creep who lusts after young man-flesh. And wondering why Adam was wasting his time.

It was probably no more than ten seconds before someone coming in off the street behind jostled me forward and fully into the shop, but it felt like an eternity. An eternity during which I was torn between two opposing actions: to turn tail and run, or to toss my head and strut my yeah-that's-right-I-*got*-some stuff to the counter and order a quadruple-shot espresso because, did I mention? I *got* it last night.

In the end, I kept my head down and walked up to the counter like it was any other day.

Sound returned, thank god, although I had the crawling sense that people were still watching.

"Hi," I said to Amalie.

She was between customers and had been absorbed in reading the paper, her elbows propped on the counter and her attention glued to it. When I approached, she looked up and did an odd little double-take before saying warily, "Hi."

You'd think there was something, anything, more exciting going on in Chipping Fairford for people to gossip about other than who answered my hotel room door last night.

"So, I guess people are judging me pretty hard right now," I said after a beat of silence.

Bring it out into the open, I thought. Confront it head on.

Amalie gave an awkward shrug, her eyes flickering down to the paper and back up.

People were *such* gossips.

"Well, I didn't sleep with him, if that's what everyone is worrying about," I said.

Amalie's jaw dropped and she recoiled. "Ray—"

"For the record, though, he's old enough. Some people might think it's problematic. But we're both adults. We shared a bed. That's it."

Amalie turned a sickly green.

I eyed her. "What?" I said. "A warm body in the night and all that..." I trailed off when she gagged. She actually gagged. "Why are you looking at me like that?" I demanded.

"You had...*him*...in the bed with you?" She sounded appalled. "Why would you do that? Ray. That's not okay."

I frowned at her.

"And maybe...maybe you shouldn't talk any more. To me."

"Uh—" Wow. "We shared a bed. Once. That's all." It had been a deeply moving and life-changing moment, but I didn't think telling her that was going to improve matters. Because Amalie was gagging again.

She really meant it, too.

"Can you please stop?" I said. "It's very offensive. Is there a bit of an age gap? Yes. But it's not that big. Come on."

"Are you kidding?" Her face scrunched up and she shuddered.

"I'm not even ten years older than him," I said indignantly.

"That's not what I heard," she said.

"I'm thirty-two! He's twenty-three. You know that. You went to school with him, didn't you?"

"Hold on." She stared at me. "Who did I go to school with?"

"Adam."

"Oh. Ohhhh. *Adam*." She said his name on a heavy exhale, then smiled, shaking her head. "You're talking about *Adam*."

"Yes. Adam. Adam Blake. Who on earth did you think I was talking abou—*oh* my *god*." My brain screeched to a halt and I replayed the conversation in my head. "Oh my god. *Who did you think we were talking about*? Don't say it. *Do not say it.*"

"The dead guy."

"What the fuck? Amalie! You think I slept with a dead guy?"

"Kinda?"

"*Why*?"

"I don't know, Ray, you've been struggling to get a date on Grindr because you won't let me do your profile—"

"Not *that* hard! I've had dates!"

She looked at me.

"I've had matches!"

She looked at me again.

"One match, fine; but I *did* have one. And, yes. *He was alive.*"

"If you say so, but you were the one who started talking about sleeping with a warm *body* the day after you were found with another corpse—"

"It's a figure of speech."

"It was not clear, Ray. And let me remind you, I have a marketing and communications degree."

"Does that include logic at all? Because I wasn't found *with* a corpse, *I* found it and I called the police! How could I sleep with a dead body—" now I gagged, "—when the police had it?"

She tapped the paper on the counter. "You could have another stashed away somewhere."

"Stashed?" I said. "Stashed?"

"So far you've had two..." She trailed off meaningfully.

"I haven't *had* two. They're not mine, are you kidding me?"

She shrugged.

I rolled my head back on my shoulders and covered my face, breathing deep. "This is insane," I said. I dropped my arms down, and that's when I caught sight of the headline splashed across the front page of the newspaper she'd been reading.

LOCAL MAN ARRESTED ON SUSPICION OF

MURDER. WHAT IS HE DOING WITH ALL THE BODIES? SOURCES SAY THERE COULD BE MORE???

I snatched the paper up and held it in front of my face. Please let this be a coincidence and some other local man had...no. No, it was me.

That was me, being 'helped' into the car by Liam Nash.

My entire body went cold.

Goosebumps cascaded over me, from my scalp to my feet.

Every hair I possessed lifted, like a hedgehog bristling.

I dropped the paper on the counter. "I wasn't arrested," I said, loud and clear. "I am not a murder suspect!"

19

I turned the paper to Amalie. "Do you see any handcuffs? No? That'll be because I am not being arrested!"

"It looks like you are, though. He's got his hand on your head. He's putting you in the back seat."

"Because he's a dick! I'm not a murder suspect!"

"Uh-huh."

"This is ridiculous. I'm going to sue. Defamation of character. Libel. Slander?"

"Come on, now. Liam's all right."

"Okay, one? No, he's not. He's a dick. And two? I was talking about this drivel." I flicked at the paper. "This nonsense. This arsehole reporter, whoever wrote it. The man I'm going to sue." I picked it up and squinted at it. "J.C. Connolly," I said.

"Don't sue Jasper, he's a lovely lad," Amalie said.

Wait. *Jasper*?

"*I'm* a lovely lad," I whisper-yelled. "He's a slanderous muppet who just cost his employer a hundred thousand pounds!"

She had the absolute gall to roll her eyes. "How d'you figure that? And if it's in print, it's libel, not slander. Slander is slagging someone off down the pub."

I jabbed at my phone. "I'm guessing. I don't know the going rate for libel these days, let me fucking ask fucking Google. Oh." I stared at the phone.

Well, I'd been joking, but...

"That solves all my problems," I said.

"What?"

"That is a nice chunk of money. I could move from this awful, awful place instead of being stuck for the rest of my life because all my money's locked into a murder house, and the idiot locals think I did it!"

"Babe," an amused voice said by my ear. "Where's my coffee? You're taking forever."

"What? Adam?" I looked over my shoulder and frowned. "Was I getting you coffee? I don't remember that. Are you sure? This is all very stressful." I passed a hand over my forehead. "I forgot. Sorry. And an Americano for Adam, thanks." I turned to him and put both hands flat on his chest. "Adam," I said urgently.

"Yes, Ray?"

I flung an arm behind me in an agitated wave, encompassing the rest of the coffee shop. "All these people think I'm a murderer."

"I heard."

"And that Liam arrested me." I grabbed the paper off the counter and pushed it into his hands.

Adam took it. His face did something complicated.

He was trying not to laugh.

"This isn't funny," I said.

"It does look like you're being arrested."

"Well, I wasn't! Unless Liam forgot to inform me of the

fact. You know what? I *hope* that is the case, since everyone thinks he did anyway. Then I'll sue him *and* Jasper, and I will definitely be able to set fire to the murder house and go live somewhere else!"

"Don't sue Jasper," Adam said, brushing a piece of hair out of my eyes and smiling down at me. "He's a lovely lad."

"*I'm* a lovely lad!"

"I'd rather you didn't threaten arson in my hearing, Mr Underwood," said another familiar voice, infinitely less welcome. "I really would have to arrest you."

I whirled around to glare at Liam. "I'll burn down my own damn house if I want to," I snapped. "Kick back and toast some marshmallows. Grill a steak, who knows? It's my house. *Liam.* Don't worry, though. I won't be claiming the insurance. I won't need to. When I'm done suing you and Jasper, I'll be a millionaire."

"It's still illegal to burn down your house, whether or not you're trying to commit insurance fraud. And it's the site of an ongoing investigation. That would be tampering. I'd have to arrest you twice." He, too, was trying not to laugh. He looked over my head. "Hey, Adam."

"You got here quickly," Adam said.

"I was coming over anyway."

"Oh, yeah?"

"Yeah, had about ten calls that a murderer was about to go off."

"You're not funny, either," I said to Liam. It was then I noticed that at least three people had their phone cameras aimed at me. I shrank back against Adam. He wrapped an arm around me. Although it chafed me to admit it, I felt safer with Adam there.

"I need to talk to you again this morning, Ray," Liam said.

Everyone shifted forward a bit in their seats.

"You're not arresting him, are you?" Adam said. Loudly.

"No."

"Why is that, Liam?"

He levelled Adam with a glare. "Because he's not a murder suspect, Adam."

"What about this?" Amalie waved the paper in Liam's face.

"Incorrect," was all he said.

"Libel," I hissed.

Liam winced.

"What *is* the procedure when it comes to libel, Detective Nash?" I said. "I'm afraid I don't know off the top of my head."

"Don't be an arse, Ray," Amalie said, sounding bored. She set my latte on the counter, Adam's Americano alongside it.

"Me? I'm the only person in here who isn't an arse! Ten minutes ago, you thought I was confessing to necrophilia with one of my murder victims!"

"All right, all right, get over it. How was I to know you were talking about sleeping with Adam?"

I opened and shut my mouth a few times. Liam narrowed his eyes at Adam, Adam tightened his arm around my waist, and Amalie held out a fist for a bump.

I drew myself up and ignored it. "More likely than me sleeping with a corpse, isn't it?"

She shrugged. If she did it again, I'd scream. "Lotta people been trying to lock that down," she said with a lascivious grin at Adam. I felt his huff of laughter ruffle the top of my head. "Yeah, I'd say it's more likely you slept with a dead guy than you snagged Adam."

I flinched.

I'd been outraged and indignant when everyone thought I was a corpse-fucking serial killer thanks to the lovely Jasper's shitty reporting. Having Amalie say in such an offhand tone that it was more likely than Adam being with someone like me hurt.

"Oh," she said. "Ray, I didn't mean—"

"Thanks, Amalie," Adam said tightly, and let me squirm out of his arms.

I collected the coffees, blushed and muttered, "Forgot to pay."

"On the house," she said.

"No. Thank you." I held my card out and it barely even trembled. She sighed and let me tap it against the card reader.

"Here ya go." I darted a glance up at Adam, then pushed his coffee at him.

"What did you want from me today, Detective?" I said, focusing on Liam. "Shall we?" I gestured to the door.

Liam stepped aside and followed me out.

On my way, I noticed a young man get up and hover awkwardly. I recognised the muscles. *Jasper.* His big eyes were round, blinking rapidly, and he looked like a guilty, guilty puppy. I wasn't going to sue the idiot, but he'd have to find that out on his own.

"What's up?" I said to Liam. Flippantly I added, "Find another body?"

He hesitated.

"You didn't." I wheezed. "Please tell me you didn't."

"Are you serious?" Adam said beside me.

"Sorry, Adam," Liam said." Can't talk about an open investigation with you when you're not a concerned party."

"I'm deeply concerned."

"Rules are rules."

"Ray will tell me later anyway," Adam said.

"Don't count on it." I broke into their glare-off. "What if you say something to your lovely lad Jasper, part-time personal trainer and, apparently, part-time intrepid reporter? He might twist it up to sell more copies, then next thing you know, the townsfolk will be coming for me with pitchforks and torches."

Adam caught my arm, turning me to face him. "Ray, we've been through this. There's nothing between me and Jas."

"I know, I—"

"Eh," Liam said.

We both looked at him.

"What does that mean?" I said.

"They've been on and off for years," Liam said. "If you're in the picture, they must be off again."

"Liam," Adam said warningly. "That's bullshit. We were never in a relationship. Just FWBs."

"Right. On-again off-again friends with benefits."

"No on, no off. Just occasional hook ups."

"Semi-regularly. For the last nine years. Sure."

"You lost your virginity at fourteen?" I said. Like that was the important thing right now. "You had a friend-with-benefits arrangement at fourteen?"

I knew Adam was more mature than me, but that felt ridiculous.

"Okay, this has been great," Adam said brightly. "Liam, thanks for shit-stirring. Nice try, but it won't work. Ray?"

"Hmm—*oh*."

When I glanced up at him, he laid one on me. A deep, wet, possessive kiss that left me staring stupidly after him as he strode down the street in the direction of the hotel, tossing a casual, "Tell me all about it tonight, babe," over his shoulder.

"Ugh," I muttered. "I hate that."

"Yeah." Liam's voice was arid. "You look utterly disgusted."

I brushed a hand over my damp mouth then discreetly adjusted myself. "Being called babe," I informed him loftily.

"Again. Clearly a real turn-off."

I glared at him. "Did you actually want something, or...?"

He grunted. "Yeah. We're going to need to look for more bodies."

"Is that why you're here? To ask permission? And can I say no?"

"I'm here because Adam called."

I frowned up at him while I sipped my coffee.

His eyes tracked down to my mouth and back up.

"Why'd Adam call? Oh my god. He called you down here to show everyone I wasn't arrested, didn't he?"

"Yup. Jasper called Adam, Adam called me."

I knew Adam hadn't asked me to get him a coffee. "I'm hardly going to complain. I think I had it under control, though."

Liam snorted.

"I did," I said.

"Ray. When I walked in you were threatening lawsuits all around, and on top of that, announcing plans to commit a major crime."

I blinked at him.

"The arson," he reminded me dryly.

"Right. Are you *sure* it's arson if I do it with no intent to claim insurance?"

"It's against the law to set fire to houses. Buildings. Property in general. I include your car."

"Why would I set fire to my car? I love my car."

"No clue. You're more of a loose cannon than I initially thought. I didn't expect to hear you planning to burn down your house, and yet here we are."

"I suppose there are rules for the disposal of personal property," I mused. "What if I wanted to, I don't know. Buy a sledgehammer and knock it down?"

Liam reached out and tested my bicep, made a considering noise. "You'll be doing it for a while."

"I'm fuelled by anger and despair right now. I doubt it'd take that long."

"Sue Jasper and use the money to hire a demo crew."

"You're the only one who hasn't told me not to sue him."

"Yeah. I'm also the only one he hasn't got fooled." Liam looked over my shoulder, his face stern. I glanced back. Jasper was gawking anxiously out the window, eyes darting from me to Liam and back.

Hmm. Was it me or was there a vibe?

"He's not quite the little angel he looks," Liam said.

Jasper was six foot three—same height as Adam. He was beautifully built, had close-cropped dark hair and wore a camo print t-shirt that said *SWEAT!!!* on it.

Neither *little* nor *angel* sprang to mind.

To my mind, at least. I couldn't speak for Liam.

Jasper did look like he was freaking out, though. I could relate. I waved. It was meant to be friendly, but I missed the mark. Jasper paled further and sat down with what must have been a heavy thump, since I saw the table shake.

By now I'd finished my coffee and my headache was back. "Can I go?" I asked Liam. "I have work to do and I'll be honest, this has been quite a shitty morning."

"Nope." He took my arm, steering me along beside him toward his car.

I hauled back and dug my heels in. "Hell, no. I am not getting in your car."

"What? Why? I'm going to drive you home."

"What do you mean, *why*? Because tomorrow I'll pick up the paper and it'll say, LOCAL CORPSE-FUCKER TAKEN IN FOR FURTHER QUESTIONING. I know Jasper is still watching." I hitched a thumb at the coffee shop behind me. "I'll walk, thank you. Also, as I'd rather not go home until you've actually done your job properly, I'll be walking to the hotel."

"I've got some more questions for you."

I chewed my lip. "I don't want to go to the station again. Is this formal?"

"No. We can do it anywhere, although I'd prefer not the middle of the street. Private would be better."

The hotel had a business centre, Adam had said. I didn't fancy it, though. Right now, the hotel was my safe place. The business centre might not be private enough, and I wasn't going to invite Liam up to my room, although the expression on Adam's face would almost be worth it.

"Fine," I said reluctantly. "Let's go to my place."

20

$\mathcal{I}$ permitted Liam to drive me after all, although first I made him go and park two streets away while I jogged down the short alley between the Co-op and the florists, and I refused to get in until there were no witnesses

"Huh," I said when we pulled up outside my house. Liam put on the handbrake and switched off the engine. I peered out the window. "I was expecting more drama."

There weren't any hoardings or plastic sheets. No barriers. No cordons. No large signs declaring MURDER MURDER CRIME STAY BACK MURDER. It hadn't been tented or anything. A couple of strips of blue and white tape formed an X over my front door, and there was a police patrol car parked in the drive.

It was a bit disappointing.

"What kind of drama were you expecting?" Liam turned to me.

"I don't know. Something like that bit at the end of *E.T.* when they tent the place. Hazmat suits all round. You know."

"We found two mummified bodies, Ray, not aliens. And the property has changed hands multiple times since it's estimated these guys died. There is a limit to what we're likely to be able to collect, in terms of forensic evidence. Now, if I'd found you standing over fresh victims with a bloody axe, we'd be a bit pickier about preserving the scene."

"If I murdered someone, you'd never know. I'd be straight down to the hardware store for an XXL storage tub and enough extra-absorbent cat litter for a panther with a nervous bowel."

Liam stared at me.

"I am so innocent," I said. "Of all crime."

"Hmm."

Now would be a good time to move the conversation on. "How are you going to search for more bodies?" I asked. "Are you going to rip up all the floors?"

I'd said I was going to burn it down, but I hadn't meant it. We were going through a rough patch right now, but I loved my little house. I didn't want to see it torn apart.

More importantly, before I let anyone start taking it apart, I wanted some reassurance that it would all be put back together again.

"A few boards will be lifted," Liam said.

"You're not going to go all Miley Cyrus on it, are you?" At his blank look, I added, "Like a wrecking ball?" I hummed a few bars.

He grimly waited for me to stop before he said, "If I recall, you were threatening to do that exact same thing yourself about ten minutes ago."

"It's my house, though."

Liam opened his door and got out. I followed. It hadn't

escaped my notice that there had been no clarity on the wrecking ball situation.

A uniformed officer was sitting in the patrol car, which blocked the door to the garage. In theory, you could fit another car in there, but in practice it was stuffed with old canvases from art college I never wanted anyone to see, gym equipment I never used, and the entire contents of my great aunt's tiny house.

When Aunt Alicia died three years ago, I was foolish enough to agree to help my dad clear her house in Banbury and prep it for sale. Dad had interpreted that as me agreeing to have him and his buddy, Marley, show up in a work van with all of Aunt Alicia's possessions, from her clothes to her furniture, crammed in the back. Despite my protests, he'd unloaded it into my garage, told me I could go through it at my leisure—*it'll be like a fun new hobby, Raymond*—and if I managed to sell anything, I should feel free to go ahead and keep the proceeds.

Needless to say, I hadn't got around to it yet.

Maybe now was the time to start.

I might need the money.

The young police officer inside the car was staring fixedly ahead. If he was aware of us, he showed no signs of it.

"Is he asleep?" I asked Liam as we drew level with the car.

Liam banged on the window. The officer flinched wildly and smacked the horn.

"Not anymore," Liam said. He tipped his head toward the front door. "Come on."

The officer slumped, wide-eyed, in his seat, a hand pressed to his chest.

"That was mean," I said to Liam.

"He's lucky I don't haul him out the car and yell at him for a bit. Supposed to be keeping watch, not dozing on the job."

"His eyes were open."

"Don't be fooled, and don't make excuses."

I dithered in front of the door, not sure what to do about the tape. Liam reached over my shoulder and pulled it down. I got my keys out and did a passable job of hiding the tremble in my hand as I unlocked it. "Why's he keeping watch?"

"He's supposed to stop sightseers from poking around the scene. It's standard procedure. Nothing to worry about."

"Okay. When's it going to stop being 'the scene' and become 'my house' again?"

"Ray, we have to conduct a thorough search of the premises."

"I know. You already told me that. I'm surprised you aren't doing it now."

I was surprised it wasn't a hive of activity. It was me, Liam, and Officer Dozy outside.

"We're a small force here. It's an interesting case, but it's not like we're investigating an open murder with a critical time element, like, say, any chance whatsoever of being able to arrest the person who did it." He gazed at me meaningfully.

I gazed back. Then the reason behind his meaningful gaze percolated. "As in...*no* chance?"

"Zero chance."

"And that would be because, considering how old the bodies are, the person who did it is...also dead?" I guessed.

Liam heaved a big, fake, put-upon sigh. "You saw them, Ray. They were essentially mummies. Of course, you've put it all together yourself, right? I'm not telling you anything you don't know here. Right?"

"Very right. Yes. I know everything. Wait. No, I don't know everything. Because it's not my crime. But I do know that the body was very, very old-looking. If I had to estimate, I'd say it was, oh..." I watched Liam's expression, adjusting my estimates as I went "...at least twenty. No, forty. More? Yes. More than fifty years old. Twice more? Are you serious? It's at least a hundred years old?"

"The lab isn't rushing the analysis on this one, but that seems to be the general consensus at the moment. Good guess."

"Thanks," I said vaguely. "Hang on, though." I hadn't waited around to get a good look at the second guy. Long enough to know I was looking at the same kind of thing—a human body in a tub—as the first guy. Who had died around a century ago. Which was really sticking. Because... "The first body was wearing bellbottom jeans and a tie-dye t-shirt," I said.

"Yep."

"The seventies was a long time ago, but it wasn't a hundred years ago."

"Your maths is impeccable."

My stomach lurched. "Liam. That doesn't add up."

"It doesn't."

"For a man who died a hundred years ago to be wearing an outfit from the seventies, that means someone dressed him up."

Liam dipped his head in a tiny nod.

"Like a doll," I said. "Oh, crap. He was a human doll?" That was the most horrific thing I'd ever heard.

"I can't speculate as to the motive behind the clothes."

"I can. I'm speculating my arse off. Creepy human doll

serial killer. Oh, fuck. It's not a murder house. It's not even a serial killer house, and I didn't think it could get worse than that. It's a human dollhouse. Liam. I'm living in the dollhouse of the dead. *Don't tell anyone.* I'll never sell it."

"I won't tell anyone, because it's speculation and it's against the rules. And you won't tell anyone that you managed to work it out all on your own, either? Will you?"

"Did you not hear me? I can't offload a dollhouse. I'm never even going to say the word again. Except...what was the other guy's outfit? I didn't see."

Liam shook his head slowly. "You don't want to know."

"I don't?" I said faintly.

"Earlier than the seventies, and it wasn't so much an outfit as a...costume."

"A costume? Like...a Halloween costume? Like Batman?"

"No, he wasn't dressed as Batman, and that's all you need to know."

I decided not to argue with him.

"As you can imagine," Liam went on, "this isn't the sort of case that a small force like ours is used to dealing with. Which is why we'll be bringing in a specialist team."

"Okay."

"We have two options there. One, we can see if we can get a cadaver dog. Two, we can get a forensics team in to do a detailed inspection. By which I mean they'll pull up some floorboards, check a few cavities. That sort of thing."

I winced at the idea of them going into the attic. It would give a hoarder nightmares. It made my garage of Aunt Alicia's stuff look like the Louvre.

"I'll have the cadaver dog, please. How does that work, anyway? They have a quick run around, sniff some stuff, give you the thumbs up or thumbs down?"

"Yep. That's about it."

"Sounds great.

"It's efficient, minimal disruption. Ideal, really."

"Definitely the dog then."

"The thing is, they are the elite of K9 officers."

"Cool." I loved dogs. I wondered if I'd get to say hi.

"Obviously, we don't have one locally. And it's not easy to book their time."

The sinking feeling in my gut told me I wasn't going to get to say hi. And the vaguely apologetic, vaguely belligerent expression on Liam's face told me they were going to tear up my floors.

"We can put a request in," he said.

I perked up.

"But it could take up to six months."

"What? To get a dog to run around my house for twenty minutes?"

"It's a bit more technical than that, Ray."

"I'd still like the dog." I said.

"On the other hand," he talked over me before I'd even finished speaking, making me blink, "we can get a consult from one of the major crimes forensics units in London. They'll be here as soon as they have an opening. It might be more invasive, but it'll be done. Better than waiting six months."

"I'm still leaning toward the dog."

"And getting it done quickly and efficiently is in everyone's best interests."

"Why do I feel like my interests aren't at the number one spot here and yours might be higher?"

"My recommendation to my boss is that, from a community policing standpoint, the best course of action is to get it done quickly and efficiently."

I glared at him. "Did I ever have a choice, or are you

torturing me? It wasn't enough fun to make Officer Dozy shit himself in his car and give me nightmares about human dolls?"

He sighed. "I'm trying to be a good guy here, Ray. I'd hoped you'd want it done quickly."

"It's not as if I want to drag it out."

Liam gave a weary grunt. "You'd be surprised at how many people enjoy being involved in this sort of thing."

"I'm surprised anyone would enjoy it at all."

"People like attention. They like to be made to feel special."

"I don't need the entire town looking at me or my house to feel special," I said. "I hate attention."

"Then you're going to hate waiting for a cadaver dog. You're going to have plenty of mornings like this morning in the coffee shop."

That gave me pause. "Nobody thinks I'm a murderer anymore at least," I said uncertainly.

"Even if no one thinks you did it, people will want to come and look themselves. Take photos of the house. Poke around. Peer through your windows." He gave me a sympathetic and not entirely genuine smile. "Be thankful this hasn't been picked up by a true crime podcast."

Seeing myself on the front page of the local paper was bad enough. Being talked about on Spotify by some arsehole who thought actual dead people and suffering was fun entertainment made my vision waver.

"Fine," I said.

Liam's mouth was already open, presumably to throw another convincing argument my way. "Fine?"

"Get the crime scene guys in. You may proceed."

"I don't actually need your permission."

"Then what was this about!" I threw my arms out.

He scowled.

"Why would you stand there taking me through options I don't even have before making me choose what you were always going to do!"

"It's called community policing," he said stiffly. "We don't just do what we like, you know. A large part of deciding how to proceed with an investigation means taking into account the effect on the victim, those involved, and the community in general."

I stared.

He scowled harder.

"You're handling me," I said, loud in the quiet room.

"Don't be ridiculous."

"No, you are. You're handling me like I'm going to make a big drama or fuss."

"I'm being professional. I'm a professional. I'm a compassionate human being. This is stressful. I can see that. Of course it is. Nobody wants you to crack under the pressure."

I stared again. He stared back.

I sucked in a breath. Adam. "Adam asked you to do it, didn't he?"

"As I said ten seconds ago, I'm a professional. I've done a victim support course *and* a seminar. I know how important it is to feel like you have some control—"

"Definitely, definitely Adam."

"Maybe I'm an excellent officer and human being?"

"You ghosted me, Liam. How great a human being can you be?"

Liam smiled with teeth. "Handling the public is all part of my job. It would be very unprofessional for me to do anything in the course of my investigation, one way or another, at the prompting of anyone other than a fellow officer, or my superior."

"Definitely not because your controlling cousin, who's trying to bang 'the public' involved, asked you to."

I'd been going for a joke to lighten the mood. I didn't like being treated like a drama queen, but I appreciated the intent behind it, to make me feel less helpless.

The joke failed to land. Liam was pissed off. "I take my job very seriously, Ray. There's a line. I'm careful with it. In a small community, you have to be. Yes, Adam called. He's concerned for you." He rolled his eyes. "Very concerned. He's nosy and controlling, and he had suggestions on how I should handle things. A lot of suggestions. However, this—" he pointed between us, "—is me trying to be a good police officer. I've got to find the balance between keeping you informed and getting the job done."

"You can be very stern."

"Ray."

"I'm kidding. Thank you for your efforts. I'd rather have it stated plainly then be led by the hand to a foregone conclusion, but I appreciate the good intentions."

He grunted, still offended and annoyed.

"How long until I can come home?"

"Depends on whether they find any more bodies."

"Ugh. Don't say that."

He pressed a smile away, flattening his lips.

"Seriously, though. Guesstimate for me."

"Say a week."

Ouch. That was going to hit me square in the wallet if I was looking at a week at a hotel.

"And how bad's the damage going to be? If they rip the floor up and punch holes in the walls, they'll fix it up, right?"

"I don't know, Ray. I haven't worked with the London guys before. They're probably fine."

Fine? How encouraging. "And you're sure a dog is absolutely off the table?"

"Yes."

"Can I hire one as an independent contractor?"

"No."

I decided to look into it as soon as I got back to the hotel.

21

For the first time since this whole unwanted period of excitement had started, Adam was not behind the front desk at the Premier Lodge. I'd expected him to be there, in part because he always seemed to be. Mostly, though, because I wanted him to be.

I was thwarted by the bright-eyed smile from the woman sitting in Adam's seat.

She stood up expectantly.

Deciding it would look weird to change direction after we'd already made eye contact, I continued on my path.

"Good afternoon, sir," she said. "How can I help you today?"

Was it afternoon already? I'd intended to ask if the business centre was available—it seemed like a breezily reasonable question—only what came out was, "Is Adam here?"

I wanted to slap myself. I really did.

When had this become acceptable? I was always asking for Adam.

I sounded like a child who'd biked over to his friend's house, tossed his bike on the lawn and scrambled breathlessly up to the front door to ask if his buddy could come out to play, like I used to do when I was ten.

When I was actually ten, if I'd cycled over to Adam's house to ask if he could come out to play, his mother would have said, sorry, he's due for a nappy change/he's breastfeeding/he's still in my uterus.

I went lightheaded at the thought.

What was I *doing*?

What the hell was I doing?

I'd come back to find Adam. I'd come here to seduce him or, more realistically, to let him seduce me.

Because it felt inevitable. He was everywhere. He wanted it, I wanted it, we were both adults. And yet, what with the second body, the serial killer accusations, and my apparently overwhelming need to have someone lie on top of me (what was even up with that), I'd managed to let my reservations fade into the background.

Just because it felt inevitable, it didn't mean it was.

I couldn't have sex with Adam. He'd become familiar because he was always around. He was always around because he wanted me, and he was a scarily perceptive man. He knew my resolve to keep him at arm's length was crumbling.

He was still the problematic guy who was way out of my league.

No matter how much I wanted (I wanted, my god I wanted) to have him and let him have me, it was a terrible idea.

Sex with anyone was a terrible idea right now. Let alone with Adam, who would, I was sure, ruin me for all other men.

"Adam's off until tonight," the receptionist said.

"Great. That's...that's great, yes, thank you."

I headed up to my room and whisked around, packing my stuff. Ten minutes later, I was back in the foyer.

"You want to check out now?" the receptionist said. "You've paid for two nights."

"Yes, right now." I tapped the desk with a nervous forefinger. "You know what, can we go a little faster? I'm in a hurry. Quicker would be better."

She kept her professional face on as she totalled up the bill and charged my card.

I didn't even check the total. I snagged the receipt from her hand as quickly as possible and bolted.

I was not running away.

That's not what this was.

Possibly you could interpret it as being conflict avoidant, but once again: dead bodies in my house. I think I deserved to avoid any more conflict.

The real issue was, I couldn't go home. I couldn't afford the astronomical cost of an open-ended hotel stay. I didn't know if the police had some sort of fund out of which they paid for people they'd ejected from their murder houses to stay somewhere else or not. Knowing my luck, if they did, they'd either put me right back here, or in a shithole of a B&B.

There was only one place left to go.

My parents.

It wasn't until I was halfway there that I wondered if I was allowed to.

I pulled over into a lay-by and called Liam.

"No, Ray," he said by way of greeting. "Astonishingly enough, we're not done yet."

"Can I leave?" I said.

"What?"

"Am I allowed to go out of town?

There was a brief silence at the other end of the line. "Where are you right now?"

"Definitely still in town."

He sighed.

"But if I were to be, say, thirty miles away, northbound on the A44, would that be illegal? Or, in this hypothetical scenario, can I keep driving?"

"By all means, keep driving."

"Okay, phew."

"Check your mirrors."

"Always do."

"You'll know it's me behind you when you see the flashing lights."

"That's a no? I'm not allowed?"

He heaved another put-upon sigh and grudgingly said, "You're not a suspect or a witness. I still strongly advise against it."

"I'm not hearing no."

"Ray. Don't run away from this."

"Who's running? I'm driving. I'm in my car. I thought I'd stay with my parents until you, uh, release the scene. I can't keep staying at the Premier Lodge."

"Where do your parents live?"

"Steeple Norton. It's a village about sixty miles north of Chipping Fairford. I'm almost there."

"I'm going to need the address. You are still part of an active investigation. Don't go on holiday abroad or anything, all right?"

"Hah. I wish."

"Ray."

"I'm going to stay with my parents until you give me the all-clear. That's it. I have clients, I have work, I have deadlines. I'm going to take over Giselle's shed—she calls it a studio—and work my arse off. That's my plan."

"Can I convince you it's a bad plan?" Liam said.

"No. It's too difficult to be there right now."

"Leaving town makes you look very suspicious."

"You literally just told me I'm not a suspect," I said indignantly.

"I meant to everyone else. You know that, don't you? Ray?"

"Can I remind you of this morning in the coffee shop? You and Adam are probably the only people in Chipping Fairford who don't think I did it, or am involved somehow."

"Come back to town, I'll find you somewhere to stay, and Jasper won't have the opportunity to get all overexcited and write any stupid articles about you fleeing the country. Because trust me, he *is* that stupid, and if he finds out you've gone, I can almost guarantee that is what will be on the front page."

"I can guarantee that I'll sue if he does."

"What about Adam?"

I sat there and failed to come up with a response.

"Ray," he said gruffly after a long, painful silence. "Come back."

"Is that a legal request?" Was that a feeble quaver I heard in my voice?

"No."

"You have my number and my email. I'll text you my parents' address. Let me know when your team's done, okay? Bye." I hung up, shot him the address, and pulled onto the road before I could second-guess myself, and do what everything in me was screaming to do: go back.

To Adam.

22

I fell asleep in my childhood bed. I went out like I'd been hit in the back of the head with a bag of wet sand. The only other time I'd fallen asleep without fidgeting and flopping around, or drifting in in and out of a queasy half-dreaming, half-waking state before finally going under, had been in Adam's arms.

Okay, that was a lie and very melodramatic. No need to romanticise things.

I'd been blackout drunk twice in my twenties. I'd also been knocked out twice; once by walking at full speed into a cupboard door a roommate left open, and once by a cricket ball.

For reference, I was *not* at a cricket match when that happened, and I don't want to talk about it.

The point was, I'd been thinking of Adam as I lay in bed, and apparently I was so obsessed with him that simply imagining that the pillow I'd tugged under the covers and furtively spooned was Adam had enabled me not only to fall asleep but to feel relaxed and safe enough that I overslept. I was hopeless.

Next thing I knew, I'd be rhapsodising about how the fork I was eating my breakfast eggs with reminded me of the fork Adam had slipped between my lips while feeding me cheesecake, and—

My father cleared his throat.

I glanced up and the kitchen swung into focus.

The radio played softly in the background. It was tuned to Classic FM—and for once the station was playing classical music rather than talking, or trying to sell me pet insurance, a new car, concert tickets to a Classic FM concert, insurance so my offspring aren't crushed by my death, Marks & Spencer food delivery, and more insurance. Also a pre-planned funeral so my offspring aren't emotionally crushed by my death. And funeral insurance.

Giselle and Dad were watching me, smiling.

"What?" I said.

"Should we leave you alone with your eggs?" Dad said. "It's nice that you're enjoying them. Quite the compliment to my cooking. But are they that good?"

I looked to Giselle in question.

"You're eye-fucking them, darling."

"Ew." Appetite gone. I dropped my fork with a clatter.

"Gigi," Dad said with a little more pain in his amusement.

Giselle sipped her coffee serenely.

Screw it, I was still hungry. I grabbed my fork and shovelled in the rest of my eggs.

"You've lost weight," Dad said. "Are you on one of those diets again?"

"Mm-hmm," I mumbled through a mouthful of toast. "Three meals of stress a day, and a little social ostracisation for a snack. Ten out of ten would recommend for swift and brutal weight loss."

Dad gazed at me levelly then returned his attention to the newspaper. "You're a graphic designer, Raymond, not a stockbroker. If it's stressing you out to the extent of losing weight, we need to talk about you changing career."

I dropped my head back on my shoulders and groaned at the ceiling. "I don't want to be a conservatory salesman."

Dad didn't glance away from the paper. He did mutter, "Why would you? It's not like there's a company waiting for you with your name already on it and everything. *Ow*."

Giselle had shoved him. "He's an *artist*, Christopher. Building conservatories would crush his spirit. We've been over this."

And over and over.

"Gigi, I've got a team. They build the things. All Ray has to do is manage the business."

"Crush. His. Spirit. Look at him."

They both looked at me.

Giselle waved an expansive hand at me, her carved wooden bracelets clacking. "Does this look like the responsible, mature business-minded man you want to let loose on your precious spreadsheets?"

I was in my washed-out old *Fraggle Rock* t-shirt and plaid pj bottoms, my hair stuck up weirdly, and my eyes were red rimmed and puffy. But still. No need to be rude. "I do run my own business, you know. I'm quite successful at it."

Dad tipped his head consideringly from side to side.

I narrowed my eyes. "So, the police found two dead bodies in my house," I said.

Giselle's hand froze in mid-air, fork halfway to her mouth. Dad fumbled the paper.

I crunched into my toast.

My parents lived an hour and forty minutes away. It

wasn't far, but it was far enough that local news from my town wasn't on their radar.

Dad read the Daily Telegraph every morning, worked a full day every day except for golf days, which were on Saturdays, Sundays, and Wednesdays, and Giselle was a full-time creative. She went from book club to watercolour class to yoga to pottery class. Out of the three of us, her schedule was the busiest. I don't know where she found the energy.

My point being, if it didn't make the national news, they weren't likely to hear of it. And I'd stuck to my initial plan of actively not enlightening them.

I loved my parents, but they had their lives and I had mine.

If I'd told them about the body, Giselle would have arrived to Emotionally Support me through my Trying Times.

Dad would have upped his awkward rumblings about how I should choose a more stable career than flighty artist, since you could weather anything with a firm foundation. I'd get all angry pointing out that I was a working graphic designer, not a flighty artist, I had a firm foundation and many, many skills beyond laying bricks even if I didn't build it with my own hands...all in all, sharing it with them wouldn't have been remotely helpful.

Adam had helped.

He'd come to check on me after the first body, and I'd run him off with my insecurities. And then he'd looked after me again with this second one, and then in the coffee shop, and I'd run away...

The big problem with Adam wasn't that he annoyed me by trying to help. It was that I let him. I welcomed it.

I wanted it.

I was clearly having a breakdown.

As was Giselle, right now, after my mic-drop comment.

"What?" she screeched. "What?"

"Huh," Dad said once I'd given them the highlights of the last couple of months, minus the sexy bits.

"When I say, *Hello, Ray. How are you? Anything interesting going on?*" Giselle continued. "That is your cue to say *Oh, not much. No, wait. I did get taken in for questioning by the police about a dead man, though.*"

"I didn't want to worry you."

"If you didn't want to worry me," she said, "you wouldn't have dropped it into conversation over the breakfast table in a weak ploy to distract your father."

I winced.

"I've come across a couple of bodies in my time," Dad mused.

Giselle whirled on him. "What?" she screeched. "Are dead people lying around all over the place and I don't notice? How come I don't find any? And when on earth did you find dead bodies?"

"Digging foundations," he said. "You have no idea what you're walking around on top of until you start digging."

Or, in my case, doing corpse pose on top of.

"You found actual dead people?" I said.

"Animals, mostly," Dad said. "And a hand."

"A hand?"

"Turned out to be a chimp's."

"Why didn't I hear about any of this?" Giselle said. "If you find a hand, Christopher, I'd like to know about it. I'm your wife."

"It was before I met you, dear. One of my early jobs."

"Where was the rest of the chimp?" I said.

"Who knows? It was an old Victorian place. Owner said

it was full of animal skins and trophy heads and such nonsense when he bought it. Fucking Victorians."

My Dad had a hate-on for Victorians that, if roused, could get him frothing at the mouth. He loathed them. To this day, I didn't know why. It was hilarious.

"This was back in the eighties, though," he said. "The police weren't all that interested, even before they figured out it was a chimp."

"No excavation? No looking around for more?"

"It was just a hand, Ray."

I stared at my father across the table.

...

...*just* a hand?

He lifted his brows.

"Right," I said. "Well, anyway. The police care about the bodies in my house, I can tell you right now they're not chimps, and I can't go home until the police have processed the scene. Again. Hopefully they'll do it right and find anything that needs to be found, and I can go back. Is it okay if I stay for a week? Maybe two? I know I sprang this on you, and you might have plans or—"

"Ray, sweetheart." Giselle reached over the table to clasp my hand and gaze at me. "Stay forever."

"Hopefully not that long, but—"

She squeezed. "We miss you. Move back home if you like. There's plenty of room."

My father blanched. I imagined I had the same wide-eyed, deer-in-headlights expression on my face.

"Lots of people have multi-generational homes," Giselle went on. "It's normal."

"I have a home, though. I was thinking a week—"

"It's an option. You don't have to decide now. At least five people in the village I can think of off the top of my head have their children living with them. Sometimes grandchildren, too."

This was escalating.

"Okay, lovely to know I could do that if I wanted, thanks."

Smiling, Giselle released me to pour another cup of tea.

I took pity on my horrified father and shook my head, emphatically mouthing, *NO.* "I'm settled where I am, and, ah. Yeah. I'll stay for a week—I'll be working, it's not a holiday, got so much work to do, you'll barely even see me—and I'll take it from there."

23

_M_y plan to take over Giselle's studio-shed were thwarted by the paper-making she'd got into since I was last home. The shed was stuffed with bags of old clothes that she was going to rag, crates of old newspapers that she was going to tear up, and bunches of dried wildflowers that she was going to pluck the petals from and embed in the finished product. At some unnamed date.

Trying to work from my childhood bedroom didn't feel great. My clients didn't know I was away from my usual desk, of course, apart from Paulina.

Back when I'd found the first body, I'd emailed her to tell her in great detail exactly how well her fabulous idea for a pity party had gone. I'd updated her about this one, too. As for my other clients, all they saw was a blank white wall and me, cool and professional as always, ready to discuss a brief or tweak a design. They didn't know I'd had to shove my bookcase full of books, Funko Pops, and priceless vintage Lego Millennium Falcon out of frame. Or that my bed was unmade and my laundry was piling up.

Five days in, I was getting antsy.

A surprise phone call from Fraser hadn't helped.

The flurry of texts he'd sent after the first body had stopped, and I should have blocked his number. Instead, I answered the call without looking—when would I learn—and the moment I heard his excited voice saying, *Ray, I heard about the second body, and we need to*— I hung up.

He left a voicemail and I deleted it. He left two more, and I blocked him.

On day one of my exile, I'd called Liam. I texted him on day two because he'd told me to stop calling him, this was official and he wasn't allowed to share stuff, Ray. I didn't contact him at all on day three, because by then I was feverishly trying to mock-up some designs for the local craft beer company that my father had pimped me out to.

"You can stop being dramatic about it any time," Dad said. "You're perfectly entitled to turn the job down if it's something you can't manage to fit in."

I dropped my shoulders in in relief, and also my arms, which had somehow begun waving in the air as I attempted to explain that just because I worked in a creative business, it didn't mean I wasn't shackled to schedules, deadlines, and a finely balanced workflow just like conservatory builders were.

"*Thank* you," I said.

"As long as you don't mind embarrassing me by pulling out of a commitment, that is."

"I never made the commitment," I said. "I can't pull out."

"I made it for you. It's called networking."

"Pimping, Dad. It's called pimping."

"Fine. I'd had a few beers in the pub, the Bears won the rugby—which you know they hardly ever do—and I had a few more, and I might have been boasting about your skills because Brian was going on and on about his grandson making the squad."

I'm sure that bragging about my skills with Photoshop really showed him. "Wow. Nice try."

He scowled. "I didn't know off the top of my head what your project rates are. I may have under-negotiated."

"I'm getting paid? I thought you were whoring me out for free."

"Raymond, I'm a businessman." He then named a sum triple my usual estimate for a simple product design.

I jumped on it.

It couldn't hurt to get a little extra into my dwindling savings account, in case of another body popping up. With the money from this job, if another one did show up, I'd be able to afford the hotel.

Best of all, getting sucked into it made for an excellent distraction. I was so busy, I didn't have a spare moment to think about Adam.

Except at night.

At night, I couldn't *stop* thinking about Adam.

On the night of Day Four, I lay in bed and stared at the ceiling. It was a full moon. I'd left the curtains open and silver light poured in. I was moonbathing. The rays fell directly on my bed, and I'd flipped the covers down, and was basking in it. I had a whimsical side.

And a guilty side.

"See you tonight, babe," Adam had said. He'd kissed me and strutted off back to the hotel, fully expecting to see me there.

And I'd bolted.

I hadn't left him a note or given him a call. I hadn't even texted him.

He hadn't called or texted me, either. And why would he? We weren't in a relationship.

Just because someone feeds you cake and calls you *babe*, it doesn't mean you're dating.

Or because they take care of you. Snuggle you into bed. Save you from angry townsfolk.

We *weren't* in a relationship.

The moon shone hard and bright on my face. I sucked in a sharp breath.

Were we in a relationship?

No.

No, I *did* have a say in it, despite how pushy Adam was, and I hadn't at any point agreed. We'd kissed. We'd slept in the same bed, once. It was hardly a commitment.

I gnawed on my lip.

He hadn't contacted me.

Which meant...which meant we weren't in a relationship.

Or it meant I'd been awful.

Oh, good lord. Had I ghosted him?

Had he ghosted me? No! There was no ghosting. We were not in a relationship. I'd know about it if we were.

Wouldn't I?

This was getting me nowhere. I was thinking in circles. Before I could think better of it, I grabbed my phone off the bedside table and opened up our last text conversation.

Our only text conversation.

It was the picture of Adam, smouldering at the camera, with the words, *For your spank bank* below. He'd taken the photo in my kitchen at one a.m. I'd watched him do it. He'd been in unforgiving strip lighting, he'd come off a long shift, and he looked spectacular.

He must have made a fortune in his modelling days.

After staring at the picture for a disgracefully long time, I heaved a sigh and started typing.

ME

Hi, hope you're well, I'm—

No. That was sad. I deleted it and stared at the ceiling some more.

Hey. What's up, I—

Nope. No. Delete. What's up? Come on, Ray.

Sorry I didn't get to see you, work emergency—

Argh.

Delete-delete-delete.

What did Adam even care? He was probably at The Lion right now with Jasper. Or at a club. Or being sexy and too young for me at a cool young-persons-only venue, like, I don't know. Experimental theatre, or board-game night at the hipster coffee shop or something.

Did I think he cared, one way or another, if I was in town? He probably hadn't even noticed I was gone. *See you tonight, babe*, had probably been nothing more than a knee-jerk, filler kind of thing to say.

I clenched my phone and tapped it gently on my forehead.

It rang.

I pulled it away and stared at the caller ID. Adam. Of course it was Adam.

...*how* was it Adam?

It was a FaceTime call.

I accepted. "Hello?"

"Switch to camera, Ray."

I clutched the phone with both hands, drinking in the sight of his face.

The lighting was low and flattering—then again, as had been established, all light was flattering to Adam. His eyes were shadowed and dark. A flush shaded the high sharp edges of his cheeks and the bridge of his nose, and his lips shone red.

He tilted his head. "Ray. Camera."

I batted at my hair, shuffled up the mattress to prop myself against the headboard, and toggled the camera on.

We stared at each other for a long, silent moment. I opened and shut my mouth helplessly. I couldn't think of anything to say

"Yeah," Adam said, his lips—so red—curled with a sharp little smile. "That's what I thought."

We stared at each other some more.

"So here I am," Adam said in a conversational tone, "lying in bed, touching myself."

What?

He hummed. "I pick up my phone and I'm looking back at our last texts, by which I mean the one text I sent you, and I see typing bubbles. But nothing came." Adam's shoulders rolled. "You were thinking about me, weren't you?"

I nodded.

"Mm. Well, I was thinking about you. I was trying not to. Got into bed, slid my boxers down and stroked my cock, Ray, trying to think about *anyone* other than you. But I couldn't. And then I discovered that you, wherever the *fuck* you are, are thinking about me." He bit his lip and his neck arched the tiniest bit. "Take your t-shirt off."

In my rush to obey, I dropped the phone. It bounced off

the mattress and fell onto the carpet with a thud. I whipped my t-shirt off and grabbed the phone off the floor.

"Lie back for me," Adam said.

I did.

Then he didn't say anything at all. He stared through the camera. He looked kinda angry. Kind of mean.

I was so hard.

Adam let out a shuddering breath. His face and upper chest filled the screen. His back

and lips parted. One arm was moving, his shoulder rolling fast. If I strained my ears, I could almost...yes. I heard the sound of skin on skin.

It sounded wet.

My mouth opened and I felt the blood rush into my face. I gripped my erection through my boxers.

Adam's angry eyes flared. He dug his teeth into his bottom lip and the picture began to jerk rhythmically.

His bright, red-gold hair was spread out over a white pillow. He raised the phone, changing the angle to show his abs tensing in a quick, undulating wave. He was thrusting up into his hand; I heard the rustle of sheets, the faint squeak of a mattress, and, much louder now, the slide of skin.

His breathing picked up.

I still wasn't doing anything except staring at him. I saw myself in the tiny rectangle at the bottom of the screen: big, startled eyes, bare chest—not quite as alluring as Adam's—and a mesmerised expression.

I licked my lips and he mirrored the movement. He aimed the camera in a quick flash lower, long enough for me to catch the impression of his fist on his cock before he slowly dragged the camera back up over his abs to his shoulders then his face. He glared right up into the lens.

I'd never seen anything so beautiful in my life.

I hadn't progressed beyond grabbing my dick, but my own breathing was as rough as his. "Adam," I said shakily.

He came.

Surprise flashed over his face and then he gave in to it. His neck arched, his chest rose, and his mouth dropped open. He gasped, eyes on mine before his lashes fluttered down to lie over cheeks that had turned poppy red as he panted, sharp and high.

The pants became deep moans and I watched, transfixed, as he relaxed, muscle by muscle. His hair was damp and lay in darkened curls on his forehead. He blinked muzzily at the camera once, then closed his eyes, turned to hide his face in the pillow, and cut the connection.

Now mine were the only breaths fracturing the moonlit room.

I dropped the phone, flopped onto my back and hauled my boxers down. At the first touch of my hand on my straining, swollen cock, I came with an anguished sob, biting into the back of my wrist.

It was the best and the worst orgasm I'd ever had.

fter days and days of waiting to hear from Adam again, because I was too chicken to contact him myself after that confusing phone call, I was finally allowed to go home.

Okay, it was only two days later, but the waiting made it feel like forever.

I was in the conservatory when Liam called. Dad had knocked it down and rebuilt it four times. In its latest iteration and at Giselle's request, it was an ornate, Georgian-style monstrosity that ran the (very average) length of the house, in which you could imagine a chiselled duke ravishing a feisty debutante behind the potted palms. *Bridgerton* was to blame for that. I was just finishing showing my designs to the representative of the craft beer company.

Normally I'd do this over Zoom. But no. My parents were determined to embarrass me. Dad invited her over. Giselle baked a cake.

I knew the client better as Naomi Reeves.

I'd gone to school with Naomi, although she was the year ahead. She was gratifyingly impressed by my work. All

I'd done was show her a slideshow of the mock-ups, and given her two branding options to choose from.

I'd worked out Dad's angle by now. Networking, my arse.

He was using me as a shiny dangling lure.

Because as well as having gone to the same school as me, Naomi *just so happened* to be the daughter of Dad's friend, Brian.

As in Brian, the proud grandfather of a potential Gloucester Bear.

Thankfully, this potential Bear was also not Naomi's son. If I had somehow aged enough without noticing to be in the age bracket where I could have fathered an enormous two-hundred-pound, twenty-year-old wannabe rugby star, I was going to dig myself a hole in the back garden, crawl into it, and let nature take its course.

Naomi was the owner of the company, and she was looking for a rebrand because she was in the middle of expanding.

Guess who wanted to build their new restaurant addition for them?

"I told you, Ray. I'm a businessman," Dad had said complacently at my accusation when I put it all together.

"You're ruthless."

The old bastard preened. "I'm doing it all for you anyway. When I die, my empire will be yours."

"I'm not going to be a builder." We'd had this argument before, again and again. "And I definitely don't want an empire."

To my surprise, Dad sighed. "I know. But you can sell it and retire early, or keep it and be a director. I don't mind."

"Why don't you retire, Dad? You've earned it. Sell up, buy a yacht, show Giselle the world."

I was being ironic. Giselle had travelled the world at

least twice before agreeing to get tethered by a middle-aged divorced man and his suspicious ten-year-old son. She'd be showing him. He had whatever the opposite of wanderlust was. He'd barely left Gloucestershire, let alone the country.

Once, when Mum was still around—mostly—and I was about eight, we'd gone to Spain for a holiday. We all got sunburned, like true English idiots. It was awful. God knows what I looked like under UV light. As far as I knew, Dad hadn't left these shores since.

Dad pulled a face. "Maybe in another ten years."

In another ten years, he'd be in his seventies.

And he'd still be pushing for business.

By the time Naomi had oohed and ahhed over my designs, I was confident that I'd secured the job, and I had three missed calls on my phone. I'd managed to ignore it vibrating in my pocket while I was doing my thing with the presentation, but now that I was sitting back letting her flip through the designs on her own, I was fretting.

I'd blocked Fraser so it couldn't be him, but...what if it was Adam?

Giselle brought in tea and cake—Christ, my parents had *no* idea how to be professional—and I seized the opportunity. As soon as Naomi and Giselle started up with the local scandal, I sloped out the door that led into the garden.

Ignoring my father, who'd spotted me making a break for it and was making hand-gestures from the kitchen window that I interpreted as, *Get back in there!* and, *Close the deal!* I jogged across the lawn to stand under the enormous western red cedar that dominated the whole garden.

It was mizzling with rain and too cold to be out here in shirtsleeves, but I welcomed the fresh air. I didn't know if it was an age thing or what, but Dad always kept the heating too damn high.

I leaned against the familiar trunk, pulled up my contacts and stared at recent calls. I hadn't had many; Adam was still listed on the screen.

I sighed, thinking of his uncharacteristic vulnerability at the end of the call. I had the feeling that people very rarely ever saw Adam vulnerable. I treasured it, even as I regretted causing it. He was so confusing.

The phone bleated in my hand and my adrenaline spiked.

"Ray," Liam said crossly when I answered.

"Detective Nash," I said, just as crossly. I was disappointed he wasn't Adam, I didn't mind admitting it. I didn't know what his deal was. "Do you have good news for me?"

"Yes. I have excellent news. You can stop texting my personal phone and asking for details I'm not at liberty to give you. The scene has been released."

"I assume that's fancy police speak for, Ray, you can come home to your own property, which you own, and once again live there."

"Yep."

There was something off in his tone.

I straightened. "Oh."

"No," Liam said.

"Oh my god."

"Do not ask me."

"I don't need to. You found something, didn't you! You found another body. Shit. *Shit.* I did the research. Three or more definitely makes it a serial killer now. I'll never sell my house!"

"Ray—"

I pushed away from the tree and began to pace. "How many? One more? Two? Are these ones wearing costumes? Why—"

"Ray! There are no more bodies. We didn't find any. And the team was, uh. They were thorough. If there had been any more bodies in there, trust me, the team would have found them."

I squinted at the rampaging tangle of Dad's climbing rose at the bottom of the garden. It had smothered the stone bird bath and was making a determined effort to strangle the small apple tree alongside it out of existence.

There was that tone of voice again.

"There are definitely no more dead bodies," I said suspiciously. "Now, are you sure? Because last time we did this dance, you half-arsed it. I can't come back here, Liam. I cannot go through this again. I am on the brink of committing double homicide as it is. Seriously. You try working from home with your parents."

Liam sounded pained. "I know you're joking and being dramatic, but please remember that I'm a police officer. You can't keep threatening to commit crime in my presence."

"So you whole-arsed it."

"Every possible nook and cranny has been inspected."

"That was oddly filthy."

"I've got some forms for you to sign. I can bring them over tomorrow. You should stay another night with your parents."

I groaned.

"Or if you're in a hurry, you can swing by the station and catch me before my shift ends. Technically you need to see the house—"

"No! No, no. I will come to you. Today. Thanks, Liam."

"Doing my job," he grunted, and hung up.

I stared out into the rain. I still couldn't put my finger on his tone, but any real curiosity was buried under the relief that I could go home.

The nightmare was over.

25

The nightmare was not over.

I packed up, thanked my parents, and was on the road an hour after Liam called, putting Steeple Norton in the rear-view mirror.

There was a jam on the motorway with a five-mile tail-back, and even though I'd left after lunch, it was close to suppertime when I drove into town and kept on going to the police station.

Liam and his forms were waiting for me at the front desk.

"Hi!" I said, breezing in with a big smile.

He dipped his chin in a curt nod.

Ah, yes. He didn't like to let people suspect that we had carnal knowledge of each other.

"You could have stayed at your parents another night," Liam said, sounding somewhat aggrieved. "I didn't realise you were going to be so late," We could have dealt with all this tomorrow."

"One more night and I'd definitely have been tempted to

homicide." I leaned against the desk and smiled. "I'm kidding."

"And yet I'm not amused."

"I want to go home, Liam. I no longer even care that there were human dolls there."

His eyes bulged.

"Sorry," I said. I wasn't supposed to know. "Dolls? No one's talking about dolls. Boring old normal dead bodies is all I'm talking about. And I'm used to the idea. I have emotionally processed it. I want to go home, have a three-hour soak in the tub, then fall into bed."

"Then let's get this done. My shift ends in three minutes, and I'll be off for the next few days."

"Clock watching, huh?"

"Yep."

"Right Where do I sign?" I scanned the paperwork, signed where I was instructed to, shook Liam's hand, and drove home.

It was a wreck.

I let myself in and looked around. What the fuck?

My furniture was shoved to the back walls, plaster dust was everywhere, the carpet was still rolled up in the sitting room—and by rolled up, I mean it was in a wadded heap—the understairs cupboard door was off its hinges and propped up against the wall.

It looked like a bunch of teenage hoodlums had been through here, not a highly trained forensics team.

It made the mess that the local crew had left in the master bedroom look like the aftereffects of a small and genteel tea party.

This looked like the aftereffects of a looting.

I dialled Liam's number.

He sent me to voicemail. The *arse*. That's what his tone was about.

I stood in my icy cold hall—they'd turned the heating off for some reason—clutching my luggage, and shivered.

If I hadn't been stuck in traffic for hours, I'd have been here after lunch and could have done something about it. But I was tired! I wanted sleep!

I could go back to Steeple Norton.

Or I could go to the Premier Lodge.

My hand tightened on the strap of my laptop bag.

I'd see Adam. Life-size, radiating warmth, in-the-flesh Adam.

And just like that I was slammed with a desperate urge to see him, feel his heat, let him take care of me. But I was too damn scared.

I'd been playing that phone sex on a loop in my head, and it had hit me that there had been something final about it.

What if I went there, ran into him, and whatever strange thing we had going on was over?

On the other hand, he might lie on top of me.

Fuck it.

I'd made enough on the craft beer job to cover another night at the Lodge.

I BLEW THROUGH THE MAIN DOORS LIKE I DIDN'T HAVE A CARE in the world. It wasn't until I saw the friendly woman who'd checked me out a week ago at the front desk that I realised

I'd once again fallen into the trap of expecting Adam to be there simply because I wanted him to be.

And to be honest with you, she wasn't all that friendly today.

In fact, as soon as she laid eyes on me, her professional smile frosted over.

"Hello," I said.

"Good evening."

"Um. I'd like to check in?"

"Do you have a reservation?"

"Oh. Right." I was more tired than I'd thought. Or too focused on getting to Adam. To the hotel, I mean. "No. Is...do you have any availability?"

"No."

I already had my credit card half out of my wallet. I glanced up at her in surprise. "Really?"

She gave me a tight smile, a grimace of straight white teeth bared in my direction.

I narrowed my eyes at her.

She narrowed hers back.

"Would you be so kind as to check?" I said.

"Of course, sir. No problem at all." She turned to the keyboard and rattled the keys with her immaculate manicure. She made a considering noise that coasted up at the end and I slumped with relief. I was being paranoid. Everyone didn't hate me. It was all fine—

"No, sorry," she said. "We are all booked out." She returned my suspicious stare with a bland smile.

"Well, then," I said. "I guess that's that."

"You can always try the one in Didcot."

I was exhausted. No, I was *offended*. When had getting a hotel room turned into a popularity contest?

I didn't know if she knew who I was and didn't want to

let a murder-house owner stay in her hotel, or if she knew who I was and this was a thing she was doing on Adam's orders, on Adam's behalf. Or if it was all in my head.

I trudged back out to the car I'd optimistically parked in guest parking, slung my bag in the back, and slumped in the seat.

Gripping the wheel, I gently bonked my forehead a few times. It didn't do much to lighten my mood or burn off any frustration but you gotta try, right?

I drove home on autopilot. I'd been planning to order room service, specifically the cake. I was home with the engine switched off before it sank in that being denied a room also meant being denied cake. I should have stopped off on the way to pick up fish and chips for supper.

I could always go and get some now? Yes. Good idea.

I fired the engine back up, changed my mind, and switched it off again.

I smothered a scream.

Okay. It was entirely possible that the stress was catching up to me. I could admit that. And I was feeling petulant. I could admit that, too. Didn't like it. Could admit it.

The last time I was in this situation, Adam had shown up and taken care of me. Allowing it had made me weak and dependent.

He was like crystal meth, wasn't he?

One hit: instant addiction.

I glared balefully at my house. When I was in my bedroom at Steeple Norton, I'd been yearning to be right here at home. Now I'd got what I wanted, I was here, and going inside seemed like way too much effort.

I'd have to have emotions and feelings.

I'd have to change my bed, after deciding which of the

graves—I'm sorry, *bedrooms*—I wanted to occupy for the night.

I'd have to throw away everything in my fridge and break open my packet of emergency Hobnobs for supper.

God, my life sucked.

(Apart from the Hobnobs.)

I much preferred it when I'd been at the hotel and had a relaxing bath, cake, and Adam.

I considered finding somewhere else to stay or even turning around and driving back to Steeple Norton, but if I couldn't face the hassle of getting out of the car, driving for another couple of hours was definitely too much effort.

I'd sleep in my car.

It wasn't as bold a statement of taking control of my unravelling life as marching in and reclaiming my house, but it was a start.

I was reclaiming the drive.

I unclipped my seatbelt and twisted around to the back. I dug through my duffle bag, found a thick hoodie, and dragged it on. Pulling the hood up and kicking my shoes off, I reclined the seat and settled in.

If I couldn't nod off by midnight, I decided, I'd regroup. Change the plan. Come up with an alternative. Grow a pair, I didn't know.

I wriggled my shoulders against the seat back, crossed my arms over my chest, and closed my eyes.

Bang bang bang.

I gasped and flailed awake, hit my elbow on the horn, and locked eyes with someone staring at me through the driver side window, a mere six inches away. I scrambled clumsily backward, nearly penetrated myself on the gearstick, and flopped in an ungainly heap in the passenger seat.

Adam cocked his head.

I laid a hand on my heaving chest and panted at the ceiling.

Rap rap rap. He knocked again, gently, with a curled knuckle.

I clambered back into the driver's seat, keeping a wary distance from the gearstick. I turned the engine on and powered down the window.

"Yes?" I said politely.

"What are you doing?"

"I was sleeping, until someone pounded on my window. What are you doing?"

"Nothing much. I was heading home at two a.m. Caught sight of a body slumped in your car. Thought I'd check it out. Call me curious."

I stared at him. He lived on the other side of town. My house wasn't on his way. "Were you coming to see me?"

"No." He gave his head a single, decisive shake.

Oh. Of course he wasn't.

"Okay, then," I said. "It's not a random body in my car, it's me. I'm not slumped, I'm sleeping. Thanks for checking, though!" I powered the window up.

Adam watched the glass rise between us with an unimpressed expression.

My cheeks were hot. Catching my bottom lip between my teeth, I chewed nervously.

Why wasn't he leaving?

Telling myself I was an idiot, I popped the locks and opened the door, swinging my legs around but not standing up.

Adam shifted back a step, continuing to *look* at me. The streetlight turned his hair an eerie glowing bronze and cast a long shadow behind him. He held out a hand.

Because I am a fool, a crazy, hopeful fool, I took it.

"You're such a dick, Ray," he said, tugging me towards him. "Seriously."

I thought I was going to get a hug or something. Nope. Once he'd yanked me clear of the car, he shoved me to one side and reached past me and into the back seat to grab my bag. He closed the car door quietly.

I'd never intended to mess with Adam's feelings. I'd been trying to protect myself. But it had started to dawn on me that he was likely getting hurt. That *I* was hurting him.

I wasn't used to being the one to hurt. I'd simply never had that kind of power before, with anyone. I didn't like the idea that I was clumsy with it.

Adam's hand rested low on my back and he nudged me up the front steps. I went easily.

26

Once inside, Adam dropped my bag by the door. I flipped on the hall light and we stared at each other.

I was jumpy and wired, and almost certain I was going to do something stupid. Yep. Definitely going to do something stupid—that was my hand, reaching out and, yep, I was touching him. I wasn't looking at him, because I'd explode if I had eye contact *and* body contact. But those were my fingers, spreading wide over his sternum and flexing lightly.

Adam took in one slow, deep breath, his head angled toward mine, then he moved into me with one long stride. He bumped me back against the wall, cushioning the back of my head with his hand. "*Ray,*" he said, voice low.

I opened my mouth, and that was when my stomach groaned.

It was the worst, gurgling moan I'd ever heard in my life.

"That wasn't me," I said automatically, and glanced up.

His golden hazel eyes were alight with humour. His smile flashed, quick and delighted and *fond*. "Jesus," he said.

"Don't ever change." He held my chin, dropped a firm kiss on my parted lips, and stepped back.

My stomach squelched again. Oh my god.

Adam headed for the kitchen and I hurried after him. When I caught up, he was rifling through the cupboards, pulling things out and setting them down on the counter.

"Put the kettle on," he said. "I'm making you pasta." He turned to me, crossed the kitchen and cupped my face. "Go and change the bed, I'll make you a big bowl of food, and you can sleep."

"Are you staying?" I remembered asking him that before, in the hotel.

"Yeah."

"*Why?*"

"Why what? Why am I staying?"

"Yes." I threw my arms out to the sides. "I don't get it!"

"I know you don't. Let's say I'm a nice guy and leave it at that."

"A nice guy with a service kink."

"I've got a few kinks. I'd be happy to share. Service isn't one of them."

I gestured expansively at him.

"What does that mean, Ray?"

"It means you're always taking care of me!"

"I'm seducing you," he said, and stroked my jaw. "You fucking idiot." He closed my mouth with a fingertip under my chin, and tapped my lips.

This man was a caretaker, through and through. "If you want to seduce me," I told him, "you don't have to cook for me. All you have to do is strip naked."

"Is that so?"

"Yes."

"Go and change the bed," he said with that fond smile again, like I was something cute.

I hadn't been upstairs alone yet since the discovery of the second body. I grabbed my bags from the hall, turned on all the lights, and pushed through the dread.

The sense of queasy violation was already fading. Perhaps because it was familiar now. I'd been through this before, after all. Both being wrangled and cared for by Adam, and having my personal space poked and pawed through by the police.

Although they'd definitely been more thorough.

It wasn't a surprise that my place didn't look show-home ready. But because it was a special unit from a major force, I'd expected a little more sophistication. Like, a soupçon.

There was printing dust everywhere. The scent of chemicals lingered in the air. Oh, and there was an enormous hole in the guest bedroom wall that I wasn't even going to think about. Certainly not tonight, anyway.

I dropped my bags in the master bedroom, put my hands on my hips, and looked around. Okay. Quick hoover. Change the bed, open the windows to ventilate the place, and I'd be good to go. I could sleep here. I could live here again. The dead guys had been here all along, they hadn't caused any trouble, and at least the police had properly checked the place out now.

If there was another body to find, they would have found it. No more nasty surprises.

I grabbed the hoover and whizzed it around the room. Someone had been rummaging around in my laundry cupboard, because everything was a haphazard jumble. I found my spare bedding set and carted it back to the bedroom. Cool night air twisted in through the open window, damp and reassuring. Instead of the indefinable odour of the Law, I smelled fresh cut grass, a hint of soil, and green growing things.

I changed the bed and hopped in the shower to give myself a quick but thorough scrubbing. I looked down at my dick. "Don't get too excited," I told it. I was half hard. "We're having pasta, and that's all."

To underscore my firm tone, I turned the shower to cold and sucked in a sharp breath when it hit me.

Erection taken care of, I rubbed myself dry, scrambled into some clean flannel pj bottoms and a t-shirt, and went out into the bedroom.

I deflated somewhat to find the room empty.

Part of me had expected to see Adam spread out naked on the clean bed, balancing the bowl of pasta on his flat stomach and offering me a fork with a come-hither look.

Or, not expected.

Hoped.

I trudged down the stairs to the kitchen. Adam wasn't naked, but he did smile and hold out a fork as I sat down at the table in front of the steaming bowl of pasta and pesto.

"Eat it, Ray," he said, after I stared at it for a full minute.

"I'm going to."

"It doesn't have death germs if that's why you're hesitating."

"I know."

He leaned over, took my fork off me, and dug in. If he tried to feed me, that would be crossing a line.

Adam popped the pasta into his own mouth. Eyes on mine, he drew the fork out slowly. He licked the end with a quick, wet flicker of tongue. "Yeah," he said. "I know you like that, you freak."

I snatched the fork off him. "I do not have a thing for cutlery." I didn't. At least I hadn't, pre-Adam. Maybe he had awakened something in me. "If you're going to fellate it right in front of me, of course I'm going to watch."

I grumpily shovelled pasta into my mouth and moaned as the flavoursome red pepper pesto burst over my taste-buds. I'd known I was hungry. I hadn't known I was this hungry.

Adam's pupil's dilated.

"You not having any?" I said through a mouthful.

He shook his head. "I don't like to eat before exercise. It gives me a stitch."

"Ah," I said, then choked when his meaning percolated.

"More Parmesan?" he asked.

I nudged my bowl closer to him, said stop when he'd liberally dusted the food with my very classy hard-cheese-style, Parmesan-adjacent foodstuff from Sainsburys—I had the palate of a barbarian—and manfully ploughed on.

When I looked up from the feeding trough, Adam was in an easy sprawl in the kitchen chair. He'd angled his body sideways and had his ridiculously long legs stretched out, ankles crossed. One arm was hooked around the back of the chair, his head had that familiar, curious tilt, and his other arm lay on the table, fingers curled around a glass of water.

He was watching me.

I watched him back. I watched in utter fascination as his cheeks flushed, making his hazel eyes stand out all the brighter. His breathing changed. It didn't get faster. It grew deeper, more controlled. The knuckles around the water glass turned white.

Very slowly, I put my fork down. I self-consciously licked my lips as I stood up. I walked around to the other side of the table, and stepped over his outstretched legs to straddle him standing up. He tipped his head back with a faint smile.

Right.

That was my move. I'd thought Adam would take it from there.

I dipped in an awkward squat, aiming for his lap, or planning on it, but I failed to commit. I sort of lurched at him then straightened again. I'd fit on his lap, but I'd probably knock the pair of us over, and while I didn't have anything against having sex on the floor usually, I—

I sucked in a sharp breath when his hands went to the back of my thighs and travelled up to cup my hips. Holding me steady, he leaned in and pressed a kiss to my stomach, eyes on my face.

I bumped my hips forward reflexively. "Oh," I said, "Sorry."

He shook his head at me, used the hands on my hips to turn me around, then pulled me down to sit on his lap, my back to his chest. Before I really registered the position, he hooked my legs to the outsides of his, then spread his thighs. Just enough to open me up and put me off-balance. An arm came around my waist and crossed up and over my chest, pressing me into him.

"Guess what we're going to do now," he breathed in my ear, then bit my earlobe.

I squirmed. "I mean, it's pretty obvious," I said. I was shooting for nonchalant. I missed it. By a mile.

Adam guided my head to the side and pressed his open mouth to my neck. He hummed. The vibration sent a shiver rippling through me. My toes curled in my socks. "We're going to talk."

"Okay," I said. "Not what I thought." I tugged at his arm. He tightened it. "Probably for the best. I've never had chair sex before. It's on my bucket list of course, but...yeah. I think this is the wrong kind of chair. And floor. It's hardwood. A softer landing would be a good idea, in case of...in case of accidents. Topplings and whatnots. And stuff."

Adam's lips continued to play over my neck. He threaded his fingers into my hair and slowly, gently, drew my head back. He licked over my Adam's apple. I made some ungodly noise that he seemed to like; he flexed beneath me.

"I want to have sex with you Ray. I think that's obvious. I've wanted it for a long time. I think that's obvious, too."

"Yes. Mostly inexplicable. But also obvious." Eventually obvious, I should have said.

His arm tightened again. "Now why'd you have to go and say something like that?"

"Huh?"

He set his teeth in my neck and bit lightly. "Why would you say inexplicable?"

I snorted. "Come on."

"*You* come on. Why?"

My cheeks began to heat with embarrassment. "You know, in case you were wondering, I'm not into humiliation and general—" my hands flailed in the air before us, "—awkwardness. Thanks all the same."

He caught my hands, twined our fingers then crossed our arms over my chest. I was immobilised. "I've got an excellent idea of what you're into, Ray," Adam said, and leaned into me until I was bending at the waist and tipped forward on his lap.

"Not cutlery," I muttered.

He sucked a kiss to the very base of my neck and held me off-balance as he said, "I'd never try to humiliate you. I know you're sensitive."

I gave an outraged gasp.

He hauled me upright and kissed me fiercely, even at the

uncomfortable angle. "You're sensitive," he said against my mouth. "I love that about you, okay?"

Was I sensitive?

Fraser used to call me touchy and irritable and hard to please. My dad always called me emotional and told me I took things too seriously, he was *joking* about my hair, Ray, stop overreacting. Giselle...well, she was always calling me artistic.

"Fine," I said. "I'm difficult and you're into it, weirdo —*mmph*." He kissed me harder.

"That," he said, "is not what I just said."

I went to speak but he pressed a finger to my lips and shushed me.

I growled and bit his finger.

Instead of flinching like a normal human being, he slipped his finger past my lips and pressed lightly on my tongue.

I went still and blinked at the kitchen in front of me. I assumed it was still there. I was suddenly so turned on that my vision had whited out.

Adam slid another finger in my mouth and kissed my jaw. "I want you. I'd very much like you to get that through your head. I think we could be great together and I want to find out. But Ray, believe it or not, I have an ego, too."

I sucked on his fingers, felt his smile curve against my cheek.

"No one likes to be rejected," he said. "I want you to tell me, Ray, is this happening or not? I don't want you to want me despite the fact I'm younger, or despite the fact Fraser cheated on you with me, or despite anything. I just want you to want me back."

He slid his fingers free, and eased me up and off his lap.

He stood and looked down at me. After a moment of silence, his smile turned tense.

I didn't know where to start.

I'd been cautious and wary. From Adam's perspective, had I been callously shutting him down?

I had the sinking feeling that my personal insecurities had, in fact, made me quite cruel.

I stepped into his personal space. "I don't get this," I said, and barrelled on when he frowned, "but I do want you. If it's any consolation, I overthink every hook-up, one way or another. I'm not as certain about things like you are. I can tell you that I do want you. Very much. More than anyone. Um. Ever."

His hand had been resting on my hip; it slid around to the small of my back and pressed me into him. He had a rueful, exasperated grin on his face. "This isn't a hook-up."

"...it isn't?"

"Nobody works this hard for a hook-up," he said grimly. "If all I want is an orgasm, I can walk into the pub and point at a guy. That'll do it."

"Wow."

"Yeah. I don't even have to try. With you, I try. And no, before you fling off in the wrong direction, you're not a challenge I must conquer to maintain my fuckboy stats. I like you. I want to take you apart. I want to feed you and calm you down when you're freaking out about whatever—"

"I'm really not that highly strung—"

"Shush, or I'll put something in your mouth again."

He sucked in a sharp breath when I cupped his dick and said, "Promise?" in a flirty voice before rearing back and saying, "Holy crap."

"Yes, I have a big dick."

"Adam, that's—"

"It's not porn big. Can we stay on topic? I—" He gasp-laughed and pulled his hips back as I ran my hand wonder-ingly down his length. He caught my hand, brought it up to his mouth and kissed my palm. "Ray. I want to have sex with you. It is not a one-night stand. I'm going to want it more than once. I don't want you because you're a challenge. God help me, I want you for your personality."

"That last bit was mean."

"I can be mean. Don't pretend you don't like it."

"As for the more than once thing, you'd better show me what you've got. Convince me to give you another go."

He smiled at me. Slow and filthy. "Okay, then," he said. He rested a hand on my chest, stopping me when I went to move forward. "If you run out on me again, Ray? I won't chase you. It's your turn."

"Okay," I said, filing that away for later.

Adam hummed. I'd wondered if he would grab me or kiss me again, or toss me over his shoulder. He didn't. He lifted his chin at the door and raised an eyebrow.

Right. Yes. Lead the way. I could absolutely do that.

27

*I*t was tough with Adam crowding me, an arm wrapped around my waist and his hips cradling my arse, thighs literally walking me forward, but I managed.

"You are very pushy," I said as we hit the landing. "Has anyone ever told you that?"

"I'm not pushy," he said. "I'm determined, I'm an opportunist, and I have a strong drive to get what I want."

"That sounds like an excellent definition of pushy to me."

"If I was pushy—" he squeezed me and rubbed his giant dick against my arse, "—we'd have done this after the first dead guy."

I struggled. He let me turn around in his arms until we were chest to chest, but he continued to walk me backwards, eyes focused and intent on my face.

I swallowed hard. His tone had been playful. I'd thought we were easing into things with all the banter. The expression on his face told me it was go-time. "You mean before or after you burned your tongue on the hot chocolate?"

"After," he said, as the backs of my knees hit the mattress. "You remember, right?"

"You having a tantrum because I called you Juni—"

He ducked down and bit my lip. Hard.

"Ow, dammit," I complained when he drew back.

"That's off-limits," he said.

I tried to be honest with myself. I did work on self-awareness. I attempted to accept even those things I felt conflicted about. Human beings are irrational, messy creatures. It's possible to feel diametrically opposed emotions at the same time.

Which was another way of saying that I'd stopped trying to convince myself I didn't like it when Adam got all commanding.

It had confused me at first—how on earth was a man almost a decade younger than me so incredibly sure of himself? Then it had rattled me—who did he think he was? Then it had aroused and seduced me.

I'd contemplated past relationships and hook-ups, imagined any of the other men I'd known treating me like Adam did. Winding me up, brazenly manipulating me. Caring for me, tucking me up in bed. Yeah, no. I'd have invited them to jog on and don't let the door hit them on the way out. Or do let it hit them, I really didn't care, as long as they were leaving

This, I concluded, was an Adam thing and not a general thing

But that didn't mean I was going to just roll over.

"You can't control me," I told him snippily.

"Mm-hmm." He fitted his hands to my waist and lifted me up onto my toes before shoving me back onto the bed. I bounced and he was crawling over me.

I scuttled backwards. "You can't silence me," I said.

Adam smiled. He pushed me flat halfway up the bed, straddled my thighs, and sat back. "We both know I can," he said.

"What a load—*oh*." Eyes locked to mine, Adam reached behind himself, grabbed his t-shirt, and dragged it up and over his head. Slowly. Arching his back.

Had that been me, I'd have come out of it with my hair half stuck down and half staticky. Adam's thick red-blond curls fell over his face in a sexy mop. They *tumbled*. He threw his t-shirt over the side of the bed and brushed his hair back off his face with one hand, bicep flexing.

"That's how I like it," he said, and patted my chest. "Nice and quiet."

I scowled. "I am stunned unto silence by your shameless exhibitionism—*oh*."

He ran his hands down his chest and sides, all the way to his waistband. Tensing his thighs, he rose to his knees. I lay under him helplessly as he looked down into my face.

He popped the button of his jeans.

A spike of adrenaline surged through me and set my heart jangling. I let out a shaky breath. To my humiliation, it had a fine edge of a whine to it.

I was...he was...he was fucking overwhelming, all right?

Adam tilted his head. His face turned a little thoughtful, a little cruel.

If he was a nice pretty boy, he'd have held me like the night in the hotel. Or he'd have said something soothing. But he liked seeing a flare of panic. Wait. What had he called it? Erotic fear.

"Oh my god," I said, gripping the duvet beneath me with both hands. "You're a sadist."

"Mhm." He gave a half-shrug and unzipped himself.

I planted my hands and feet and went to scramble backward, but he simply knee-walked after me, and reached down to cup my cheek. He bent to kiss me.

"Relax, Ray," he said, once our lips had parted with a soft sound.

"You relax," I told him shrilly, and grabbed his thighs.

My heart was still pounding. The hand Adam had on my jaw slid down over my throat, along my collarbone, and stopped over my chest.

Adam frowned a tiny bit, then that fond look mixed with the predatory cast on his face.

It was a lot.

He lowered down and stretched out over me, easing his body against mine with small adjustments until he was comfortable. He curled his arms up around my head. I was completely caged by him.

I squirmed my own arms free and cupped his beautiful face, gazing up into his darkened eyes. I stroked a thumb over his bottom lip.

He smiled and darted his tongue out to lick it.

Craning up, I kissed him. He made a half-surprised, half-encouraging noise. Was this the first time I had taken the initiative and been the one to close the distance between us?

I thought perhaps it was.

I pressed my shaking mouth to his. I mean, I had game. Usually. I had way more game than this. But with Adam, I was apparently a Madonna song. I smiled and snorted a small laugh at the stupid thought. Adam's lips followed the curve of my own.

"What?" he murmured.

The frantic pounding of my heart had settled to a honey-slow beat, a pulse I felt everywhere.

"Nothing," I said.

"Tell me, Ray."

"You're not the boss of me, I—"

"Please." He licked out at my bottom lip.

I kissed him again and said, "It's stupid. I just... I'm a sophisticated man, right? An experienced lover."

He started shaking against me.

"And you've got me so crazy I'm hearing *Like a Virgin* in my head, and—okay, why the hilarity?"

"S-s-sophisticated lover," he giggled.

"Uh, yes?"

He giggled harder.

I pushed him up and away. "I'll have you know that I am very good in bed, and confident in my ability to pleasure a man." Ew. Why had I phrased it like that?

"You are a delight," he said. "I never know which way you're going to jump." He caught my hands and stretched them up and over my head to the full extent. "But sophisticated?"

I wrinkled my nose at him and sighed. "Fine. Maybe not."

He nudged my head to the side and nibbled at my neck. "I'm intrigued by the like a virgin thing, though," he said, and flexed his entire body against mine. His breath was hot over my skin, and he scraped his teeth along a tendon.

I let out a noise that sounded like, *haaah*, and humped up involuntarily as he rubbed over me.

"Yeah?" he said, sounding interested.

"What do you mean, intrigued? You want to role-play or something?" My legs came up and around his narrow hips as he began to rock into me.

Adam was leaning into one arm, leaving a hand free to stroke back my hair. He traced my eyebrow thoughtfully, drifted a fingertip down my nose and over my lips. "If you want to."

"Me? No. I've never...I mean, I don't want to. Do you?"

"I meant I like that I make you feel that way."

"Oh. You do. Shiny and—*oh*. Oh. *Oh*, Adam."

He'd widened his knees and rocked down hard against me. His face was flushed, eyes sparkling. I had a tendency to blotch and my ears went oddly red when I was turned on. My face was so hot, you could likely see me from space. Adam seemed to like it. At least, he couldn't seem to look away.

I panted hard as he worked his hips against me. I dragged my hands down his hot, damp back, and moaned when my fingers slipped into the deep dimples at the base of his spine. "Hhhn," I muttered, and grabbed his waistband. I tugged. "Off. Off, off, off."

"Yeah." He pushed up and back, finished unzipping himself and hauled his jeans down to his knees. He made short work of my pjs, pushing my hands away when I started fumbling. "Lift up," he snapped.

I did, and he whisked my pj bottoms down my thighs.

He shoved his boxer briefs down, lay back on top of me and ground in.

My head fell back and I stared up at the ceiling. His body was heavy and hot and hard. He was hard all over. He rocked into me, sliding his cock over mine, alongside mine. My breath sharpened and punctuated the air with broken, staccato gasps. I caught his rhythm and we moved together in a dazzling sort of harmony.

The pleasure was intense, and more immediate than I knew what to do with. I held on and was surrounded in every way by him—his heat, his scent, his relentless movement. His breathing was low and harsh but controlled. At least in comparison to mine. I was going to lose it. Everything tightened. My thighs and stomach muscles clenched in rhythmic pulses and my balls lit up. I was going to lose it, I was going to—

Adam rolled off me and onto his back. His belt buckle jangled and I reeled, my body screaming at the sudden lack of sensation.

He sprawled back on the pillows, looking debauched. His curls were dishevelled and dark with sweat, his body glittered in the light, and he was holding his cock in one big hand, a light grimace on his face.

"Wha—" I swallowed my dry croak. "What are you doing?" I said indignantly. "Why did you stop?"

"Was gonna come," he said, sounding as wrecked as I did.

I reached out and curled my hand tentatively around his. "Good?"

His fingers tensed under mine and he hissed. His throat bobbed. "I want to come inside you, Ray," he said, voice low. "Will you let me do that?" He turned onto his side, gave his hips a pushy roll into my hand. His flushed cheeks and half-closed eyes made him look almost drunk. His swollen mouth looked obscene. "Let me show you?" he said.

"Yes." I plastered myself against him. "Yes, please."

He pulled his bottom lip between his teeth and made a satisfied noise, like a low rumble. I felt it in his chest against mine. He skated a hand down my side, drifted it over my arse and down to grasp my thigh. He dragged it up over his hip as best he could while we were still tangled in our clothes.

"Yeah?" he said, hitching against me in tiny pulses. The bedclothes rustled beneath us. "You going to let me in? Open you up, nice and slow until you're begging me for it?"

"I might not beg, but absolutely—"

"You might not?" he said in reproving disbelief, drawing his head back to look down his nose at me, all arrogant. "We'll see, I suppose."

"Yep."

"I think I'll make you beg. I think you'd like that." He used his weight to tip me back at an angle. "I'll make you desperate for me, Ray." His eyes glinted.

I didn't know quite how to tell him, but I was about as desperate as I could get by this point. Any more desperate, and I'd combust right here. It was all I could do not to reach down, grab him, and sit on him.

He stroked in wide circles over my arse. The circles began to narrow. He dragged hot fingers against my skin, then eased them between my cheeks. He hummed when I flinched and thrust against him involuntarily.

I caved.

"Okay, " I said, "you're right. I'll beg. Please put your beautiful big dick in me, Adam."

He grinned. "I'd say you're easy, but holy *shit* it's taken me months to get you where I want you. Once I've got your pants down, though? Then you're easy for me."

I opened my mouth to shoot back an indignant response, but where was the lie? "You should see how easy I get when my pants are all the way off as well as down," I hinted.

Adam writhed himself out of his jeans.

That's the only way I can describe it.

He flexed his large body, dragging his jeans the rest of the way down, and squirmed them off. He lay before me and quirked a brow.

I skimmed a hand over the flat plane of his abs. His cock jumped and he hissed.

"You're the most beautiful thing I've ever seen," I told him.

His eyes met mine with a hint of vulnerability. I was reminded of the way he'd turned away at the end of the phone sex.

"You're also bossy, annoying as hell, and I like you. A lot." I had a horrifying feeling that *I like you* didn't begin to cover it.

Adam held my gaze.

"I've already had a better time with you than in any relationship I've ever had," I continued. I patted his stomach. "Even if the sex turns out to be a bit of a damp squib?" His eyes narrowed to gleaming, dangerous slits. "I'd still want you around. To know you."

I had the feeling that people lost their minds over Adam.

I couldn't deny that I was doing it right now. He was beautiful.

But I really, stupidly for my heart and ego, really did like him. He wasn't a beautiful thing to me. I'd made a mistake saying that. I meant it as he was the most beautiful person. Of course he heard it all the time. Of course he'd think that I was talking about his body. I wasn't.

Adam sat up, and took hold of my t-shirt. He drew it up and over my head, the fabric brushing over my skin and making me shiver. He smiled when, yep, my hair stood up in a puff of static. He smoothed it down, and cupped the back of my neck. "Get the condom and lubricant." he said.

"Yes," I said, sitting there with my pjs still around my knees. Then, "No. Oh, no."

"What's wrong?"

I grabbed him by the shoulders. "I don't have any!"

"Okay, calm down." He was trying not to laugh.

"No, I won't calm down. Don't tell me to calm down. Do

you know how long it's been since I was even close to anyone?"

"I'm guessing a long time."

"A long time! It's been a long time! And now there's you? And I don't...oh no...oh, seriously, fuck my life. Fuck it."

Adam pushed me flat, kissed me hard, and rolled off the bed. "I'd rather fuck you," he said. "And I'll get on that in a minute. You get naked for me. I've got condoms."

"Of course you have." I yelped when he pinched my toe as he passed.

"Naked," he said. "Right now." I watched him go. All sleek muscles and dangerous grace, and his round arse flexing as he—

"Ray."

"Naked. Yes. On it."

*a*dam ran down the stairs, and I got busy untangling myself from my clothes. My erection had faded to a dull throb. I made the tactical error of darting into the bathroom before Adam came back. I flushed the toilet, washed my hands, and glanced up at the mirror.

I moaned in horror.

My cheeks were hectic and blotchy with arousal. My hair, even after Adam had smoothed it down, was a disaster. My eyes were wide and panicked with pupils so blown I looked high, and my lips were kiss-bitten and—I licked them—actually not far off sore.

I looked a desperate, half-crazed mess. I clutched the sink. What was I *doing*? How could he—

"Oh, no," Adam said behind me. I watched his reflection stride across the room in the mirror. "None of that." He grabbed my hand and hauled me after him.

"I just—" I said as I stumbled into the bedroom. "It doesn't make sense." I whapped his chest with the back of a hand when he turned to face me. "Me wanting you? Obvious. You wanting this?"

He wrapped an arm around my waist and fell backward onto the bed, taking us both down. "You're cute and sexy and a hot mess and I dig it," he said. "I love the way you analyse things, by which I mean over-analyse *everything*, and I love the way you get all up in your head." He tapped my forehead, turned me onto my stomach and straddled the back of my thighs. He bent down and set his teeth to the base of my neck. "I love that I can pull you right out of your thoughts and make you do nothing but *feel*."

I was about to demand what the hell he meant by that when I heard the faint rip of plastic and then a large warm hand touched my butt. He squeezed gently, gave it a soothing rub. I whimpered. I have no words to describe the noise I made when he slipped his fingers between my cheeks and rubbed gently at my hole.

"There," he said in satisfaction. "Right there, huh?"

I mumbled something incoherent into the pillow, and demandingly pushed up into his hands.

He laughed. The bed shifted under me as he stretched over and snagged the other pillow. Patting my hip, he murmured, "Lift up for me."

I did, and he slid the pillow under my hips. I humped it and lurched forward when he gave me a brisk spank. "No humping the bed," he said.

"No promises," I replied.

"I'll roll you over and make you watch me while I finger you open," he warned.

"I will do my very best not to hump the bed," I replied quickly.

"That's what I thought. Although, we will be doing that soon. You'll be putting it off, not avoiding it entirely. In fact, I'm going to make you watch me do all sorts of filthy things to you."

"You are?" I cleared my throat. "What would...? What do you mean? I should probably know what to expect."

Adam stroked a proprietary hand over both my buttocks. "Well," he said, and slipped a finger inside me without warning. I gasped and jolted under him. He spanked me lightly again and I bit the inside of my cheek in a vain attempt to not moan. "I'll spread you out. You're a squirmer, and I'd have to hold you down for it, but I don't think that'll pose too much of a problem. I'm bigger. Stronger. Heavier. I'll spread you out, legs nice and wide so I see everything, and I'll make you watch while I do this." He was sliding in and out tenderly. Too tenderly. I found myself pushing back with impatience. "And I'll enjoy watching you get all embarrassed about it."

"I won't be embarrassed." I would be *so* embarrassed.

"Right," he said. "I remember. You're a sophisticated lover."

Adam added another finger, and pushed deeper. I hitched a leg up in reaction, rocking down into the pillow.

"Ray," he said in that warning voice again.

"I can't help it," I snapped. "It feels too good."

He pressed a hand to the small of my back and held me down. "How does this feel?" He thrust in hard and fast a few times, then slowed to a languorous, gentle stir.

"Like you should get in me," I babbled. "I'm good to go, come on, let's get this party started."

"The party is in progress," he said with an amused snort. "Try to keep up."

"More," I said.

He leaned more of his weight into the hand effortlessly pinning me down, and changed the angle with each stroke until my breath stuttered. Bright sensation streaked through my pelvis. He nudged my prostate a few times, and then very deliberately avoided it.

"Is this the part where I'm supposed to be begging?" I said. I dug my forehead into the pillow, my neck arched, and I was panting hard. I kept trying to spread my legs and push back up into his hands, but his weight on my thighs made it impossible.

"You're already begging," he said. "This is the part where I'm telling you all about the things I'm going to make you watch me do."

"Is it? Sorry. I got bored with all the chit-chat. Oh!" He bit my arse, hard.

"I'll make you watch while I touch myself," he said. "And I won't let you do anything. You won't be allowed to touch me or yourself. You'll have to sit there and watch."

Unless he tied me down, I wouldn't be able to *not* touch him.

"I think I'd like to strip for you."

"I think I'd like that, too."

"I'd put on some music—" he twisted his fingers inside me and I shuddered out a long, breathless moan, "—and I'd take my clothes off sloooowly. I'd wear something pretty for you under my jeans. A little surprise. If I was in the mood, I'd wear something with lace on it. I'd—Ray."

I lay there, shaking against the damp sheets. I buried my face in the pillow.

"Ray," he said, and moved over me to dip down and place his lips at my ear. "Did you just come?"

I sighed. "Yes," I said unhappily.

He gave a huff of laughter that I felt over the side of my face, pushed a hand up through the back of my hair, and kissed my hot damp neck. "You are perfect," he said. "What am I going to do with you?"

"I liked the sound of the striptease."

"Then I'll do that for you. I'll go full Magic Mike."

"Oh, god," I said, and my traitorous dick gave a feeble attempt at an encore.

"Ray," he said. There was something almost wondering in his voice.

"You can still fuck me," I said, and pulled my face out of the pillow.

He hesitated. "You're not too sensitive?"

"Sensitive, yes. Too sensitive?" How could I blush even more, seriously? "I don't mind it."

"I'm shooting for something a bit better than, *You can fuck me, I don't mind it.*"

I scowled. "I like it."

"Interesting." He tugged at me, encouraging me to turn over.

I did. Reluctantly. I refused to meet his gaze, mortified by the mess I'd made, until he said, quietly, "Please look at me."

I did.

"Hi." Adam bit his lip. "That was the hottest thing I've ever experienced. I want you to know that."

"Me prematurely ejaculating? Wow, you're easy to please."

"You coming untouched," he said. "Apart from grinding against the pillow, of course."

"I wasn't *grinding*, you were *shoving* me back and forth..." I trailed off under his bright, intense gaze. He ran his fingers through the mess on my stomach. I grimaced.

"No?" he said on a laugh.

I shook my head.

"Stay there. I'm going to clean you up. Then I'm going to get you hard again. And then I'll fuck you."

I opened and shut my mouth a few times. "Sounds like a plan," was the best I could come up with.

I was still grappling to get myself back together when Adam returned. I'd half-expected him to drop a cold washcloth on me to make me yelp, but instead, still gloriously naked, he sat on the side of the bed.

He leaned over me, planting a hand beside my head, and smiled down at me. He did that a lot.

I didn't hate it.

"How are you doing?" he asked. He trailed his gaze down to my stomach, and must have seen the grimace again from the corner of his eye because his lips twitched with amusement. He flattened the warm wet cloth over my abs...well, my abdominal area...and wiped in soothing circles. "This I find intriguing by the way," he said. "I had you pegged for a guy who likes to get dirty."

"Oh, I do. I don't like to lie around in it after."

"Would you? If I asked you to?" He glanced up at me briefly, then back to the soothing circling of the washcloth.

"What?" I pushed up into the touch. It was nice. No one had rubbed my stomach since I had appendicitis when I was seven, and my mother said it was just a stomach ache and it would go away if I stopped complaining about it. Boy, was she wrong. It exploded. This was nicer. "Lie around in it? In...my..." I waved a hand.

"Come on, Ray. You've got to say it."

"I can say it."

"Then say it, sophisticated lover of mine."

"In my semen."

He gave a sharp crack of laughter. "Sexy."

"Accurate."

"And? Would you?"

"Why would you want me to?"

"Answer the question."

"Yes. Of course I would." I'd do anything at all he asked me to, sexually speaking. As long as it was super gay. I did have enough self-preservation not to tell him that, though.

"If I showed up with a tub of chocolate body paint?"

The hairs on my body prickled. "Gross. But yes."

"Would you lie there pulling faces while I painted you?"

"I'd try not to."

"What if I brought a bottle of honey?"

"For some reason sounds less gross than body paint? Don't know why."

"Hmm. What about coconut oil? What if I wanted to give you a full body massage and then slide around on you?"

Goosebumps rushed over me. What on earth...? "You are so much kinkier than I imagined," I said. "Give it a try and find out, I suppose."

"All right. Let's pencil that in for next Tuesday. For now, back to the original question. How are you doing?"

He pulled the cloth away.

"Squeaky clean, thank you."

"That's not what I was asking, Ray."

"I am getting impatient. There was mention of you fucking me a while back. Do we have a timeline on that yet, or...?"

He threw the washcloth at the bathroom door, climbed on the bed, and shuffled me around until I was lying in the middle. He stretched out over me.

"Are we done negotiating kinks?" I said.

"No. But you're not shaking any more, and you're looking at me like you want to kiss my face off. I think we're good to go."

"What? I wasn't *shaking*. What?"

He rubbed a hand up and down my arm and didn't

respond. Scowling, I cupped his cheek and brought him closer.

"I like your face," I told him somewhat grumpily.

"Good to hear."

I kissed him, bit him on the chin, and said, "Will you please, please fuck me?"

"My pleasure," he said.

Adam gathered my hands in his and stretched my arms out over my head. He kneed my thighs apart and slipped between them. I immediately yanked against his hold. "Condom," I said.

"It's on."

"It is?"

He pulled one of my hands down, lifted up enough that I could get it between our bodies, and drew back a little. "See?"

I patted him on the condom-covered dick. "Proceed."

"How did you not notice me putting it on?" he asked, hauling my arm back up. He pulled it tighter and I was deliciously stretched.

"I was looking at your face."

"My face which you like."

"That's the one."

"More than my dick."

"I mean...let's hold off on any grand sweeping statements until I have actual experience of your dick. We haven't really become acquainted yet."

His smile edged with that little flicker of meanness that saved him from being too much perfection in one package. He reached down, positioned himself between my legs and, holding my wide gaze, thrust in in one smooth, merciless glide.

"Ohhh," I said. Yes, he'd prepared me better than I'd

ever been prepared in my life and he slid in like I'd been created to his proportions but that didn't mean I didn't feel it. I did. From my scalp to the soles of my feet, I felt it.

It was nothing like him fingering me open. That had been overwhelming. This—our eyes locked, him buried deep inside, the careful, relentless possession that he'd been taking since we walked into the bedroom what felt like a lifetime ago—this was beyond overwhelming.

Something inside me shifted. My vision flickered. My heart threw out a succession of out-of-rhythm beats.

And then he started to move, still gazing down at me.

There was triumph there. Like I said, he wasn't perfect. Part of him had won something he'd been hunting down for a while now and he wasn't afraid to show it. His eyes gleamed with satisfaction. And then he came out and said it, because that's the kind of man he was. "I've got you," he said.

It sounded like something else altogether.

Our bodies were pressed as close together as they could be, and he barely even drew his hips back. He wasn't pounding or hammering into me. It would have been easier to bear if he had been. Familiar territory. Just the way it goes. I'd have hooked my legs around his hips, held on, and done my best to give it back to him in a sweaty, athletic ride.

Instead, he slipped a hand beneath me at the small of my back and used it to tug me up and into him as he flexed, rolling his hips, circling and grinding them into me. He caught me at the right angle, glided over my prostate, and to my mortification, I wailed.

Adam's eyes were wide as he stared down into my face. "Again," he said, and pulsed against me.

I choked at the sensation, squeezing my eyes shut and clenching down. I heard his deep groan somewhere beneath the open-mouthed panting I was making, a sound which got louder and louder and took on a seeking tilt upwards.

Adam let go of my hands to plant his fists beside my shoulders. He kept relentlessly stroking into me. The bed creaked. His cheeks were rosy bright, his eyes fierce, his hips relentless, shoving at mine, moving me against the sheets. My whole body was sensitised, and even the brush of cotton over my back and buttocks was adding to the overwhelm.

He ducked his head, angling it to one side, and laid his lips against mine. He didn't kiss me. It was a wise choice, the way I was absolutely unravelling beneath him. I'd never been so undone or wild in my life. Our lips brushed against each other with his jolting movements. We shared breath.

Whenever I closed my eyes, he whispered against my mouth, "Open, open, Ray, please. I want to see you, I need to see you, need you so much." And I'd look up again, and again, and he was always watching and chasing my pleasure, not his, adjusting and giving and giving and giving.

His arms were shaking and through the sex haze I could tell by the concentration on his face he was trying not to tip over the edge. He dropped down to his elbows.

I clasped his hot, damp neck with both hands and pressed our foreheads together, working my hips against his, squeezing down, doing everything I could to push him over. "Yes, yes," I said, "Come on, come on, come—"

He moaned and stuttered against me in hard, tight pulses. My eyes stretched wider as I felt his heat inside. I threw my arms around him and held on. He almost sobbed with it. "Ray," he said. "*Ray.*"

I smoothed my hands down his back and grasped his arse, dragging him in even harder.

He gave three sharp pants, and came to a quivering stop, his face in my neck, his weight fully on me.

My blood was thundering through my veins. My dick ached. I was close, I was close, I was—

Adam gripped my hips and held on as he rolled us, then shoved at my shoulders until I sat up. His cheeks were hectic with colour and he was flushed all the way down his chest. He took hold of my dick and pulled the orgasm clean out of me in two strokes.

I arched my back, made one of those awful, shiveringly needy noises that I couldn't hold in, and I came.

Adam stared at me as if he couldn't look away.

If that was his idea of everyday sex, if he *did* try anything kinky, I wasn't sure I'd survive it.

29

*A*dam appeared in the kitchen the next morning as I raised my third cup of coffee to my lips. I had pillow creases, bedhead, and bags under my eyes from being shagged twice more during the night.

Adam was radiant.

He glowed with vitality; his skin was rosy from the shower, his eyes were clear, and his still-damp, copper-blond curls were carelessly pushed back. His body was loose and oozing satisfaction.

The arsehole.

He grinned at me as he strode over to the coffee machine. I was slumped in a kitchen chair, clutching my coffee mug with both hands.

"Morning," he said, dropping in a pod and pressing the button.

I grunted.

He rummaged around in the fridge, added a generous splash of milk to his coffee, and sauntered over to the table.

He did not sit down in the chair I pushed out for him using a toe, somehow managing not to complain when my thigh muscle, which had had the workout of a lifetime, cramped. He came all the way around and perched his pert bottom on the table right beside me. All his radiant heat washed over me. He took a big gulp of his coffee, watching me over the rim.

We took stock of each other.

"What?" I said after a long silent minute, during which he was content to simply watch me, and I had about a thousand flashbacks from the night before that scorched my cheeks.

"Not a morning person?"

"Morning person, yes. Stay up all night person? No."

Adam drained his coffee, set it on the table, and slid a hand under my jaw. He stroked his thumb back and forth over my chin, gazing at me consideringly before he made a small *huh* sound. I don't know what that was all about. I was on the point of asking him when the doorbell rang.

"Ugh," I said. "What d'you want to bet that's your cousin?"

"Why would Liam be calling on you at nine a.m.?"

"I may or may not have left him about five voicemails last night. I may or may not have been calling him names in those voicemails."

He grinned. "I'll get it," he said.

"Thank you." A fourth coffee wasn't the smartest move in the world, but three hadn't made a dent on the exhaustion. I was aware that it was more emotional than physical. I shuffled over to the coffee machine and had a clear view right through the hall to the front door where Adam stood.

His wide shoulders blocked whoever was on the doorstep. They didn't do a thing to block the voice.

"Adam?" Fraser said. "What are you doing here?"

Every single good feeling that had been simmering in

me since Adam took me apart then held me in his arms vanished at the sound of Fraser's familiar voice.

Stiff-legged, I walked out of the kitchen and to the front door. Adam's tall, solid body was filling the doorway. I had to step to one side before I could see through to Fraser.

He looked the same—an inch or two shorter than Adam. Dark blond hair in a stylish cut, blue eyes behind fashionable black-rimmed glasses, a runner's lean-muscled body. Standing on my doorstep like he'd forgotten his keys and was about to come on in, throw his bag down in the hall, and ask what was for supper.

Fraser's attention was on me as I approached. Adam's back muscles tensed.

"Ray," Fraser said. His gaze flicked from Adam to me. He quirked a brow and pointed between us. "Don't tell me you two...?"

The silence was appalling.

"Are you serious?" Fraser said. "Ray, I didn't know you had it in you. Nice."

Adam slammed the door in Fraser's face, whirled around and grabbed my shoulders.

"What—" I got out, and that was all I managed before Adam dragged me up against his hot body and kissed me.

I moaned as his tongue slid over mine and he straight-up fucked my mouth. He wrangled me around, shoved me up against the door and held me against it, not even giving me space to breathe. Our teeth clashed, his fingers gripped so hard I thought he'd leave bruises, and he leaned into me as if he was trying to fuse us together from the knees up.

"Adam." I panted hard when he tore his lips from mine. "What is happening? I—*ohhh*." He pushed a hand down the front of my sweatpants and gripped my cock possessively. "Adam," I said. "Adam, what—*uhhhn*."

He dragged his fist down the length of my rapidly filling dick, and licked into my mouth.

The sound of the doorbell two feet from my ear broke me out of the overwhelming sexual haze that Adam seemed determined to plunge me into. Once I'd heard the doorbell, it registered that Fraser was also pounding on the door.

I tipped my head back, pulling my mouth out of reach, and gasped for air. "Adam," I said.

He chased my mouth, and when I twisted away he scowled and went for my neck instead.

The bastard. He *knew* I was extra sensitive there.

He scraped his teeth down the taut and quivering tendon, then drew skin into his mouth and sucked, hard.

I yelped, getting a fist in his hair and pulling him back.

"Stop," I said.

He glared down at me, his beautiful face stormy and fierce.

My neck throbbed where he'd no doubt put his mark on me. My head pounded.

No, wait. That was still the door.

"Hang on a sec." I turned in his arms, opened the door, and all but yelled, "Yes, WHAT?" at Fraser.

Fraser was red, eyes sparking angrily, and he glared at Adam over my shoulder. I risked a glance behind me. Adam was glaring back.

He also had an arm around me and one hand resting low on my stomach. I grabbed it to prevent it going further south. I had a fair idea what was going on with him, even though it made no sense at all, but I wasn't keen to have him handle my junk in public to make his point. On the doorstep. With people watching.

"Very classy, Ray," Fraser sneered.

"Thanks," I said. "Was that all? It was? Great. Goodbye." I went to close the door.

"Wait," Fraser said. He ruffled a hand through the back of his hair and dropped his arm to his side. "Let's start again."

"I'd rather not," I said. "If you'd like to remove yourself from my property, that'd be great."

"Well," he said with a short laugh, and a flick of his eyes to the left. "Kinda mine, too."

I flat-out gaped at him. Kinda his? How did he come to that batshit conclusion?

Adam made a small sound behind me. Like a cross-between an *aha* and a grunt of satisfaction. The tension in his body didn't go away, but it definitely eased.

"We can all talk inside," Fraser said, already stepping forward.

Adam's long arm came over my shoulder and stopped Fraser in his tracks.

"Who's we?" I said.

Fraser gave a short laugh. "Ray, we've been over this. Come on."

"I haven't spoken to you in over a year! I don't know what you're talking about."

"Okay, very funny. I've been texting you. I called you. Left voicemails?"

"I know. I don't know what about, though. I blocked your number."

Adam snorted with amusement.

Fraser had the audacity to look indignant. "You blocked my member?"

"Uh...yes? "

"Why would you do that?"

I said slowly, "You cheated on me with an unknown

amount of men the whole time we were together, and when I threw you out, you moved to Wantage. I assumed that meant we were done?"

Fraser flushed. "And now you're the one sleeping with Adam. What is that about, anyway, some kind of revenge?"

I laughed. "You know, the fact Adam was stupid enough to sleep with you in the first place was a big old mark in the con column. *Ow.*"

Adam had pinched my belly fat. I sucked in my gut and twisted my neck to scowl up at him.

"You had a pro-con list?" he said, a smile flirting over his mouth.

"....maybe."

"I'm going to need to see that list."

"Ha ha, no." Never.

It was in my journal, along with all sorts of incriminating shit and way too much gushing about his beautiful face and the way he made me feel *seen*. I'd burn it first. I'd be upset, because it was finest Italian leather and a gift from a dear friend. I'd still set it on fire before I let Adam read a word.

"Can you two dial it down, please?" Fraser said with a brittle laugh. "You're making everyone uncomfortable."

I blinked and looked away from Adam. "Who's everyone?"

"If you'd read my texts or listened to my voicemails, you'd know. I told you I was coming by today with a photographer and journalist."

"And I told you I blocked your cheating arse. Wait. Journalist? Photographer?"

"Please, Ray. Stop being such a drama queen. Can we discuss this inside like grown-ups?"

It did sound preferable to standing here putting on a

show for the two women standing behind Fraser and the couple of neighbours who'd come out to see what was going on.

They were probably hoping for another body.

"I suppose—"

"No," Adam interrupted. "You cannot."

"It's not your house," Fraser said though a tight smile.

"I don't care. I say you can't come in. Access to the property is denied."

"Is he in charge?" Fraser demanded, poking a rigid finger in Adam's direction.

"No," I said.

"Yeah, he's in charge, all right." Fraser's tight smile twisted. "You like that, do you, Ray? Being told what to do? Perhaps I should have tried it."

I stiffened. "No need to get personal."

"Does he make you call him sir?" Fraser went on.

"Uh...he gave it a shot the once but I declined?"

Fraser ignored me. "That's what Adam likes. Right, Adam? Like it when the guy you're taking calls you sir? Calls you daddy?"

My mouth dropped. "Did Fraser call you daddy?" I said to Adam.

Adam tapped my mouth closed. "He called me whatever I told him to."

"I'm not calling you that."

"I know," Adam said with a blinding smile.

"Except if you got me drunk. I might do it then."

His gaze moved over my face. "Noted."

"Super drunk. But that's not my thing."

"I know what your thing is, Ray," he said, sweet as honey. "You're not that complicated."

"And if I did want to call him daddy," I whirled on

Fraser, "it's my business, not yours. If I want to be tied down and spanked until I'm sobbing—" Adam's hand on my stomach flexed, "—also not your business. Don't you try to kink-shame me, thank you very much."

Adam shook against me. He was laughing. Fraser's face was red and tight with anger. I'd had enough.

"Are you going to tell me what you're here for? "I said. "Or would you please go?"

"Let me in and we can discuss it like adults," Fraser said through gritted teeth.

"You've already proven you're not capable of that. Good-bye, Fraser." I stepped back and went to close the door.

"Wait."

Adam groaned in my ear—not the sexy kind of groan—when I paused and arched a brow.

"All I want is to get a few pictures of the house," Fraser said. "Let me do a walkthrough."

"Why?"

"These guys are doing a piece."

"A piece?"

"Ray, he wants to cash in on the bodies," Adam sighed. "Try to keep up."

"It's rather hard, actually, when I'm sandwiched between the two of you like this."

"No," Adam snapped.

"Huh?"

"I was talking to him."

I glanced at Fraser, who was eyeing us. "Ew, no," I said. "If I was going to have a threesome, it'd be with him and Liam."

"Liam is still my cousin, babe," Adam said.

"With him and Jasper," I corrected. "I meant to say Jasper. Who is also...right, yes. Jasper is a journalist. The only journalist I'd be interested in talking to if there was even any kind of story here, which there isn't."

Fraser looked surprised, then sneered. "His fuckbuddy, Jasper?"

"Have you seen him?" I said. To be clear, I absolutely did not want a threesome with anyone, I was confident Adam knew that, but it was worth it to watch as Fraser's sneer was wiped away by a flash of pure jealousy. "And how did you even hear about the whole dead body situation, anyway?" I said.

"I read the local news. I'm still local."

"Regardless, I'm afraid you've wasted your time coming here. I have zero interest in being in the paper again, what with not being an attention ho."

Fraser had the audacity to press a hand to his own chest and act all wounded. "I'm not an attention ho!"

"You are a huge attention ho. Please. You slept with at least five other men that I know of while you were with me."

"It was an open relationship," Fraser said to the journalist, who'd gone from scrolling through her phone beside Fraser, looking bored, to shifting impatiently from one stiletto to the next. "On-again off-again."

I narrowed my eyes at him. "I wish you'd have told me that," I said. "I'd never have asked you to move in."

Fraser grinned triumphantly and turned to the journalist. "Like I said, it was my home. I always knew something was off about it, though. Especially the bedrooms."

"That was probably guilt from fucking randos in my bed," I said.

"Oh, calm down, Ray. It was my bed, too."

My blood pressure sky rocketed. "It was not! I bought it on sale from John Lewis, it took me six months to find that bedding set, and it's my house! You lived here for a year!" I looked over at the journalist, who was watching us carefully. "He didn't even contribute to the utilities or the groceries."

He hadn't contributed to my life at all, I realised. Unlike Adam, who had done nothing but try to contribute. From the very start.

"Do you want to move in with me?" I said, turning my face up to Adam.

He gave a startled laugh. "Do I want to move into your murder house with you?"

"When you put it like that, yeah. Stupid question."

"You just want me around to scare the ghosts."

"That never crossed my mind. I wasn't thinking. It just fell out."

"Guys, seriously," Fraser said. "Are you letting me in or not?"

"Not," I said. "This isn't your house, this has nothing to do with you."

The journalist muscled Fraser aside, and stuck out a hand. I unthinkingly shook. "Kate Chisholm," she said. "I'm with the *Wantage Gazette*. Mr Underwood, what were your first thoughts on finding the bodies?"

"What the fuck, mainly," I started to say. Adam's arm around my waist tightened. "You can read about it in my upcoming exclusive interview with Jasper Connolly of the *Chipping Fairford Inquirer*."

"Can I ask—"

"I'm sorry, no."

She gave me a calculating smile. "I'll have to ask Fraser if you don't give me anything."

I shrugged. "If that's going to satisfy your editor," I said. "*Cheater who lived there for a few months says he always knew something was off* doesn't sound like much of a headline to me, but what do I know? Excuse me." I stepped back, Adam giving ground, and closed the door.

"Wait," I said, and opened it again. "Please get off my property or I'll notify the police! Have a lovely day."

I shut the door and turned to face Adam. "What was that?" I asked.

"The shit-stirring of a desperate attention ho."

"No, I got that." I hitched a thumb behind us. "But what was all...you know." I waved both hands at him. "That. The whole shock and awesome kissing thing."

"What can I say? I'm young. My hormones got the better of me."

"Right."

We stared at each other. For once, I wasn't the only uncomfortable one in the room. Registering that made my own discomfort ratchet up a few hundred percent.

Three hundred percent at least.

Then I remembered that I had asked Adam to move in with me, and my discomfort shot into the red zone.

I had asked Adam to move in with me.

The morning after.

In front of the last man I'd lived with.

Who'd cheated on me.

With Adam.

Who I slept with once, and apparently he banged the sense clean out of me because, again, I *just asked him to move in with me the morning after*.

What the hell was Adam feeling awkward about? He couldn't top that. Nobody in the history of awkward could top that.

We fidgeted at each other and the silence dragged on. When I glanced up at him, his eyes were boring into mine. I couldn't maintain eye contact. And I couldn't stop looking back up.

Oh, this was horrendous.

Adam was swagger and confidence and always in control. Seeing him uncomfortable was so unusual. It made me feel tender toward him, like the phone sex had, like I wanted to—

I made a move toward him. He stuffed his hands in his pockets and turned for the kitchen. Had he seen me move, or...?

"Listen," he said. "I've got work. I'm late, in fact. I'd better head out." He grabbed his keys and wallet and motorcycle helmet from the kitchen counter.

"Oh," I said, following him to the front door again. "Did you—*mmph*."

He held my jaw, kissed me softly, drew back and stared at my face like he was going to be quizzed on it later.

I gave him a tentative smile. We were going to be all right. Right?

Maybe not. He released the tender hold on my face, slapped me on the arse, whisked out the door, and roared off on his motorcycle.

And that was the last I saw or heard of him.

30

*T*he most disturbing thing about returning home after it had been ransacked by a forensics team and had a second body carried out, was how quickly I got over it.

I didn't know if that was thanks to the epic night of sex with Adam which had realigned my reality and put things into perspective, or if Fraser showing up and making claims about it had made me realise how much I loved my little house, despite its quirks.

Or maybe I was just a pro. You know. At having dead bodies discovered in my house. And at being disappointed in men. Like Fraser.

And like Adam, who, seriously? It had been a *week*?

And like Detective Liam Nash, who was disappointing me right now.

"Nothing?" I demanded. "You've got no clue whatsoever?"

Liam sighed in resignation.

"How can you have nothing?" I said.

"You know why, Ray. You know how old those bodies are. How can you expect me to have anything?" he countered.

I cocked a hip. "You're a detective? It's your job?"

I'd been on Zoom with Paulina when the doorbell went. Needless to say, I'd ignored it, until I glanced out of the window and saw Liam's familiar car parked outside my house.

When I'd groaned and told her it was the fuzz at the door, she blew me a kiss, told me to go and to call her back when I was done. I'd been telling her about Adam, and she wasn't going to let me off.

I made it to the front steps before Liam had climbed back into his car.

He must have run down the drive to get there so fast.

"Hi!" I shouted when he was half in, half out of the car. "Liam!"

"Oh, good," he said. "You're in after all. I thought I'd missed you."

"Yeah, you wish," I said as he stomped back up to the house. I waved him in. "What have you got for me?"

His nostrils flared. "Is there any chance I can convince you to treat me as an officer of the law rather than a friend when I'm on duty?" He said it without much hope.

I scoffed.

"Didn't think so." He followed me to the kitchen without any fuss when I told him I'd picked up a box of donuts that morning and tapped out after two, meaning there were four left, lounging around and waiting to be eaten.

He stared at the donuts, his expression flashing through hunger, suspicion and amusement. It was quite the face journey for such a rugged man, who usually looked like he was carved out of granite.

"Did you buy these to bribe me?" he said.

Why lie?

"Yes. I was going to bring them by the station after my meeting."

He gave me an unimpressed look. "A half-eaten box of donuts isn't much of a bribe. And I'm deeply offended at the whole cop-and-donut thing. Are you aware that this is Chipping Fairford, not New York?"

"Don't force yourself," I said cheerfully, and tugged the box away. "Hello, lunch."

He hooked a finger over the edge of the box and tugged it back toward him. "I didn't say I didn't want one."

I grinned at him. "Coffee or tea to wash it down?"

"Coffee," he said.

He polished off three donuts one after the other under my wide-eyed gaze and when I asked him to hold up his end of the deal, the bastard gave me nothing.

"I told you with the first body, Ray," he said, sitting back and lacing his hands over his flat stomach—how? Three donuts! Three! "—it's a cold case, and despite what people think about police and crimes and mysteries, it's not that easy. Sometimes the evidence simply isn't there to be found. And again, as I've told you more than once, I can't discuss the case in any detail with you."

"You told me they were dolls."

"You deduced that on your own."

I wasn't that smart. He'd led me to that conclusion. "We discussed it in detail when you had me in the interrogation room," I said resentfully.

"I never had you in an interrogation room," Liam replied. "That was my office. As I told you at the time."

"You should fire your interior designer. It looked like an interrogation room."

"Right. I'll let my boss know that the station needs a new decorator. And that was me investigating, not gossiping."

"I get it," I said, and leaned my butt against the kitchen counter. "No big deal. Two dead guys in my house. Worse, two human dolls. I get ostracised by the community as a serial killer. My gross ex tries to sell 'his story' to the papers. My house needs renovating because of your wrecking crew —I'm sorry, did I mispronounce *forensics team*?—and I'll have to live here for the rest of my natural life because I'll never be able to sell it. I get nothing. It's fine."

"I wouldn't say nothing." Liam's eyes took on a teasing light. "You got Adam out of it."

"Hah," I barked a hollow laugh.

He blinked at me in surprise. "What does that mean?"

"I'd say Adam got *me* out of it." I shifted uncomfortably and wrapped my arms around myself. "Then Adam declined to come back for seconds."

Liam stared. "Are you sure you've got that right? He's crazy about you, Ray. Any crazier, and I'd be here with a restraining order all filled out and ready for you to sign."

"He'd have to come near me or at least text me before a restraining order is in order. Wouldn't he?"

"He's avoiding you?"

"Yes."

"Interesting."

"Embarrassing, actually. I thought...you know what, never mind what I thought."

Liam opened his mouth to reply.

"I asked him to move in with me," I blurted.

Liam began to smile. "Ray Underwood. You don't hang about, do you? Was this before or after you consummated your love?"

I pulled a face. "Consummated?"

He raised a brow.

"After," I grumbled. "Consummated our *love*. Again, hah. The love part was very one-sided. He likes me fine, but I—"

I felt my pupils shrink in horror as I locked eyes with Liam.

The first time I'd admitted that I was in love with Adam —to myself, let alone anyone else—and it was to his cousin.

"I didn't say that," I shot out.

"What, Ray? You didn't confess that you love Adam?"

I pointed at him. "You are evil."

He stroked his chin thoughtfully. "You're denying that you love him, then?"

I dropped my gaze and fumed at the floor. "You can't prove anything."

'I don't need to prove anything."

"Good. You can't."

"You're denying him. You're denying that you love him."

He made it a statement. Flat.

I agreed, but my voice quavered up at the end. "Yes?"

"You don't love him, in fact."

"Yes."

"Yes, you do love him? Or yes, you don't? Make up your mind, Mr Underwood."

"I dooo...n't."

"You dooon't?"

"You heard me."

"Let's recap. You don't, in fact, love Adam. You used him. You like him, he's a fun hook-up, you like him taking care of you and that's all there is to it. Am I right?"

I opened and shut my mouth. "No!" I forced out, indignant. Used him? "*Used* him? How dare you!"

"You'd hardly be the first man to do it."

"I didn't! I didn't do it!" I clutched the edge of the kitchen table. "I'm innocent!"

He barrelled on, "Adam's a good-looking young man. He —" Liam broke off when I made a rude noise. "You disagree?"

"Yes. Hell, yes. He's not good-looking, are you an idiot? He's beautiful. He's the most beautiful person I've met in real life!"

"We're related. I don't see him quite like that."

"You have eyes, haven't you?"

"I do, in fact, have eyes. Yes."

"Besides, it's not just his face and his body, although I could look at him all day long. Aaall day long. He's so kind. Except when he's being a bitch. But I like that part of him anyway."

"But you were happy to use him."

"What? No!"

"Then you do love him?"

"Of course I do!" I shouted. The glasses in the cupboard behind me rattled. "Yes! I love him. I love him a lot. I've never loved anyone like it. Why are you torturing me like this? How dare you!"

Liam, the shit, was full-on laughing at my big, incoherent, romantic declaration.

I glared down my nose at him. "I feel sorry for all criminals who cross your path."

He waited.

"I love Adam," I said, and slumped. The energy drained out of me. I could almost hear the gurgle as it circled my metaphorical drain. "Fuck my life," I said. "Seriously. Fuck it. Also, you."

"No, thanks. Adam would kill me, my good friend Detective Sergeant Patel would arrest him, and it would all get very messy."

"Why is he avoiding me, Liam?" I asked.

Liam gave me a sympathetic smile. "I don't know. What was the last thing you said to him?"

"I told you, I asked him to move in with me."

"Hard to see how he could take that wrong." Liam mused.

"Oh dear."

He quirked a brow.

"It wasn't the most romantic of circumstances. When I asked him. It was kind of a knee-jerk reaction."

Liam dismissed this. "We all say stupid stuff during sex."

"It wasn't during sex. It was, uh. When Fraser showed up."

"Fraser, your ex? Fraser, the thirty-five-year-old guy who had sex with my twenty-two-year-old-cousin?"

"I'm thirty-three next month," I said with some trepidation.

Liam said, "I know both of you. Trust me on this, Adam is not the immature one."

I was going to argue, but I didn't have a leg to stand on. "It probably wasn't the right time to ask him to move in, was it?" I said, then carried on without waiting for an answer. "No, it wasn't. I knew if the second I'd said it."

"Yeah, I doubt it made him feel good. He's a prideful man. And no one likes feeling like the prize in a pissing contest."

"You've got that wrong," I said, thinking of Adam mauling me up against the front door. "I was the prize." I squinted when Liam gave me a disbelieving look. "Okay, I know how that sounds. I don't mean it like everyone was fighting over me, but..." I trailed off.

Adam *had* had that unsettling hint of vulnerability about him again when he'd staked his claim, along with an almost frantic desperation.

I chewed this over while Liam eyed up the last donut and eventually caved.

I had been trapped between Fraser and Adam, in more ways than one. Me on my doorstep. Fraser, my past, in front of me in the drive. Adam, my future, behind me and still in the house.

I'd been flustered and angry with Fraser, and still vibrating from the night before with Adam. And then from Adam's passionate claim.

It hadn't crossed my mind that Fraser wasn't just my past, he was Adam's, too.

I didn't know what emotional baggage Fraser had left with Adam. And I never thought for a second that Adam could imagine I'd compare the two of them and find him lacking in any way.

It was fairly clear, what with me insisting Fraser get off my property, that I wasn't looking to get back together with him. But Fraser was an attractive man. He was older than Adam, he had a very well-paid job, he was established in life.

I supposed that if Adam had even the slightest doubt about whether or not I saw him as a serious romantic prospect or a sexy young thing for sexy times only, it could have felt like a competition that he couldn't win.

Which was ridiculous.

And here was another thing. I was annoyed, upset, unsettled that Adam hadn't contacted me. He hadn't come by. He hadn't texted or called. I had, foolishly, expected him to.

I gripped the sides of the kitchen counter, butt still

leaning against the cupboards. It was like when I went to stay at my parents. My fingers tightened until the counter was biting into my palm.

He hadn't called me then. He hadn't called me until he'd caught me trying to text.

Every single time we'd interacted, he'd come to take care of me. He'd come with a purpose. It was never, not once, for sex.

We'd ended up kissing or almost having sex, and just the once we'd had it, but his reason for coming after me had always been to see if I was all right and to bully me into accepting care.

He'd never come after me for the sole purpose of seducing me.

I'd waited a week. I could wait another thousand weeks.

Adam wasn't coming.

Adam wasn't going to show up until I needed him. Until he had a reason.

I'd misunderstood his confidence. Adam wasn't afraid of anything. He took what he wanted and he moved on. He was brave. He was demanding.

But when it came to him and me...maybe he was as uncertain as I was?

I looked at him and thought, how can this beautiful boy possibly want me? Perhaps he looked at me and thought, how can this average older man want me?

I already knew Adam had a complicated relationship with his looks. It had to do something to you, to be consistently judged for your appearance, whichever end of the spectrum you fell on.

Adam knew that people wanted him.

Had he ever thought that people wanted to *keep* him?

Because I did.

I'd keep him forever, if I got the chance.

And it didn't have a damn thing to do with how he looked. I was a graphic designer. Fine, I was an *artist*. I knew about lighting and angles and harmonious shapes and spaces. I could appreciate them, but I didn't get caught up in them. I was interested in what lay beyond them. What they meant. After the initial bedazzlement, it was the Adam behind the beauty that had captivated me.

He had absolutely no reason to think that.

As far as Adam was concerned, he came after me every time I needed him. He provided comfort or help. Bossily and in a domineering way because I wasn't fooling myself here. He was a bossy bastard. He liked to get his way. He'd made overture after overture, and I....I'd never reciprocated.

I'd only ever put myself in his space when I needed a hotel room, not him.

I'd never reached out.

I'd accepted his advances; I hadn't genuinely signalled that I was very much in favour of more, had I?

Apart, that is, from the aforementioned ill-timed asking him to move in with me. Now that Liam had mentioned it, that could very well have been seen as a way to rub Fraser's nose in the fact that now *I* was the one getting it from Adam.

"As fascinating as it is watching you have some kind of revelation over there," Liam's voice jolted me out of my reverie, "my shift is over and now, thanks to you, I have to go to the gym and lift weights for the next six hours to work those donuts off."

"Right, of course. You're welcome."

Liam was already standing by the doorway. I hadn't even noticed him get up.

"The bodies," I said, although it didn't seem even remotely important anymore. Not compared to Adam thinking for a second that I didn't want him. Didn't love him. "Where did we land on...? You know what? I don't care anymore."

Liam's brows rose. "You don't care?" he said. "You?"

"Nope. Forget about it." I bustled over to him and guided him out of the doorway into the hall.

"Forget about it? Ray, you have called me and texted me and talked my ear off about this for months now, and not once has it sunk in that I've told you all I can and that's all there is. And now you're saying *forget about it*?" He was leaning back, making me work to shove him ahead of me.

I reached out and opened the front door. "Well," I said, "consider it well and truly sunk. It is what it is, right?" I clapped him on the shoulder.

"Yes, but—"

"Don't worry about it. We'll see what forensics comes up with. These things take months. Sometimes years. We may never know."

"That's..." He drew himself up indignantly. "That's what I keep telling you!"

I tapped my ear. "I do listen. Now, thanks for stopping by, but if you don't mind, I have important business to attend to."

I started to shut the door on his red and annoyed face.

"Is this Adam business?" he said suspiciously.

"It's my business." Yes, it was Adam business. Liam had already squeezed a love confession out of me. I'd like to tell Adam myself without Liam knowing about that, too. Or giving him a heads-up, which he totally would.

Liam held the door open with the flat of his hand. "You be good to him, okay?"

"I intend to be very good to him," I said. "Very good. Repeatedly. And I'd like to get on that—also on him—so if you'd....there we go. Thanks, Liam." I poked him out of the way and closed the door on his face, laughing at his expression.

He thumped the door once in farewell and I heard his footsteps retreating down the path.

Right. I blew out a breath. Time to get proactive about this whole relationship stuff.

31

*I*t didn't take me long to decide how to do it.

I was going to be romantic as hell.

Thanks to Dad sticking me with that craft beer design job, I had the funds.

Once I'd checked the hotel website and saw the price, I amended that to I *just about* had the funds.

Adam was worth it.

I smiled dopily at the website and clicked the BOOK NOW button. He was worth everything. Anything.

Catching sight of my reflection in the window behind my computer, I scowled. Keep it together, Ray, I told myself, and immediately started smiling again.

Well, I was trying.

Realising that I'd kept Paulina waiting for a whole hour and a half, I called her back as soon as the payment went through. Even though she wouldn't dump me for ducking off a call, I was a professional. I told her enough about Adam to satisfy her curiosity, we wrangled over the design brief, and once I hung up, I started to fret.

I buried myself in more work, but it was no good. I grew more and more nervous as the day dragged on.

I was a worrier by nature. If this went sideways, I didn't know how I'd get over it.

Still, even when my nerves threatened to get the better of me, I grimly pushed on. I wrapped up work, packed an overnight bag, swung by the pharmacy, and headed over to the hotel.

I knew it was possible that Adam would see the booking, but I'd confirmed with Liam that Adam was on the night shift, and I was safely checked in and ensconced in the room before Adam even showed up to work.

There was one downside to my grand plan: I was knackered.

It's not every day you realise that you're in love.

I'd been running on adrenaline and nerves from the moment I'd declared myself in the kitchen with Liam. I'd also travelled the full length of the confidence spectrum, from swaggering around, thinking, *Yeah! Gonna get my man!* to slumping around, thinking, *Shit. What if...?*

Waiting until Adam's shift finished at midnight gave me an agonising eight hours of hanging around in the honeymoon suite, wringing my hands and second-guessing myself.

I had my phone with me, but I wasn't a teenager. Instagram could only interest me for so long.

At half ten, I ran myself a bubble bath. I was jittery and not in the mood to relax, even though I'd brought my lavender bath oils. After a few minutes of lying there listening to the low hum of the extractor fan and the blood rushing in my ears, I gave up on the idea of forcing myself to get in the mood, and climbed out.

The mood might not be happening, but I groomed until

I was shaved and moisturised like I'd never been before, and minty fresh. I was thorough enough that I dragged it out until midnight, which I thought was the perfect time to call down for a snack.

Doing my best to ignore the faint trembling in my hands, I sat primly on the edge of the bed and dialled room service.

Please please let Adam answer, I thought. I had a plan for if he did and a plan for if he didn't, but I definitely preferred it if—

"Reception, how can I help you this evening?"

I opened my mouth and a dry croak came out.

Great.

Fab start.

Adam repeated the question in his deep, steady voice.

I clenched my fist on my bouncing knee. I could do this. I was doing it. Right now. "Yes. Okay. I'd like to order a meal?"

There was the faintest hesitation at the other end before Adam replied, "Of course, sir. What would you like?"

If I strained my ears, I could hear the clicking of keys. He was looking up the room, I knew it. I knew it for sure when I heard his shaky breath.

"Um," I said, as if thinking it over. "I would like the steak. The steak's good, right?"

"We have not had any complaints about the steak."

"Well then. Let's have that. With a side of fries and onion rings."

"Anything else? Something for dessert?"

"I'll take the chocolate cake. Make that two pieces of chocolate cake."

"Anything else?"

"Yes. I am very particular about my cake."

"I see."

"It's got to be served right, you understand."

"The chocolate fudge cake can be served as is, or hot with a scoop of vanilla ice cream," he said.

"Sounds nice. But I was thinking more of the presentation."

"I'm sure we can oblige."

"I do hope so. I'd like it served a la naked abs, preferably on a six-foot-three blond with a hint of ginger? It's specific, I know. Do you happen to have one of those lying around?"

"'I'm sure we can find something to suit."

"Great!" I said. "Send it all up! On second thought, hold the steak. I'm more of a dessert guy. All I want is the cake."

"Certainly, Mr Underwood," he said with an edge. "Two pieces of cake, served on a bed of abdominals, six-foot-three blond, should be there in ten minutes."

"Thanks!" I said, hung up, and bent over at the waist to breathe into the paper bag from the pharmacy with the condoms and lube in.

In my head, the whole cake thing was a sassy and fun request. Spoken out loud, I realised it could also be inter-preted as the request of a deranged cannibal. While I was fairly certain Adam would take it the right way, I felt like a bumbling idiot.

I pretty much had myself under control when a knock came at the door.

I rushed over, threw all pretence of cool out the window, and snatched the door open.

It wasn't Adam.

It was a young woman with shaded ombre hair in a high ponytail that went from black roots to almost white-blond tips. Not a hint of red or copper. And even in four-inch stilettos, she didn't quite hit five feet five inches.

"Here you are, sir," she said with a big wink, holding out a tray.

I took in a sharp breath, and swallowed hard. "Thanks," I tried to say, but it came out as a tragic wheeze.

Her face fell and she glanced off to the side.

I took the tray and tugged. She let go. I wished she hadn't. My hands had started shaking again, rattling the contents of the tray. It wasn't from excitement and nerves. It was shock and disappointment.

I hadn't realised that, deep down under the panic, I'd thought it was going to work. I'd been sure it was going to work.

I conjured up a smile, and nodded at her. "Thank you," I said, and backed into the room, shutting the door.

I stood there blankly, clutching the clinking tray.

Well, shit.

The door beeped open. Adam strode in. "For god's sake, Ray," he said. He leaned his upper body back out into the hallway and I heard him murmur, "He's not crying, okay?" before he shut the door again.

I stared at him helplessly as he crossed the room to me.

"What am I going to do with you?" The sound of rattling plates and cutlery picked up. Adam bit back a smile. "Are you nervous?"

"No. Why? Do I look nervous?" I frowned at the trembling crockery.

"You look devastated, according to Misha."

"Just...hungry for cake."

"For cake, hmm?" He very gently took the tray off me and strode over to set it on the desk. He turned and rested his arse against the desktop.

"Yes. This is low blood sugar."

"You'd better come over here and do something about it,

don't you think?" Keeping his eyes on mine, he picked up the napkin-rolled cutlery and took out a fork. My breathing picked up as he removed the cover off the cake, slid the fork through, and picked up a piece.

He put it in his mouth, and slowly pulled the fork back out.

What was with him and cutlery?

What was with *me* and cutlery? I didn't remember moving, but one minute I was staring at him across the room, and the next minute I was standing in front of him, my socked feet touching the tips of his shoes.

Adam tilted his head and looked down into my face. He licked at the corner of his mouth, and went to cut another piece of cake.

He stilled when I took hold of his wrist.

"I believe I asked for it served a la abdominals," I said, again going for sassy but failing miserably. One, because my voice was reedy. Two, because, oh my god, stop sounding like a *cannibal*. Three, because he snatched my hand and held it between his own.

"Jesus, Ray. Your hand is freezing!" He chafed it.

"Oh, you know," I said breezily. "I'm having a bit of a fight, flight, or freeze reaction here. It'll pass." I kept my gaze down and tangled my fingers through his.

"What's going on?" Adam murmured.

I hummed, turned his hand over, and started playing with it. He let me, watching as I drew a circle over his palm, slipped my fingers through his and back out again. "Not much." I stalled.

"Did you find another dead guy?" he said sympathetically.

"Don't even joke about it," I said, glancing up. Our eyes

clashed. I quickly glanced away. He looked amused. Tender. Wary.

And so patient.

Liam really had hit it on the nose when he said I was not the mature one in this relationship, hadn't he?

"No more dead guys, " I said.

His free hand came to rest on my chest. "You just fancied a night away from home? Decided to treat yourself to the honeymoon suite? At the Premier Lodge?"

"Yes. Something like that. Something completely normal like that. Like a normal person would do."

He waited, but I was still freaking out quietly.

"Well, then," he said. He pulled his hand away and undid his tie.

I still couldn't quite meet his eyes again—I would absolutely and definitely grow a pair in a minute. Demand he date me. Throw the condoms and lube at him. Something classy.

But right now, my gaze was stuck to his neck. He left the tie hanging loose and popped the top button of his white shirt.

Then the next button.

Then the next.

He kept on popping buttons until his shirt was hanging open. I'd been trying to be sexy about the whole eating the cake off his abs thing, but with both cake and abs in view, I was feeling less theoretical about it.

Adam took my hips in a firm grasp, and pulled me into him. My body was pressed against his. There was only the thin layer of my t-shirt between us. I tipped my head back and met his steady gaze.

"Are you ready to talk?" he said.

"I love you."

His mouth dropped open.

Okay, I *was* going to ease into it slightly more gracefully than that.

A bolt of horror washed through me when I said it, just as it had when I'd confessed it to Liam. It was washed away just as quickly by a sense of rightness. Of fate.

It didn't matter how Adam responded, I'd said it.

I'd laid it out there.

And okay, I'd sort of flung a love confession at him out of the blue and I could probably have gone with a soft opening, like, hey, do you want to date? But it was fine.

Why wasn't he saying anything?

I didn't know whose heart was beating the fastest at that point.

A faint noise came from Adam's throat.

I bit my lip in anticipation, but it must have been air escaping. He didn't say anything.

He just stared at me.

I felt my face change from bold to hopeful and then twist into a grimace as heat flooded my cheeks.

"Um," I said. "So that burst out unexpectedly."

His fingers tightened on my hips. If I'd had any idea of putting some distance between us, I set it aside. I wasn't going anywhere. I'd have to pry him off first.

That was encouraging, yes?

I leaned back enough to flatten my hands over his hot, tense chest. "Not like the whole move-in-with-me thing burst out. Sorry about that. I definitely don't know where that came from. I mean, I'd still like it but—nope." I shook my head.

"No?" he said faintly.

"No! I will not get off track. I love you. It popped out but it was deliberate. I planned it."

"You...?"

"Planned it. I was always going to tell you tonight. It was going to be less of an ambush, though. It wasn't a mistake. I think we need to be clear on that. I came here with the sole purpose of telling you I love you."

His fingers tightened again, almost painfully. He swallowed. The sound was loud in the otherwise silent room.

They had great double glazing here. Dad would be impressed. Couldn't hear even the buzz of traffic outside.

Okay, I didn't give a shit about the double glazing and I definitely didn't want to be thinking about my dad.

I bumped my hips into Adam's. "That's about it. I never said it was a complicated plan. I've been thinking about us. A lot."

"Us," he said.

"You know, you're not responding quite how I anticipated? And there is more to the speech, but I'm not sure at this point that you want to hear it?"

He barely even let me finish. "I want to hear it."

"In a general, *I'm curious as to what nonsense he's coming out* with kind of way? Or in an, *I am invested in the outcome* kind of way?" I drew a big circle over his chest, staring at it as if absorbed. Bullseye, right over his heart. "Because I'll tell you either way, I think you deserve that, but it turns out this is harder than I thought it would be. Didn't think that was possible, because I thought it was going to be nightmare hard, but there you go." I patted his chest.

"Why do I deserve it?"

"It came to my attention that I haven't treated you terribly well."

He frowned. "That's not true."

I reached up, cupped his face, and looked him in the eye. "I didn't treat you like you deserve to be treated."

He still looked puzzled.

I eased my hold and stroked a thumb over his bottom lip. "You are so, so beautiful," I said. His mouth curved and his tongue flicked out. "But I need you to know that I love you despite that."

He gazed at me sombrely. "Ray," he whispered. "Are you trying to tell me that you love me for my personality?"

"Yes," I slumped with relief. "Exactly, thank you. At first, I'll admit it, I was dazzled."

He bit my thumb lightly and smiled around it. "Dazzled?"

"Yes." This was getting awkward. I pushed on. "And I definitely thought about your beautiful face and your flawless skin, and your curls and your abs—"

"A lot of thinking," he murmured. His long body was relaxed now, all the tension having left it. He was still throwing off heat. I was still a chilled and sweating mess. I leaned into him gratefully.

"And wanking," I said.

He choked out a laugh.

I nodded. "Like you wouldn't believe. I almost chafed."

"I am...flattered?"

"I imagine a lot of people get chafed over you."

He grimaced. "Thanks."

"No," I patted his chest again. "No, no. That's...I'm trying to say that obviously I was gross and objectifying you for a while there—"

"Are you sure this is the speech you planned?" he said, voice vibrating with amusement. His eyes gleamed down at me. "Is it a first draft? Did you read it back at any point? Give it a quick run through at all? Because so far—"

"Obviously I didn't plan to ramble and insult you, it was

all much more straightforward in my head. I may be freestyling. Shh. Let me get this out."

He caught my wrist, dragged my hand down over his abs and pressed it into his erection. "Why don't you?" he said.

I laughed, high and nervous. "Yes. But. I respond to beauty and aesthetics and shit because it's kind of my jam. Graphic designer and all." I pointed at my chest.

He slid a finger under my chin, tipped my face up to his and dropped a bright kiss on my surprised lips. "Artist," he whispered.

"Eh—"

"Artist," he said firmly. "Please continue with the worst wooing speech ever spoken. Where did we leave off? Right. A crowd of anonymous strangers wanking themselves sore over me."

"I knew the second I said it that it wasn't coming out right." I planted both hands on his chest and pushed back. He let me go, but not far. "You have done nothing but be kind and thoughtful and take care of me. Whenever I needed you, there you were. You never asked anything of me. You never demanded anything of me. And I kept using you whenever you showed up and offered yourself and I feel awful about it."

"I like taking care of you, Ray."

"You are very selfless and giving."

His lips twitched. "You're the first person to say that to me."

"Everyone else you've ever been with must be stupid, then," I shot back.

"No," he said, still thoughtful. "They just never saw me for me."

"Like I said. Stupid."

"Dazzled," he said, and leaned back into his hands. His abdominal muscles tensed. "By all of this."

"I want to be the one giving to you," I said. "For once, please let me. Make your demands."

"I don't have any demands," he said quietly.

"Adam—"

"I don't have any demands," he said, "because you've already given me everything I never thought I'd get from you."

I cocked my head.

"Maybe next time you have a big speech," he started, popping the top button of his trousers. "Ray. Ray."

"Huh?"

"Eyes up here."

"Like you didn't know that unbuttoning would distract me—"

He undid his belt and drew it sloooolwly through the loops, then slooooowly coiled it and set it on the desk.

"As I was saying—" he continued, his cheeks beginning to flush, "—next time you have a big speech prepared, might I suggest some index cards? Jot down a few bullet points. You can refer back to them. Stay on track."

"Okay," I agreed. I'd agree to anything at that point. "But you'll have to be fully clothed, because even index cards can't save me from that."

He stalked toward me with his trousers undone and shirt flapping, like Mr Darcy striding through the misty fields at dawn in his swirling greatcoat.

If I'd tried that move, my trousers would have fallen down around my ankles. Then again, Adam's impressive erection was doing a great job of holding things up.

"You love me," he said, coming to a stop in front of me as I bumped into the bed.

"Yes." It was the easiest thing in the world to say. I didn't know why it had taken me so long.

"That's all I ever need you to give me," he said. "If I have that?" He ran a knuckle up my neck, then curled a hand around my nape and leaned down to press his forehead to mine, "I can take the rest."

Holy shit. I gasped, and he caught it in his mouth. He kissed me hard, then lifted me up to my toes and tossed me backwards.

32

*H*e put a knee to the mattress and followed me down, crawling over me. I scooted up the bed, Adam knee-walking over me until we reached the top.

To my surprise, instead of dropping down and getting on with business, he sat back. I was trapped between his muscled thighs. He was sitting on my slightly less-muscled thighs.

We looked at each other.

I genuinely didn't know what he saw in me. My chest was heaving, I knew my face was blotchy, and I lay there beneath his regard, frozen. He was over me, beautiful and golden, thoughtful and watching.

"I love you," I said, running my palms up his thighs. "I don't know if it's too soon or not, and I get that it probably is? But I think you deserve to know. I love you. I appreciate you for everything you are, and...yeah." I bit my lip, worried at it. "That's really the only important bullet point on my index card."

He reached down and eased my lip from between my

teeth. With a gentle fingertip, he traced around my mouth, his eyes following the movement.

"I want to date you," I said, then shook my head at once.

"No?" he murmured.

"Dating is what you do when you're on an app. I want a relationship with you. I don't want to meet for dinner or drinks, or sext each other. It's not about finding out if we're compatible or what we want from the relationship. I know what I want. I want you in my life. Properly."

"Mm?" He was still tracing my lips. His pupils were deep and dark against the bright hazel, and he had that delicious flush over his cheekbones.

I flexed beneath him.

He arched his back and dragged his shirt off, tossing it over the side of the bed.

"I want—" I broke off in a gasp when he shoved my t-shirt up under my armpits and bent down to lick a nipple. I went to hold his head. He snagged my hands and held them down. "I want you to move in. You don't have to do it right away, if that's going too fast. Whenever you're ready. I want to wake up with you. And go to sleep with you. And *ohhhh* my god." He shifted over me.

He pushed my t-shirt up and over my head, knelt up and slapped my thigh. "Get these off," he clipped out.

"Okie doke."

He cracked a laugh and helped me drag my pyjama bottoms down and off. Then he resumed his position, sitting on my thighs. Except instead of holding my hands, he was holding my cock and thumbing the head. "Carry on," he said politely.

My voice came out broken. "Uhhh. That's really. That's my pitch. That's really all there—oh god yes, there. *There.*

Right there." My stomach muscles drew in tight as he stroked me. And then let me go with a playfully cruel smile on his face.

I humped up beneath him, and caught him by surprise. "Hah," I said, knocking him over and rolling on top. It was a short-lived victory. He continued the roll and I was pinned beneath him again. "Crap."

"Nice try," he said.

"The pitch or the move?"

He considered. "Both."

We fell into silence and stared at each other again. "Sooo," I said. I hooked a leg up around his hip. "Thoughts?"

"I think I'm going to fuck you."

"Or..."

He smiled, slow and filthy. "You want to fuck me?" He drew my hand back until it was resting on his tight, round arse. My fingers spasmed and dug in.

Adam laughed. "That's a yes," he said.

I opened my hand and stroked over his buttock instead. "Actually, it's a no."

He didn't seem too devastated. Adam might be flexible, but he'd made it clear from the first that he had a strong preference to being on top.

"I was wondering..."

"Mm?" He grasped my thigh and pulled me down a little. I now had both legs around his narrow hips, and he was resting between them, propping his weight on his elbows.

"If maybe, uh..."

"Ask me, Ray," he said. "There isn't anything you can't ask me for."

"If instead of fucking me, you'd like to...if you could..." I pushed a tangle of red-blond curls back from his forehead, then let my fingers slip down to hold the side of his face. "If you'd like to make love to me instead?"

He gazed down at me in astonishment.

"No?" I said. "That's fine. Just because I love you it doesn't mean you have to love me back. People are on their own timetables. I know that. They don't always run, you know. Side by side."

"Yes," he said meaningfully. "I do know."

"Fucking it is," I said, trying not to be disappointed.

"Ray," he said, exasperated. "I've been in love with you for months."

"Wha—?"

"Infatuated with you for years. In love with you for months."

"Since when?"

"Since you actually deigned to talk to me. Let me in. Let me close."

I stared. "And infatuated? For *years*?"

"The first time I saw you, I was eighteen. The whole time I was working at the Co-op, I used to hope that you'd come in when I was on the till. Better yet when I was stocking shelves, and you'd have to brush past me. I won't tell you I fell in love. Again, I was eighteen. I'd shag anyone."

"Like Fraser."

"Yeah. That was a few years later, but, yeah. As we have established, I didn't know about you two. And then I did, and I came to apologise. And, baby. Your face. Your beautiful face." He ran a curled knuckle along my cheekbone. "You made me grow up. I'd never seen anyone so hurt. I'd never been the one to hurt another person like that."

I reached up and cupped his cheek.

He smiled. "I used to see you around a lot."

"I don't remember seeing you."

"You wouldn't. I didn't exactly come over to say hi. Never could dig up the courage. And I never did forget you. Even when I went back to Cambridge to finish my degree. When I came back home, Fraser was gone and you were still here. Ray, you're something else. You giant weirdo. I love you too."

I'd scowled at the *giant weirdo*, so was caught out with a stupid expression on my face when the love of my life told me he loved me too. "Really?" I said, voice going high.

"Yeah. If you're still interested in making love, we can get started. Because I don't know about you, but my dick is about to explode." He rocked against me. "We're in the honeymoon suite. We've got it all night. There's cake for dessert. Unless you want to start with it a la abdominals?"

"Maybe another time." Make that never. I'd changed my mind. I respected cake. I respected abdominals. I didn't see any reason to mash the two together. "Another time for the cake, I mean." I took hold of his cock. "I'd hate for anything to explode. You'd probably charge me extra for the cleaning bill."

"I absolutely would," he agreed.

I squirmed out from under him, pushing and shoving. He flopped back elegantly and ran a hand down his own chest and abs to play with his dick. I turned back, lube and condom in hand, and froze.

The corner of his mouth lifted. Eyes burning, he continued to stroke up and down his erection with long, lazy pulls and a deft flick of his wrist. "Yeah?" he said, low.

"You're young," I said.

"Ray, can we be done with this once and for all? Yes, I'm younger than you but—"

"I mean, keep going with that—" I waved at him, "—and you'll be good to go again in...?"

He ran his gaze over me. "Twenty minutes."

My brows lifted. "Really? Wow."

"I don't know, I've not timed it. You want to find out?" He never stopped stroking.

"Yes." I stretched out beside him, propping my head on a hand and watching as he pleasured himself.

It didn't take long. His abs were tensing and releasing within minutes, his face flushed, eyes locked on the side of my face. I darted a glance up at him every now and then but was mostly mesmerised by the way he handled himself. Graceful, and with confidence, and how the hell did I get this lucky?

"Ray," he panted.

"Yeah," I said, "Come on."

"Ray, touch me. Please, I—"

I slid my hand over his and he came straight away. My own dick kicked at the sight of his perspiration-damp body gleaming against the sheets, his hips pumping up into the air, his beautiful cock jerking in my hand.

"Oh my god," I said, sounding high and startled. "I think I'm gonna—"

Adam pushed me onto my back and pinned me down by lying on top of me. He was damp and spent against my own hard cock.

"I'm definitely gonna—" I gasped out, and felt it start. I yelped when he lifted away enough to get between us and tug my balls down.

I glared up at him, betrayed. "*Ow!*"

His eyes glittered feverishly. "You don't get to come until I'm inside you," he said.

"That is very bossy." I tried to hide how thrilled I was,

but I don't think he bought it. I writhed with discomfort beneath him.

He groaned and jerked against me. "Uhhhn. Hold still."

"*You* hold still," I said, and cupped his arse. He was like hot damp silk under my palms.

He squeezed my bollocks again.

"Seriously, though," I said. "*Ow.*"

He eased up. "Shh," he murmured, and kissed my neck. "Let me take care of you, Ray. I want to take care of you." His voice was slow and deep, edging toward slurring.

He was about to fall asleep. "Okay, Adam," I said. "In a minute. I'm not going anywhere."

He hummed with satisfaction against me. My breath stuttered a little. His large body went lax against mine and he slipped into sleep.

He took me under with him.

I woke some time later—I didn't know how long, but I had the sense that it was an hour or two—to his soft face and warm eyes over mine. He'd woken me up with butterfly kisses, I realised, when another drifted over my lips.

He must have got up at some point, to clean us both and to turn off the bedside lamps. The lamp on the desk was still on, sending a gentle glow our way.

"Hello," I said.

He angled his head and kissed me deeper.

I threaded my hands through his hair and held him there. He moved over me and between my thighs. He touched me gently between my cheeks. "Yes?" he whispered.

"Yes," I said, and hissed when he stroked me there. He'd already found the lubricant, and I glanced down to see that he had a condom on. "Been waiting long?" I said with a smile.

"My whole life," he replied, and slipped a finger inside.

My neck arched in response and I tightened my grip in his hair.

"God, Ray," he said. "You're so responsive."

Was I? No one had said that before. Maybe it was him, the way he touched me, the way I wanted him. "More," I said. "Hurry, hurry."

"No chance," he said. "I'm going to make you shake for me, and beg, and—"

I gripped his face and tilted it down so he was looking me in the eye. "I will do all of those things for you, I have no doubt many, many times. But need I remind you what happened last time?"

He hid a smile. At least, he tried to.

"Yeah," I said. "Congratulations. You're too sexy and I can't control myself around you. If you want me to come with you inside?" I pinched his arse. "Get in."

Adam obliged. He went slow but it burned. It must have shown on my face. He slowed down and wouldn't let me hurry him after that, opening me up on his cock with slow, leisurely thrusts that had me panting blankly at the ceiling.

I tugged and pulled him, trying to get closer. He laughed and held me down, made me take it at his pace, ignoring my swearing until he was seated deep, deep inside.

Then he stretched out over me, giving me all of his weight, his eyes dark and knowing, and began to move. Long, rolling thrusts of his hips. Unrelenting eye contact.

He rocked into me over and over. Now and then he dipped down to slide his tongue into my mouth and let me suck on it, but he always pulled back to watch, like I was something he didn't want to miss, like seeing me come apart beneath him was something he couldn't look away from.

I'd never had an orgasm while looking directly into someone's eyes before. It was overwhelming, and intimate, and the surge of emotion that crashed through me even before the physical pleasure did had moisture gathering at the corners of my eyes.

Adam bent down and kissed it away. "Are you crying?" he asked.

"Pfft. No."

"It's okay to cry."

"I know. But I'm not."

He ran his thumbs over my damp cheeks.

"I'm happy," I told him.

A wide smile broke over his face. "Yeah?"

"You make me happy. I don't even care about my murder house anymore because it brought me to you. And I love you."

"I love you."

I stretched luxuriously beneath him. "Mm. What time is it?"

His face took on a mischievous cast. "It's one thirty."

"Ooh. Plenty of time for more—"

"In the afternoon."

My voice dried up and I stared at him. "What?"

"It's one thirty in the afternoon."

We'd slept the whole night away. And the morning.

"Don't you dare," I said.

"Ray." He pulled a mock-apologetic face. "You know checkout is at ten a.m. I'm going to have to charge you for an extra night."

"You're a dick," I said.

"It's company policy. Late checkout only goes—ahhh!" He giggled when I started pinching his butt, then shoving at him.

"You should have woken me up!"

"You should have set an alarm!"

I growled at him and bit his neck.

He moaned, allowing me to wrestle him flat. "I'll cover it," he said. "This one's on me."

"Bet your arse it is," I said. I scrambled on top in a flurry of knees and elbows, and we stayed there until checkout the next morning.

EPILOGUE

*H*e didn't move in with me right away.

If it had been down to me, we'd have checked out of the Premier Lodge—preferably for the last time ever—swung by Adam's house to pick up his stuff, and moved him in that day.

Adam, being the mature and responsible one, held off. He wasn't being coy; he had decisions to make about his future. I promised myself I wouldn't hold him back. He was bright and talented and beautiful. He deserved the world, and if he wanted to go out there and grab it with both hands, I wouldn't stop him.

He wasn't as impressed as I'd expected him to be when I nobly told him this.

He said he was exactly where he wanted to be (which, when he said it, was on top of me) his hands were full enough, thank you (of my arse) and he'd move in as soon as his application to get a master's degree in architecture at Cambridge was accepted. If it wasn't, he'd have to look at London or move north for a few years, and heads up, he'd be taking me with him.

He'd said this last bit challengingly. He had to know I'd follow him anywhere. I told him anyway.

He was accepted, of course. We popped champagne, he moved in, and it was great. He commuted to Cambridge to study, and he came home to me every night. He did all those things to me he had promised to do, including the strip-tease, and life was good.

I even made headway on my house renovations. I'd been encouraged by how spectacularly my love life renovations had gone.

Before I got stuck into it, I gave Jasper the in-depth interview I'd told Fraser I was going to give, and I even let him take photographs before I gutted the place.

Giselle was about as suspicious of Adam's advent in my life as I had been of hers, but it didn't take him long to win her over. Dad, in contrast, loved Adam from the start.

He loved Adam for making me happy, he loved Adam because here, at last, was a man Dad could talk to about proper man-things, like construction. Sometimes, Adam brought Liam around, and then Dad could talk rugby, too. It was a dream come true.

Most of all, Dad loved Adam because under the combined pressure, I caved and let Dad build me a conservatory.

"It makes sense, Ray," he told me. "It'll raise the value of the property and add some interest to a very run-of-the-mill Cotswolds cottage."

I thought that my cottage was already about as interesting as I could stand for it to be. I agreed on the condition that Dad could build it, but Adam had to design it. That had the pair of them happily conspiring for months.

In late spring, Dad and his right-hand man, Marley, came up to break ground. Adam and I had been together for almost a year, and I could barely even remember what my house had been like without him in it. Echoing. Empty. Just me and the dead guys.

On the day the building began, Adam was doing something technical on his enormous computer in our joint office. I was standing at the kitchen sink, thinking about the antique drafting table I'd bought as a surprise for Adam as soon as I'd said yes to the conservatory. It was actually going to be a conservatory/office for him. I couldn't wait to see his face when I showed him my design for it, once the exterior structure was up. I'd done a 3D render and everything.

Dad and Marley started up the digger. They'd been at this conservatory business for longer than I'd been alive and they still argued over who got to operate the thing. After their usual heated debate, Marley won the coin toss, and Dad had to stand there, hands on hips, yelling instructions that Marley ignored, because, *I know what I am doing, Chris.*

I heard the digger rattling away as I did the drying up, saw the arm go up and down a few times, registered a bit more yelling, and then the arm stopped and the digger turned off.

I looked out.

Marley dismounted and they stood side by side, staring down at the ground. The foundations had been marked out with string. Dad had laid it all out yesterday. I'd caught Adam sneaking out that morning to double check Dad had done it right.

I watched them, and frowned when they didn't move. Slinging the damp tea towel over my shoulder, I went out the back door.

"Dad?" I called. "What is it?"

I joined them and we all stood there, staring down at the dark, moist earth of the trench.

"Huh," I said.

"Yuh," Dad said.

"That's not a chimp," I said after another moment.

"It's not just a hand, either."

Adam came out and wandered over to join us. "What's going on?" he said. "What are you all looking at?" He came to stand beside me and peered down.

"Maybe call Liam?" I said to him. "We found another —oh."

Adam crashed to the ground in a dead faint.

Dad and Marley looked at him with mild surprise. "Did you know he was squeamish?" Dad said.

"I had no clue," I marvelled, dropping to my knees and checking Adam's pulse before I sat on the damp ground and lifted his head out of the dirt and onto my lap. He moaned faintly.

"Good job all he does is design the buildings rather than build them," Dad said. Clearly, Adam's stock had taken something of a dip in the face of his 'squeamishness'. "You don't faint when you find dead people, do you, Ray?" Dad continued, judgement heavy in his voice.

I scowled at him. "I literally just found one, Dad. Right in front of you. I very emphatically did not faint. You watched me not faint." Adam moaned again. I stroked his cheek. "It's okay," I said. "It's okay. It's a body, nothing to worry about."

"You didn't find it," Marley said. "I found it."

"Regardless, there was no fainting from me," I said.

"Don't even start, Marley," Dad said, talking over me. "I found it and you know it. Don't you go claiming it as yours."

"Uh, I'm the one digging the holes, Chris."

"I'm the one telling you where to dig, Marley."

"Ray?" Adam said. "What's going on? Why are they shouting?"

"Shh, it's nothing. They're arseholes. Leave them to it." I shifted a bit, shoving a hand into my back pocket to get my phone.

Adam gazed up at me, eyes dark. "Did I faint?"

"Only a little, it's fine."

"I've never fainted before."

"It's a startling thing. Seeing a face where you don't expect it. You'll get used to it."

Adam was rallying. "I don't want to get used to it, thanks. I was less startled by the face and more by the fact it's a clown," he said. "I fucking hate clowns."

The digger had broken right through the tub. You couldn't see all of the body, but you could see enough to tell that it was dressed as a clown.

This wasn't a happy, smiling, kids party clown's costume, either. This was a creepy, late 1800s-style carnival clown in a striped onesie, pointy little shoes with ruffles on, and a chalky white makeup job with red circles on his cheeks. Any minute now, Dad was going to notice that it looked Victorian, and then he'd really kick off.

I was inappropriately delighted at Adam's confession. "Are you scared of clowns?"

He scrambled to his feet. "No."

He kept me between the trench and him, though, I couldn't help but notice. "You are. You are scared of clowns! You cliché!"

Adam looked down his nose at me. "I am not scared of anything and you know it."

"Okay. Stay right there. I'm going to call Liam."

Adam's eyes widened and he lunged to keep me between him and the clown when I moved.

I grinned at him.

He glared, put his shoulders back, and stalked over to me. I *oofed* a little when he wound an arm around my waist, pulled me in close, and deliberately arranged us with him between me and the dead-clown doll. He paled, but was determined.

"Are you protecting me from the clown?" I said.

"Yes." He was trembling. "I couldn't be there for you the last two times. I'm here for you now. I'll always be here for you."

"That is the most romantic thing you've ever done for me."

He smiled down at me in that intense, focused way he had, the way that stirred up the ever-glowing embers of my desire for him. Which felt inappropriate, to be honest. One, dead guy dressed up as a clown. Two, my Dad was right there.

"Look at what this guy's wearing," Marley said in a thoughtful tone of voice. "I can't quite put my finger on the period. What do you think, Chris? Victorian?"

Marley was a bastard. He *knew* what would happen next.

"Let's take this inside," I said, grabbing Adam's hand. "Come on, quickly, before Dad loses his shit."

"What?" Dad was saying. "Fucking Victorians."

Adam and I fast-walked for the back door.

"Ray!" Dad yelled behind me. "Raymond! The killer was a Victorian. What the fuck was wrong with those fuckers?"

As soon as we made it into the kitchen, I called Liam. Another doll.

He was going to love this.

EPILOGUE TWO

A *Chipping Fairford Inquirer* Exclusive!!!
Local man arrested on suspicion of being serial killer again!
Is his Dad in on it???
Exclusive Expose by J.C. Connolly

A *Chipping Fairford Inquirer* Apology!!!
How I got it wrong again, local man definitely not a killer, or
arrested, still wasn't even born when murderer on the
rampage and neither was his Dad! (sorry, Ray)
Exclusive Apology by J.C. Connolly

END

ALSO BY ISABEL MURRAY

Romantic Comedy

Not That Impossible

Worth the Wait

Merman Romance

Catch and Release

Fantasy Romance

Gary of a Hundred Days

CATCH AND RELEASE EXCERPT

Chapter One

"The fuck is it?" Jerry said.

I shrugged. The mystery lump that had caught his attention lay two hundred feet from where we stood on the beach. A semi-solid curtain of driving rain hung between it and us. If he couldn't see what it was, how was I supposed to?

"Come on," he said, and bustled off.

Jerry Barnes was fifty-eight years old. He'd lived every single one of those years in a little harbour town tucked away in a fold of land between Scotland and England, and yet the man still got excited by every seaweed-wrapped heap of driftwood that was coughed up by the tide.

"Joe!" he said, prancing ahead in his bright yellow wellies. "Come on!"

Seriously. He had twenty years on me, and he moved like I had twenty on him.

I couldn't conjure that amount of energy and enthusiasm even five coffees into my morning.

Especially not for something that was bound to be either boring or disgusting, depending on how dead it was, and how long it had been that way.

I followed him, but only because Jerry was still carrying my tackle box.

Since I'd moved to Lynwick six years ago, I'd built myself quite the reputation. I was well-known around these parts for being the worst fisherman to cast a line on the east coast. For some unfathomable reason, Jerry took it as a personal challenge.

Jerry owned and operated a mid-size trawler, the *Mary Jane*, with his brothers. That morning, he'd spotted me on his way home from the harbour. As usual when I didn't see him first and have time for evasive manoeuvres, he came rushing over to impart the wisdom of his family's many, many generations of fishermen.

This morning's pearl had been, "Only thing you're gonna catch if you try casting in this wind is yourself, Joe."

I was well aware. It had already taken me half an hour of fumbling with numb fingers and rapidly vanishing patience to detach the hook from the seat of my trousers.

I wasn't a complete idiot. The weather had been *fine* when I started.

Jerry had helpfully collapsed my rod and packed it away for me, even though I hadn't actually agreed to stop fishing. He let me have the rod back and hefted up my tackle box before I could grab it. I had the sinking feeling that he was about to do something awkward, like offer me lessons again, when he was distracted.

Though the tide was high, it was on the turn. Sullen waves sucked back toward the horizon, hissing angrily under a dark metal sky. A distant liner slid ominously along the skyline, heading for Norway, or America, or maybe

Antarctica. I didn't see Jerry reach the tangled mass that had been abandoned by last night's storm but when I glanced over at him, he was motionless, frizzy ginger hair whipping about his head.

I hesitated at this un-Jerry-like lack of animation.

"Well?" I called. "What is it?"

Jerry flapped his arms in an oddly helpless gesture. If he gave any answer, it was lost to the wind.

"What?" I shouted.

He turned to face me. His stone-green eyes were wide and his bushy eyebrows were halfway up his craggy forehead. An expression of excited guilt sat queasily on his face. "It's a body!" he yelled after a brief pause.

"Of what? Not a dolphin?" It was big enough and then some. This close, I could see that the large mass had been all but cocooned in a knotted and tangled monofilament net.

"Noooo," Jerry said as I came to stand beside him.

I dropped my fishing rod alongside the tackle box. "Oh, shit."

It was a man.

A pale, pale man. His skin was the fairest I'd ever seen. Who knew how long he'd been in the water? Although, there was no obvious bloat. Nothing was sloughing off. Maybe he was naturally pale?

He was big, even prone and half curled. One leg lay straight; the other was hitched up protectively into his body. He lay on his side. A thickly muscled right arm covered his head and obscured his face. His left arm was tucked beneath him.

"His hair's blue," Jerry said, and flipped a lock of it with the toe of his boot, like he was turning shells. "Really blue."

I nudged him, hard.

"Ow," Jerry said.

"Don't be disrespectful."

"He's dead, mate. Think he cares?"

"I know *I* do."

Jerry sleeved scattered seawater and rain from his face. "Reckon he's one of them club kids, then?"

I frowned. "Club kids?"

"Yeah." Jerry flailed his hands in the air around his head and whooped.

I stared at him.

"Dancers," he said. "Dancey clubs. Raves. You ever been to one?"

"Have *you*?"

"Nah. I'd feel a right prat, going into one o' them places. Used to want to, though. Back in the day." He sighed wistfully. "Never did get around to it. Think I missed the boat on that one. So. You reckon? Club kid?"

"...because his hair is blue?"

Sometimes, I struggled to follow Jerry's train of thought. I hadn't decided if our communication misfires were a generational thing, a local thing, or a Jerry thing.

Jerry grunted.

Blue hair wasn't all that unusual, even around here. Neither was pink, purple, or green. I didn't know why it said alternative club lifestyle to Jerry. The sixtysomething librarian in the next town over, which was twice the size of Lynwick and had a permanent library rather than a retro-fitted bus full of books that parked outside the pub once a week, had hair that she dyed an extraordinarily fake flat green. She wore it in a beehive. I thought it looked kind of amazing. Extra amazing when she shoved pencils in there.

The body's hair was also amazing, but nothing about it looked fake. It shone in a dark, wet snarl of indigo and cobalt, lying in long, thick ropes over his upper chest and face.

"Big 'un, isn't he?" Jerry said. "I'm thinking six four? Six five?"

"Yeah. Easy." He was closer to seven feet than six. I gazed down at him. "Who do you think he is?"

"He's not local, I can tell you that." Jerry squatted to pull at the net entangling the man. "There's no one around these parts the size of him." Jerry tipped his head to one side and paused thoughtfully. "Got a nice arse, though," he said.

I did a slow pan and gaped at him. So far as I knew, Jerry was straight.

So far as his *wife* knew, Jerry was straight.

He nodded at me encouragingly. "Right?"

I scanned the man without meaning to. A pale gleam of wet, white buttock peeked out through the holes in the net. Okay, yes. He had a nice arse.

For a corpse.

"Even I want to slap it." Jerry bent down.

I snagged him by the back of his collar and hauled him up. "Jerry, don't you dare get bi-curious and start slapping a dead man's arse."

Jerry batted my hands away. "Holy shit," he said. "Holy motherfucking shit."

"If you're having a gay crisis, I don't want to hear about it."

"Merman."

"I swear to God... Jerry. What the hell?"

"He's a...he's a..." Jerry bounced. "Merman!"

"Are you broken?" I dug around for my phone. I was going to call Marcy.

Jerry grabbed my face, angled it toward the body, and shouted, "Merman!"

"I don't see any tail."

"Okay, but what about that?"

"That's a penis."

Oh.

It sure was.

Large. Thick.

Hard.

...Wait.

When had he rolled over? He was now lying flat to the dark and sodden sand. Hadn't he been on his side? And his leg, had it moved? Wasn't it hitched up, covering his groin, and weren't his arms...?

"That's an erection," Jerry corrected me. "Probably rigor mortis."

I couldn't swear to it, but I didn't think an erection was part of the rigor mortis experience. Then again, my forensic knowledge had been acquired while squinting at the screen during the obligatory morgue scene in every crime show ever filmed, and waiting for it to pass. What did I know?

"Anyway, I'm talking about this." Jerry squatted down again, his hold on my face taking me with him. And, coincidentally, putting me eye level with the penis.

Jerry squeezed my jaw and redirected my gaze.

"Is it just me," he said, "or does the dead guy have gills?"

ABOUT THE AUTHOR

Isabel Murray is a writer, a reader, and a lover of love. She couldn't stick to a subgenre if her life depended on it, but MM romance is her jam. She lives in the UK, reads way too much, and cannot be trusted anywhere near chocolate.

You can find Isabel at her website, or on Goodreads, Amazon, and Bookbub.

www.isabelmurrayauthor.wordpress.com